Silk caught a gl‍‍‍‍‍‍‍‍‍‍‍‍‍‍‍‍‍‍‍‍ ock-
ets on Aerwin's cl‍‍‍‍‍‍‍‍‍‍‍‍‍‍‍‍ s of
a golden chain, has‍‍‍‍‍‍‍‍‍‍‍‍‍‍ pocket, had spilled
loose in their struggle. Just as Aerwin followed his gaze,
he stepped forward and crouched down, reaching to
grab the trailing chain and pull it free.

Her reaction was a fraction of a moment too late.
Silk caught the chain and tugged, and it came out of
her pocket. Along with it came a jade amulet in the
shape of a dragon.

"This is Marc's," he accused, eyes coming up to fix
hers with a cold glare. "*This* is why you fragged us?"

"You have no idea how completely," Aerwin said
softly, with a poisonous smile.

Suddenly the night turned to day as a blazing light
stabbed down from the sky. Though Silk's optics compensated for the glare, he was momentarily dazzled,
and reflexively sought the source of the light.

Aerwin's kick sent his pistol flying, but Silk held on
to the amulet. He dove to the side as her weapon
cleared its holster. There was no cover on the slope,
nowhere to hide as the dark-clad woman leveled her
gun directly at him, no way she could miss at this distance. Silk had seen her take down far harder targets.

The shot that came, however, wasn't from Aerwin's
gun but from farther up the slope, and it sent her staggering back. Silk followed the sound of the shot and saw
Mustang standing less than fifteen meters away, fierce
determination creasing her face as she scrambled down
the slope toward them. He saw that the light was coming
from a helicopter hovering overhead, its searchlight
sweeping the side of the mountain.

"Drop your weapons!" a voice boomed in English.
"Drop your weapons and put your hands on your heads!"

FALLEN ANGELS

A Shadowrun™ Novel

STEPHEN KENSON

A ROC BOOK

ROC
Published by New American Library, a division of
Penguin Group (USA) Inc., 375 Hudson Street,
New York, New York 10014, USA
Penguin Group (Canada), 90 Eglinton Avenue East, Suite 700, Toronto,
Ontario M4P 2Y3, Canada (a division of Pearson Penguin Canada Inc.)
Penguin Books Ltd., 80 Strand, London WC2R 0RL, England
Penguin Ireland, 25 St. Stephen's Green, Dublin 2,
Ireland (a division of Penguin Books Ltd.)
Penguin Group (Australia), 250 Camberwell Road, Camberwell, Victoria 3124,
Australia (a division of Pearson Australia Group Pty. Ltd.)
Penguin Books India Pvt. Ltd., 11 Community Centre, Panchsheel Park,
New Delhi - 110 017, India
Penguin Group (NZ), cnr Airborne and Rosedale Roads, Albany,
Auckland 1310, New Zealand (a division of Pearson New Zealand Ltd.)
Penguin Books (South Africa) (Pty.) Ltd., 24 Sturdee Avenue,
Rosebank, Johannesburg 2196, South Africa

Penguin Books Ltd., Registered Offices:
80 Strand, London WC2R 0RL, England

First published by Roc, an imprint of New American Library,
a division of Penguin Group (USA) Inc.

First Printing, March 2006
10 9 8 7 6 5 4 3 2 1

![ROC] REGISTERED TRADEMARK—MARCA REGISTRADA

Printed in the United States of America

To my friends; my parents, George and Lynn; and to Christopher, most of all.

ACKNOWLEDGMENTS

When you write in the Sixth World of Shadowrun®, you stand on the shoulders of giants. My deepest thanks to Mike Mulvihill for his trust and guidance, to Sharon Turner Mulvihill for her input and expert editing, and to Bob Charrette, Tom Dowd, Paul Hume, and Jordan Weisman for starting it all, and each helping in his own way to bring the Sixth World to glorious and gritty life. Without them, this book wouldn't exist, and I would have missed out on a whole lot of fun along the way.

TRANS-POLAR
ALEUT

ATHABASKAN
COUNCIL

QUÉBEC

SALISH-
SHIDHE
COUNCIL

ALGONKIAN-MANITOU
COUNCIL

Seattle

TIR
TAIRNGIRE

SIOUX
NATION

UNITED CANADIAN
AND AMERICAN
STATES (U.C.A.S.)

UTE
NATION

Denver

CALIFORNIA
FREE STATE

PUEBLO
CORPORATE
COUNCIL

CONFEDERATED
AMERICAN STATES

AZTLAN

CARIBBEAN LEAGUE

NORTH AMERICA
AS OF 2060

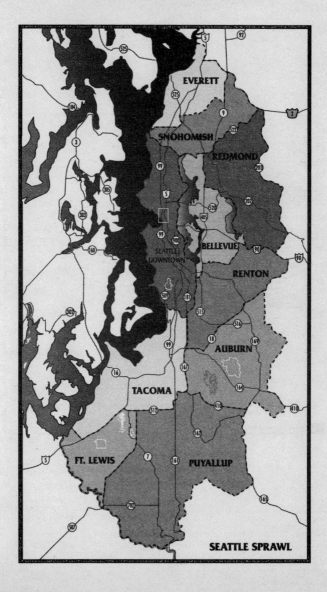

SEATTLE SPRAWL

PROLOGUE

Even the elves of Tir Tairngire feared the wilderness, and with good reason. They were haunted, those forests and mountains. They had been transformed—by the wild, untamed force of magic, the power unleashed in the Awakening in 2011—into places out of legend . . . places not at all friendly to visitors.

The inhabitants of the Land of Promise knew better than most just how unpredictable, how capricious, magic could be. So they stayed clear of the deep forests and the smoking mountains. One such isolated area was an ideal place to perform the work going on that night, but the remoteness of the wilderness location only served to increase the nervousness of the woman called Mustang. She stood on the rocky slope of the mountainside—looking out over the dark forest that stretched in all directions, and the tattered clouds veiling the half-lit face of the waning moon—and tried not to worry about what was going on in a nearby cave.

The wind moaned, whipping loose strands of hair across her face, and she turned up the collar of her jacket, wishing for something warmer than synthleather and ballistic armor lining. She zipped the jacket up as high as it would go, cradling a sleek automatic pistol in her right hand.

A faint sound, a glimpse of movement out of the corner of her eye, and the gun swung up and around, laser sight showing as a faint red gleam in the darkness, painting a targeting dot on the shadowy figure approaching close at hand.

"Easy!" came a low voice from the shadows. Mustang slowly lowered her weapon, but kept it ready in her hand.

"You shouldn't sneak up on me like that," she scolded, looking back out over the dark vista.

"Sorry, force of habit." He moved closer, until he was standing just behind her shoulder. "When I can't surprise someone, it's time to get out of this business."

Mustang snorted faintly. "I wonder if it isn't that time already," she muttered. "I have a bad feeling about this, Silk."

Her companion rested his hand gently on her shoulder.

"It'll be fine," he reassured her. "We're almost finished. Once Marc has taken care of his business, we can get the frag out of this place. I know I won't miss it."

"I think I will, in a way." Mustang drew a deep breath and let it out in a slow sigh. "It's not like most people believe, some faerie-tale kingdom, but it is . . . magical."

"Sure, if you happen to have been born with pointed ears," Silk said derisively. "I didn't see too much of the 'magical land' in the slums of Portland, did you?"

She shook her head slowly. "No, but still . . . it's like there's something in the air here."

"Well, I think you might have a somewhat biased view of elf culture," Silk replied, his voice gently mocking.

Mustang just smiled. He was right about that. She would never look at Tir Tairngire, or elves, in quite the same way ever again. Her life would never be the same as it was before they came here—assuming they made it out alive.

Silk gently squeezed her shoulder. "Don't worry," he said, reading her look of concern. "He's going to be fine. He knows what he's doing."

So he says, she thought, turning to face Silk. "It's not him I'm worried about," she said, and Silk nodded grimly.

"I know. But she wants out just as much as he does."

"Does she? I still don't know for sure."

"We needed her help."

"No. It was just easier with her help," Mustang countered.

Silk shrugged. "So, it was easier. Since when have you had a problem with an opportunity to do things the easy way?"

"Mostly when it involves people I can't trust."

"Hey, that's life in the shadows," Silk said. "Can we really trust *anybody*?"

Mustang stared over Silk's shoulder at the cave entrance that was guarded by the dark crags of the mountains on either side. "One of us should be in there."

Silk shook his head slowly. "I feel the same way,

but Marc doesn't need the extra distraction, and you don't want to interrupt a wizard while he's working."

"It should have been me," Mustang insisted, "or you, not her."

"I think he wants you out of danger," Silk replied, "and I think he trusts me least of all. I'm not an elf, and I'm not . . ." Mustang's eyes narrowed, and Silk just shrugged and left the rest of the comment unspoken. "I think he's a little jealous of me," he concluded instead. "He sees me as competition. I know, I know," he continued before Mustang could reply, "I'm not, but he doesn't seem to know that. We work well together. It's easy to mistake that for something else."

She looked longingly at the cave entrance, her thoughts far away.

"You really do love him, don't you?"

Mustang's gaze jerked back to Silk. The bald statement shocked her like a wave of cold water.

"Yeah, I really do." It was the first time she'd admitted it to anyone else and acknowledged that this was more than just another mission—that, after this, things wouldn't be the same.

She looked at the cave entrance again.

"Silk," she said, and he turned to look. Red-gold light was pulsing from the entrance, growing brighter, like a miniature dawn coming up inside the dark mouth of the cavern. Light poured out and illuminated the ledge as the sound of chanting echoed down the mountain, the sound growing in intensity with the light.

Mustang had taken three running steps before Silk managed to grab her arm. She angrily tried to jerk free.

"We can't interrupt!" Silk gritted out. "He said to stay here, no matter what happens!"

She stopped struggling and stayed where she was. The chanting died away, but the light remained, glowing steadily, brightly.

"What about that light? It'll be visible for miles."

"There's nobody around for miles," Silk countered.

"Patrols," she said stubbornly.

"We'll be done and gone long before a patrol could get here. Will you just take it easy?"

Mustang sighed, her burst of energy leaking away. "You're right. I just wish it was over."

"What are you going to do when it is?"

She shook her head slowly. "I don't know. Depends on what the company does, I guess." Silk nodded in agreement. It always depended on what the company wanted.

"Well, you know if I can help . . ." he began, but a flicker of movement in the cave caught their attention. A shadowy figure dashed from the entrance.

"Aerwin!" Silk shouted, but the slim figure didn't stop—didn't even slow—as she flew toward the tree line.

"Marc!" Mustang cried, and ran for the cave. Silk hesitated for a second, afraid of what Mustang would find, then took off after the woman who had rushed down the slope.

Aerwin had a good lead on Silk, but the rocky slope of the mountain was treacherous, and even she couldn't move too quickly. He thanked the implanted optics that magnified what little light came from the stars and veiled moon and allowed him to see as clearly as if it was daylight, avoiding obstacles and keeping track of the lithe figure in black moving in the shadows ahead.

Silk put on a burst of speed and veered to the left, heading up a low ridge, then flinging himself off the edge. He tackled his quarry in midair, and they tumbled down the slope in a shower of loose stones.

Aerwin scrambled to her feet. Silk took them out from under her with a sweep of his leg. She rolled to one side as he allowed his momentum to carry him in the opposite direction, and they both reached for their weapons. The optical signal processor at the base of his spine made Silk just a bit faster than his opponent. His weapon cleared the holster, the laser sight painting a vivid red dot on the pale face in front of him, the elf's smooth skin gleaming almost like pearl in the moonlight.

"Don't," was all he said, and Aerwin slowly lifted her hand from her pistol. "Stay down," he told her, careful to keep the gun level as he pressed his other hand against the ground and slowly stood up. The woman's dark eyes never left his, never flinched as the glare of the laser crossed them.

"What the frag is going on?" Silk asked, afraid he already knew the answer. "You were playing us? This was just a setup? Why?"

"We can make a deal . . ." she began, and Silk fought the urge to squeeze the trigger. Not until he found out what was going on.

"Shut up," he said. "No deals. That was obviously a mistake the first time, and it's not going to happen again. I'm going to ask one more time: why?"

Aerwin remained still and silent, but Silk's enhanced vision caught a gleam of something in one of the pockets on her close-fitting dark pants—a few links of a golden chain, hastily shoved into her pocket, had spilled loose in their struggle. Just as Aerwin followed his gaze, he stepped forward and crouched down, reaching to grab the trailing chain and pull it free.

Her reaction was a fraction of a moment too late. Silk caught the chain and tugged, and it came out of her pocket. Along with it came a jade amulet in the shape of a dragon.

"This is Marc's," he accused, eyes coming up to fix hers with a cold glare. "*This* is why you fragged us?"

"You have no idea how completely," Aerwin said softly, with a poisonous smile.

Suddenly the night turned to day as a blazing light stabbed down from the sky. Though Silk's optics compensated for the glare, he was momentarily dazzled, and reflexively sought the source of the light.

Aerwin's kick sent his pistol flying, but Silk held onto the amulet. He dove to the side as her weapon cleared its holster. There was no cover on the slope, nowhere to hide as the dark-clad woman leveled her gun directly at him, no way she could miss at this distance. Silk had seen her take down far harder targets.

The shot that came, however, wasn't from Aerwin's gun but from farther up the slope, and it sent her staggering back. Silk followed the sound of the shot and saw Mustang standing less than fifteen meters away, fierce determination creasing her face as she scrambled down the slope toward them. He saw that the light was coming from a helicopter hovering overhead, its searchlight sweeping the side of the mountain.

"Drop your weapons!" a voice boomed in English.

"Drop your weapons and put your hands on your heads!"

In one sweeping glance, Aerwin took in Silk lying on the ground, Mustang approaching, and the chopper as it banked around for another pass. She didn't even hesitate before bolting again for the tree line. Silk could see that she was holding her left arm stiffly, but it barely slowed her movement.

Mustang reached him just as he got to his feet. "Are you—?"

"I'm fine," he said. "Let's get out of here."

"Are you crazy? We can still catch her!" She started after Aerwin, but again Silk grabbed her arm.

"We can't," he said. "It's a setup. Any second now, this place is going to be swarming with Tir patrols! We have to get out of here!"

"Silk, she—" Mustang's voice broke.

"I know!" he interrupted. "There's nothing we can do, Stang! We've got to get out of here!"

Mustang looked at him for a long moment, her face streaked with tears, and took a deep breath. For that moment, Silk was sure she was going to fight him, insist on going after Aerwin regardless of the consequences. Then she let her breath out in a shuddering sigh.

"You're right," she said. "Let's go."

When the helicopter's searchlight swept over the area again, the shadowy figures were gone. All that remained was the flickering red-orange glow coming from the mouth of the cave high along the slope of the mountain, the wilderness and the haunted night.

1

Kellan Colt crouched beside the high chain-link
fence surrounding the corporate office facility in
Bellevue, all but invisible in the shadows pooled outside the ring of illumination cast by the halogen flood-
lights. She checked the fence carefully, gently touching
a voltage tester to the metal mesh. It wasn't live.
There were no signs saying it was, but some corporations ignored niceties like notifying potential intruders
about their security, so it always paid to check. She
glanced up at the strands of razor wire topping the
fence. Not the most sophisticated deterrent, but still
not easy to overcome for a person working alone.

Kellan was used to being on her own. From the
time her mother left her with an aunt who cared more
about her next drink and her next sim than family,
Kellan had taken care of herself. She learned that you
had to look out for number one, and it was a lesson
that had been reinforced by living and working in the
shadows, the spaces between "proper" and "recognized" society.

She was on her own with her aunt. As soon as she
could, she took off into the shadows of Kansas City,
and she was on her own there. She worked with other

runaways and small-time shadowrunners, but everyone looked out for their own interests. Then she got the mysterious package, containing some running gear, the amulet she always wore, and a note. "This stuff belonged to your mother. Thought you might want it," it said. No signature, no explanation. Nothing except for a postmark showing that the package had originated in the Seattle Metroplex.

So Kellan set out with the last of her credit for Seattle, and was on her own there, for a while at least. She met new people in the shadows, made connections. Even then, she discovered the need to watch her back. She learned that she had the talent for magic, and began taking lessons from the troll mage Lothan, but she also ran up against Lothan on a job, discovering he hadn't told her or anyone else the whole truth about the run. That was the way it worked: nobody told the whole truth unless they had to, and everyone had an agenda of their own. Everyone looked out for number one. Even if you worked with a team, you still had to work alone. Like Kellan was alone. That was the way it was, she told herself, that was the way it had to be.

She focused on that sense of solitude. She found that the feeling of being detached from the world around her made the magic easier. She drew on that feeling as she spoke the words of a spell Lothan had taught her, sensing the mana, the magical power flow around her. That power bent and warped light, reshaped shadow. As the last whispered syllables faded from her lips, Kellan faded from view.

She took the compact bolt cutters from the sheath strapped to her thigh. What they lacked in leverage, they more than made up for in the specialization of their cutting edges—spun diamond monofilament. They quickly, silently snipped through the chain links as if the fence were made of cobwebs. In mere moments, Kellan cut an opening large enough to crawl through. She slipped through the hole and into the compound.

If her information on the timing of the security sweeps of the grounds was accurate, she had only a few moments to wait. She glanced down at the barely visible phosphorescent glow of the chronometer on the back of her glove, which she had synched to the schedule she'd acquired. It had to be accurate, because if it wasn't, she was as good as caught. Her spell would protect her from casual notice, but the facility's cameras almost certainly had infrared capabilities. Her employer would deny any knowledge of her existence, of course—easy to do since Kellan had no real idea who her employer was. Anonymity was all-important in the shadows.

She watched as the seconds ticked past, her body tense. Just a few more and . . . now!

Kellan bolted away from the fence and headed for the side of the building, moving as quietly as she could, as quickly as she dared. Her gear was strapped on tight; the only sound she made was the whispering tread of soft-soled boots along the concrete. She pressed up against the cool outer wall, barely breathing hard, and glanced down at the time readout again. She'd made it with seconds to spare. Now came the tricky part.

Moving along the wall, she reached a side entrance shown on the building schematics—a standard steel fire door. Beside the door, a narrow card slot was faintly illuminated by a burning point of red light set into the frame of the maglock. Kellan moved directly in front of the lock and took a passkey from a pocket of her jacket. This handy tool consisted of a circuit-imbedded plastic card trailing wires to a small keypad. She slotted the card, and the keypad flickered to life.

She could easily use the passkey to scramble the lock and open the door quickly, but that would likely trigger alarms set to watch for any malfunction in the building's maglocks. The trick was to let the passkey cycle through possible combinations, until it found the right one to open the lock without arousing any suspicion. Unfortunately, the potential number of combinations was immense. Unless the passkey hit on the right one quickly, Kellan would have to try something else to get in, or abandon the run altogether. She waited in silence as the glowing numbers cycled on the passkey's screen.

The seconds seemed to crawl past, unbearably slowly. Kellan barely allowed herself to breathe, her senses straining to detect any sign that she'd been spotted, watching for any approaching trouble. The numbers flashed past at computer-processing speeds, too quickly for human eyes to read.

Suddenly, without warning, the numbers stopped. The light over the card slot changed from red to green, and there was a faint click as the lock disengaged. Kellan's breath whooshed out in a sigh of relief. Taking hold of the edge of the door in one gloved hand, she eased it open just enough to slide through, pulling it gently closed behind her.

The hallway was lit by the dull, whitewash glow of phosphorescent bulbs, every other one turned off to conserve power at night. The walls were nondescript and sterile. No signs marked the way, but Kellan knew

what she was looking for. She headed down the hall
to where it intersected another and turned to the right.

Just as she turned the corner, a dwarf in a dark blue
uniform stepped into the hall. Kellan started,
panicking—until she remembered she was as invisible
to the security guard as she'd been to the cameras
outside. He wore his dark brown hair in a long braid
and had a full beard, a fashion popular among dwarfs.
An almost invisible throat mic extended from over
one pointed ear, and the butt of a pistol jutted away
from his hip. As he pulled the door closed behind
him, he turned to scan the hallway. He was . . .

He was looking right at her.

Drek! Kellan thought as the dwarf reached for his
weapon, at the same time calling out, "Intruder at the
east entrance!"

As he grabbed his gun, Kellan snatched a short
metal rod from her belt. With a flick of her wrist, it
extended to almost a full meter in length, its tip crackling with blue sparks. She slammed it into the dwarf's
arm as he brought up his pistol. There was a crackle
and a yelp of pain as nerveless fingers dropped the
gun. The dwarf stumbled back, clutching his arm
where the stun baton had touched it.

Kellan pressed her advantage, slamming the tip of
the baton into the dwarf's chest. There was another
crack and the smell of ozone as the security guard
pitched backward onto the floor, muscles twitching.
At the same moment, alarms began to sound throughout the building.

Kellan left the dwarf where he lay and took off back
down the hall from which she came. She barreled into
the door at full speed, but only ended up bruising her
shoulder as she bounced off it.

"Ow!" she swore. The building was on alert, so now the door was locked down. Quickly, she slotted her passkey and punched the override button. It scrambled the maglock; the time for stealth was over. The security door released, and Kellan kicked it open, bolting back across the compound toward her hole in the fence.

She'd made it about halfway when a burst of automatic gunfire ricocheted off the pavement nearby, sending up sparks. Several uniformed security guards were headed her way.

"Stop!" one of them yelled, and Kellan could see two were wearing infrared goggles. The third either had implanted thermal optics or was relying on the other two to tell him where their target stood. Still, if she could reach cover beyond the fence, she might be able to escape. She kept going.

"Stop!" the guard shouted again, punctuating the order with additional bursts of gunfire. Kellan was gathering herself to dive through the fence when she felt a sharp pain in her lower back that knocked her to the ground and made her cry out. *Dammit!*

Kellan ripped the electrode net from her head and tossed it aside. The pain in her back immediately began to fade as the simsense signal was cut off, her surroundings shifting from a corporate office compound at night to the living room of her small apartment. She looked at the woman sitting in the chair to the left of her couch.

"Congratulations," she said dryly. "You're dead."

"I shouldn't be," Kellan retorted, frustration making her voice sharp. She picked up a plastic squeeze bottle from the floor next to her and took a long drink of filtered water, rinsing the dryness out of her mouth before she swallowed. "My invisibility spell—"

"Isn't effective against a metahuman with thermographic vision, like a dwarf," the other woman interjected.

"Right," Kellan said. "I didn't think of that. Sorry, Midnight. Let me give it another try." She reached for the trode net.

"I think that's enough for now," Midnight said. "Plus, we've got more to go over." She tapped the slim datapad resting across her knees.

Kellan sighed. Training sessions with Midnight were difficult, maybe even more so than lessons with Lothan. Whereas the old troll mage had an ego the size of an arcology and loved nothing more than to hear himself talk, Midnight was a woman of few words but penetrating insight. She didn't sugarcoat things, and always told her *exactly* what she thought Kellan was doing wrong. She was always right, too.

However, unlike Lothan, Midnight didn't consider it to be a character-building exercise to let Kellan figure out for herself the right way of doing things. She was as free with advice and suggestions as she was with criticism, and when Kellan did something right, she was quick to praise. Her analysis of Kellan's performance in the latest simulation was typical: blunt and honest, sparing neither praise nor criticism where they were due.

Kellan listened carefully. Midnight knew the ins and outs of breaking and entering better than anyone she knew. She had been in the business . . . well, Kellan didn't really know how long. Midnight didn't talk much about her past—not a lot of people working in the shadows did. Still, she had the kind of reputation you didn't get overnight, and Lothan, himself a very veteran shadowrunner, seemed to have known Midnight for a long time. Since Midnight was an elf, it was difficult to tell how old she was. She could pass for only a few years older than Kellan, but she could be as old as Lothan, maybe older.

"It's important to know your limitations," Midnight was saying. "Magic is a useful tool, but it's no substitute for preparation, or old-fashioned stealth and discretion. You may not always be able to rely on it to accomplish your goals."

Kellan nodded. "Maybe there's a variant invisibility spell that works against thermographics. I could ask Lothan—"

"You're not getting my point, Kellan," Midnight interrupted. "The solution isn't more magic, it's more awareness of your situation, and planning for every contingency. Being discovered in the facility was a distinct possibility from the start, but when it happened, you weren't prepared. You let your magic make you overconfident." At Kellan's sheepish look, Midnight shrugged and smiled.

"Don't worry about it. You did a lot of things right. You've come a long way since we started working together. I think your mother would be proud of you."

Kellan beamed momentarily at the mention of her mother, then her expression became wistful.

"Do you think so?" she asked, and Midnight nodded.

"I do," she replied firmly. "You really do take after her, and I like to think of what we're doing as my way of paying her back for everything she helped teach me."

"I wish she was around," Kellan said, "or at least that I knew what happened to her."

"I know," Midnight said sympathetically. "I know."

Kellan thought about the mother she hardly knew, who had placed her in the care of an alcoholic aunt, showing up only occasionally and always leaving too soon. Kellan now knew it was because her mother had been a shadowrunner, too, working outside the law. She couldn't settle down for too long in one place, or take care of a young child. Still, she sent money when she could, and messages for Kellan.

Then one day the money, the messages and the visits just stopped. Her mother sent no explanation, and Kellan's aunt offered none. She grew even more resentful of the burden she felt Kellan represented, and had made her feelings clear to Kellan at every opportunity.

When Kellan discovered that Midnight had worked with her mother—had, in fact, learned the ropes of shadowrunning from her—Kellan felt like she'd finally found a real connection to her mother, apart from the few possessions she'd inherited. Kellan had hoped that Midnight knew what became of her mother, but Midnight had lost contact with Mustang over the years.

"All right," Kellan sighed, "let me try this again."

After Midnight left, Kellan gratefully crawled into bed to get a few hours' sleep. In her dreams, she made her way through the test again: approaching the perimeter fence, carefully cutting a way in, slipping invisibly into the compound. She crouched alongside the security door, the passkey working through the combinations.

The door clicked and a bright, shining light poured out around its edges, flooding into the dimness outside. Kellan felt the amulet she wore at her throat become warm, tingling against her skin. She thought she heard someone calling her name from the other side of the door.

"Kellan . . . Kellan . . ."

As if in a trance, she swung the door open, then threw her arm up to shield her eyes from the blazing light; it was like looking directly into the sun. She squinted into the glare, trying to make out the shadowy figure she thought was standing there.

"Kellan . . ." the voice called again. It sounded like a man's voice, but Kellan couldn't make it out clearly, didn't recognize it.

"Come to me . . ." the voice said sweetly.

"Kellan . . ." another voice spoke from behind her and Kellan spun, turning away from the light, framed by it in the doorway.

Someone stood behind her, raising a slim pistol level with Kellan's midsection.

"Congratulations," she said dryly. "You're dead."

The gun went off with a bang, and Kellan woke with a start.

2

"Lothan, what do you know about dreams?" Kellan asked, keeping her gaze on the symbols she was chalking on the freshly cleaned floor of Lothan's basement ritual space.

The troll wizard raised one shaggy white eyebrow, glancing up from the book he was reading. The fabric-bound volume looked comically small cradled in his big hands.

"Dreams?" he asked. "What about them?"

"Well, do they . . . mean anything?"

"That depends on what you mean by meaning, so to speak," Lothan rumbled. He set the book down on a workbench crowded with crystals, plastic bags containing colored powder, and other books and bric-a-brac, giving the subject his full attention. "There are many different levels of meaning." Kellan could sense Lothan shifting into what their mutual associate Jackie called "pontificate mode," an attitude he often adopted when expounding on one subject or another.

"Dreams can certainly have psychological meanings—the expression of the deep archetypes of the psyche—and those symbols and archetypes in turn often have magical meaning—"

"Like visions?"

Lothan harrumphed at the interruption, his broad mouth pursing into an expression of disapproval. "Hardly," he said. "I mean the symbolism from dreams is often quite similar to that of the astral plane, particularly the metaplanes, and an understanding of that imagery can be useful to the practitioner in understanding the experience of metaplanar journeys and the like."

"So dreams can't predict the future—even, you know, *our* dreams?"

"There's no indication the dreams of the Awakened are any more powerful or meaningful than those of mundanes," Lothan said with a shake of his horned head. "Despite considerable folklore and urban myth supporting the theory, no study to date has turned up a truly reliable magical means of predicting the future—in or out of dreams, at least for more than a few seconds—with any real degree of reliability. It has to do with the field of probability, which expands as you go further out . . ." Lothan trailed off.

"I'm sorry, am I boring you?" her teacher asked. Kellan didn't think he'd seen her roll her eyes. She quickly shook her head.

"No, it's just . . ."

"Kellan, have you been having some unusual dreams lately?"

"What? No. No, I was just wondering. I've been doing some reading, and I'd heard some things, you know, about dreams."

Lothan raised an eyebrow, and then waved his hand dismissively. "Well, you shouldn't believe everything you read—or hear, for that matter."

"Unless it comes from you, of course," Kellan interjected slyly, and the troll smiled, showing off the short tusks jutting up over his upper lip.

"Of course. I am, after all, the definitive authority on . . . well, most everything."

"Of course," Kellan said, bending over the chalk diagram again. Lothan stood up from the broad stool where he was sitting, and looked over her shoulder.

"Nearly finished?"

"Almost," she said, as Lothan moved around the edges of what she had drawn on the floor.

It was a circle three meters across, consisting of an inner and outer ring with a space between them as wide as the length of Kellan's hand. Into that space Kellan was chalking magical symbols oriented toward the four cardinal directions. Inside the inner circle was a five-pointed star, the points just touching the inner line. In each of the star's points was another magical symbol. Outside the circle, in the east, was a smaller triangle, about half a meter on a side. Symbols were drawn at each point and along each side of the triangle as well. Kellan had been working on the diagram for most of the afternoon, knowing it would soon be washed away, and all of her work with it.

She'd asked Lothan once why mages went through all the trouble of drawing ritual circles by hand. Why didn't they just have them embroidered onto rugs, or digitized and printed out on paper for use when they were needed? Lothan's answer had been typical.

"Because it's not the *symbols* that really matter," he said. "It's the intent that goes into creating them. It's the *act* of creating the circle that makes it a circle of power, not chalk marks on stone, or ink on paper. It's the difference between drawing or painting a landscape and printing out a picture you downloaded off the Net: the digital file you print out is just a file, but the artwork contains a part of *you*. It's connected to you, unique, *alive* in a magical sense. The same is true of the circle. Some soulless printout is of no more use magically than simply throwing paint on the floor and calling it a pattern. Less even, since at least the thrown paint has some amount of intention behind it."

"It's just a lot of work," was Kellan's only response.

"Naturally," Lothan said with a tusky smile, "which is one of the reasons why mages have apprentices."

So Kellan learned to draw and paint the ritual diagrams by hand, consulting books for the right symbols, putting her intention behind placing each one precisely and in the right order. She filled in the last symbol in the west and drew a solid line, connecting the inner and outer lines of the circle, tapping the chalk against the floor like a punctuation mark ending a sentence.

"There," she said, standing up and stretching her cramped legs.

Lothan paced slowly around the perimeter of the circle, careful not to scuff any of the chalk marks, his hands clasped behind his back, bending down occasionally to examine Kellan's work.

"Hmmm," he murmured, glancing first one way and then the other. "Hmmm."

Kellan waited patiently. Lothan's inspections used to unnerve her, until she figured out that that was what they were supposed to do. Lothan paid close enough attention to know already if she'd made any major mistakes. He just liked to take his time and make her sweat. So Kellan waited, standing quietly until he was done.

"It will do," he pronounced finally. "Yes, I think it

will do well enough. You have prepared the ritual?"
he asked.

"Wouldn't have done all of this work if I hadn't,"
Kellan replied, retrieving the datapad leaning next to
her bag.

"Oh, but you would have," Lothan muttered, loud
enough for Kellan to hear. He would have made her
draw out the circle whether she was ready to use it
or not, and she knew it.

"Very well, then," Lothan said. "Begin." The troll
wizard settled back down on the broad stool in the
corner of the room, perched like a massive gargoyle
in the shadows, to watch Kellan work.

She dimmed the lights in the room and placed a
candle in each quarter of the circle. With the barest
effort of will, she ignited the wicks, shedding a golden
glow over the chalk marks. The flickering shadows
seemed to make the symbols come alive and stand out
in stark relief against the gray floor, faintly shimmering with power. It could have been dismissed as a
trick of the light, but Kellan took it as a positive sign
that everything was in place.

She made sure the small basement window was
open just a crack to admit the evening air, and took
quick inventory of her supplies: charcoal burner,
parchment paper and a jar of granular incense she'd
ground and mixed herself. Once she stepped into the
circle, she couldn't step back out again to get something she forgot without interrupting the ritual. If that
happened, she'd have to start all over again.

Kellan stepped over the outer and inner lines of the
circle, careful not to disturb them. She crouched down
in the center of the circle, putting everything into
place, then stood, took a deep breath and centered

herself. She let the breath out with a slow sigh and drew in another, then another, before she turned to face the eastern quarter of the circle.

"Hail, O powers of the east," she intoned. "I call upon the element of air to be present here within my circle, for air is the power I summon tonight. Be present here, and truly do my will." The candles flickered for a moment as a breeze coming from the open window stirred their flames, but none of them went out. Kellan turned toward the south, raising her arms, hands open, palms up.

"Hail, O powers of the south," she said. "I call upon the element of fire to be present here within my circle. Air is the power I summon tonight; give your passion to my effort. Be present here, and truly do my will." The candle flames grew brighter and taller for a moment, filling the circle with their glow, then shrank back to their former size. Kellan turned toward the west, arms spread wide, palms facing out.

"Hail, O powers of the west. I call upon the element of water to be present here within my circle. Air is the power I summon tonight; give your depth to my effort. Be present here, and truly do my will." The shadows swam and flickered, like reflections off a shimmering pool at night, before passing and returning the circle to its steady glow.

Finally, Kellan turned to the north, intoning, "Hail, O powers of the north. I call upon the element of earth to be present here within my circle. Air is the power I summon tonight; give your strength to my effort. Be present here, and truly do my will."

The circle cast, Kellan felt rather than saw a looming presence all around her, the protective power of the wards she invoked to focus the energies she would raise, contain them, and protect her from any outside influence.

Kellan lit the charcoal at the bottom of the burner with a pass of her hand, quickly setting it to glowing. Then she shook a small amount of incense onto it from her hand, sending a steady stream of sweet, pungent smoke rising into the air like a curling serpent.

When Lothan first introduced Kellan to conjuring, she told him she wasn't entirely comfortable with the idea of calling up spirits and commanding them to do her bidding. Although she considered herself a practical person, Kellan couldn't help but wonder: if spirits acted like intelligent beings, able to understand and carry out orders, then how did they feel about being whistled up to do a mage's dirty work? Wasn't forcing them into service wrong?

After making some crack about how that didn't differ very much from the job description of a shadowrunner, Lothan had patiently explained that servitor spirits such as elementals, while intelligent, were not necessarily any more self-aware than sophisticated computer programs (though Kellan wondered about those sometimes, too). Spirits were *made* to serve, in Lothan's expert opinion. It was only those times when the summoner was careless or overeager, when spirits escaped from their bindings and became something more, that they acquired that spark of sentience, of will, perhaps from the very ritual intended to place them into service.

In the end, Lothan said it didn't matter to him whether Kellan wanted to learn conjuring or not. He was perfectly content to teach her nothing but spells, or limit his lessons to banishing and defending against hostile spirits rather than summoning them. It was a decision Kellan needed to make for herself, not one she could be forced into, if she was ever going to be able to do the rituals properly.

In the end, it was Lothan's willingness *not* to teach her that convinced Kellan that she ought to learn. The old troll was just a little too happy to keep the secrets of conjuring to himself, to not pass on some of his carefully hoarded knowledge and experience. Kellan knew Lothan liked to play his cards close to the vest. She also knew you didn't pass up something that could give you an edge in the shadows, because you could be sure the other guy wouldn't, and then you'd be yesterday's news.

So she decided to take Lothan at his word and at least *try* learning the basics of spirit summoning. She couldn't judge it until she'd at least tried it for herself, and she didn't want Lothan quietly lording his superior knowledge over her for all time. So she learned to summon watchers, simple-minded spirits used to spy and carry messages and such. Then she learned to summon the spirits of the elements, and put that knowledge to work.

Kellan quickly lost track of time in the warm haze of the incense smoke as she chanted, her voice rising and falling like waves, like wind rippling across water. The air was still and close, the candles giving off a surprising amount of warmth inside the confines of the circle. Whenever the smoke rising from the burner began to thin out, Kellan added another pinch of incense from her jar, until the room was almost filled with the smoke, and she could barely make out Lothan looming in the haze.

A cool breeze from the open window stirred the warm, still air, making the smoke from the incense swirl and dance. Kellan focused on the chant, and on the tingling energy she felt building up, flowing up her legs, all along her body, down her arms to her finger-tips, up to set her head buzzing. She felt a subtle pres-sure at the base of her skull, a feeling in the back of her mind like a thought just out of reach, waiting to be remembered. She held on to that feeling and con-tinued the chant, letting it build before she held her hands out toward the incense burner and focused all her attention beyond it to the triangle drawn outside of her circle.

She spoke the final invoking words of the spell, and felt the gathered power rush out of her, like a spring suddenly released. A wind moaned and whis-tled through the window, and the smoke gathered, pulled toward the space above the triangle like a magnet to metal, spinning slowly around a central point about a meter off the floor. The small cloud began spinning faster, reeling in more and more of the smoke.

"Be here now!" Kellan commanded, and there was a crack like thunder, loud in the enclosed room. The swirling cloud of smoke hovering in the air at arm's length from the incense burner opened glowing eyes of electric blue, the color of the edge of a lightning bolt, bright against the dark gray mist. It hovered there, looking at Kellan, and for a moment she felt like the energy she had released was trying to push its way back into her brain. She resisted, not looking away from the hovering spirit, and the pressure sud-denly stopped. The glowing eyes seemed to blink, and the swirling cloud resolved itself into a rippling collection of mist, hovering, waiting. Waiting for her to command it.

Kellan realized she was holding her breath and let it out in a sigh, brushing the back of one hand across her forehead to wipe away the sweat that had gathered there. She looked over at Lothan and a wide grin spread across her face. Her teacher only raised an eyebrow and got up from his stool with a slightly bored, jaded look. He stepped closer to the hovering spirit and looked it over. He held his left hand open and moved it around the outermost edges of the spirit's misty form, and wrinkled his prominent nose as he sniffed the air. If the spirit noticed any of this testing, it didn't react, and kept its eyes on Kellan.

Finally, Lothan straightened up. "Congratulations," he said. "You have successfully summoned a complete, albeit minor, air elemental. The spirit clearly bears the stamp of your aura, so I would say it is properly bound in your service."

Kellan glanced from Lothan to the hovering spirit. It remained impassive, waiting for her to command it.

"What do I do now?" she asked.

"You can dismiss it," Lothan said. "I think we've done enough for tonight. You can call it again as you need it with far less effort than it took to summon and bind it. Go ahead." He returned to his stool while Kellan took a deep breath, recalling the techniques she'd studied and practiced under Lothan's supervision.

It was almost like relaxing a muscle. She didn't need to speak, but simply turn her attention to the spirit and will it away, sending it back to where it came from, to await her call again. She felt a flicker of acknowledgement across the ether, almost like a spiritual nod; then the glowing eyes vanished and the cloud of mist seemed to collapse in on itself. It swirled, like it was being sucked into a hole in the air and suddenly, with an almost audible pop, it was gone. Kellan looked down. The incense burner had gone cold. The air in the basement was as crisp and clean as she'd ever known it to be, with a faint tang of ozone—like the clean smell after a rainstorm—the only scent remaining.

Lothan nodded approvingly. "Good," he said rising from his seat. "Now you can clean up and put things away before you go." He turned to leave, but Kellan stopped him.

"What about the circle?" she asked.

"What about it?"

"Well, it can be reused . . ." she began, and Lothan shook his head.

"I prefer a clean working space, so for your next lesson you'll just have to start over again." He paused by the stairs to toss Kellan a cleaning rag hanging from one side of the workbench. "It's good practice."

Kellan was left to scrub the chalk marks from the floor and to put away all the equipment in its proper place in the workshop. She looked forward to the time when she could afford a work space of her own, rather than having to use Lothan's. She would certainly leave *her* ritual circles in place until she needed to draw a new one. Hours of preparation and ritual, just to wipe it all away!

She relived the feeling when the air elemental regarded her and she knew—she *knew* she had it, that it was obedient to her will, there to do as *she* commanded. She couldn't stop herself from feeling a surge

of pride, and she grinned as she scrubbed the floor.
She could see why Lothan considered conjuring
important and why he seemed to enjoy it. *Still,* she
thought wistfully, *next time I'm going to summon a
spirit that can clean up for me.*

3

As soon as she was finished cleaning up, Kellan stuck her head into Lothan's study to say good night before shouldering her bag of gear and heading out the door. She was about to kick her motorcycle to life when her phone rang.

"Yeah?" she asked. There was no ID on the display, which was standard operating procedure for the kind of calls Kellan got.

"I've got us a job," Midnight said without preamble. "You feeling up for it?"

Kellan smiled fiercely. "Where and when do you want me to meet you?" Midnight gave her the place and time, and Kellan agreed to be there. Snapping the phone closed, she kicked her bike to life and roared off into the night. Her blood was pumping even more than it had during the summoning. This was a kind of magic, too—shadowrunner magic. There was a job to do, and Kellan had never felt more ready.

The place was a nightclub called the Alabaster Maiden, on 12th and East Mercer downtown, a modest drive from Lothan's place. Kellan had heard of it, but had never been there. Since it was fairly early in the evening (in shadowrunner time) when she arrived, the club was still pretty quiet.

She found a place to park her bike and headed up the club's broad stone steps. A young elf woman, her blond hair streaked with fluorescent pink, checked the ID on Kellan's credstick and deducted the cover charge. Kellan's ID didn't give her real name, and also said she was over twenty-one—to facilitate business in Seattle's nightspots. The elf waved her in without a second glance.

The broad foyer was floored in black marble, with tall greenery in granite planters flanking the entrances and exits. They were checking coats to one side, but Kellan kept hers on and climbed the second set of steps leading up to the club itself.

In the entryway stood the nightclub's namesake, a life-sized statue of a woman made of almost translucent white stone. She stood as if poised to come to life and move, glancing over one shoulder, a wry, almost smug look on her face. She wore close-fitting leathers and a revealing top under a short jacket, and her wavy hair cascaded past her shoulders.

Kellan looked up at the statue, standing on a waist-high pedestal of black marble, and wondered. Urban legend said the Alabaster Maiden was actually one of Seattle's first street magicians, back in the years just after the Awakening. According to the story, she overreached her powers one day and was accidentally turned to stone. The club owner bought the statue at auction and arranged to have it displayed; as memorial, warning or revenge, no one knew.

Thinking for a moment what it must be like to be petrified, trapped, for decades, Kellan started to peer closer at the statue. She summoned her inner vision to look, not with her physical eyes, but with her mystic senses.

"Kellan." The sound of her name and a gentle touch on her arm jolted Kellan back to the present. She spun to see Midnight standing there.

"I didn't think you saw me," she smiled, and Kellan blushed in spite of herself.

"I didn't," she replied. "I was just . . . thinking."

"Quite a piece of work, isn't it?"

Kellan glanced back at the statue. "Yeah."

"You think the rumors are true?" Midnight asked, leading Kellan toward a cluster of tables off to the side of the lounge area.

"I really don't know. Do you?"

"I try not to listen to rumors," the elf replied.

A nearly full glass of white wine stood on the table. Midnight slid into the upholstered bench seat behind the table, leaving the wrought-iron chair opposite it for Kellan, who shook her head when Midnight asked if she wanted anything. A tiny shake of Midnight's head in the direction of the bar received a slight nod in return from the bartender.

"So," Kellan asked, setting her bag next to her chair, "what's cooking?"

Midnight took a sip of her wine and leaned forward across the table. "A client of a certain cyberclinic is interested in having all records of an extended visit there eliminated. And not just any cyberclinic," Midnight continued. "A top-of-the-line clinic specializing in . . . discreet operations."

"If they're so discreet, then why . . . ?"

Midnight shrugged. "My guess is our client prefers to not take any chances," she said.

"So we're just supposed to erase information?"

"That's it."

"I assume it has to be an inside job?"

"Yes. The datastores are protected offline—no Matrix access. We need to get inside, get access to the data and delete certain files."

"Sounds simple enough."

Midnight smiled faintly. "I wouldn't quite call it simple, Kellan, but I think it's something we can do."

"Sounds to me like something *you* can do," Kellan said, cocking an eyebrow at Midnight. "Getting inside a secure building and deleting data is right up your alley. What do you need me along for?"

"Magic," Midnight said simply. "Everybody's making more use of magic in security these days, and according to my information, this clinic can afford some decent magical safeguards. So I need someone who knows the Art and can work backup to respond to whatever magical security they might have. That's you. While I have my talents, magic has never been one of them."

Makes sense, Kellan thought. It was true that those with the means were beginning to rely on a combination of magic and technology to provide security, taking a layered approach and hoping the mundane measures would stymie the Awakened, while the magical security did the same to the mundane experts like Midnight who were able to overcome most technological measures.

"Plus," Midnight continued, "you've got solid computer skills—you know how to handle data, and you can take care of yourself if there's trouble."

"Wouldn't you be better off with a real decker?" Kellan asked. Midnight was right—she'd always had solid computer skills, and had invested in a decent cyberdeck and software since coming to Seattle. But Kellan knew her abilities fell far short of those of a professional decker like Jackie Ozone or any of the other codeslingers she knew.

"I think you're up to handling this one."

"And the client?" Kellan asked.

"Prefers to remain anonymous, of course."

"But if we're supposed to delete the client's info . . ."

Midnight smiled and raised her eyebrow. "Who said it was the *client's* files we're being hired to eliminate?"

Kellan snorted softly. "Good point." Blind and double-blind. No real surprise, either, since anonymity and deniability were primary concerns in the shadows. Corporations, governments and many other organizations hired shadowrunners because runners were difficult to trace, and so insulated their employer in the event the runners got caught or decided to make more money by selling out to the competition. Midnight probably didn't know who their employer was, either; most times, there were multiple layers of deniability between the fixer, who arranged for the talent, the runners and the client, who usually preferred to not know who was hired to do the job.

"So what's it pay and how soon do we do it?" Kellan asked. Midnight named a figure, and Kellan's eyes widened involuntarily. It was more nuyen than she'd ever made on a single run.

"That's your cut," the elf said, "assuming you're interested."

"How soon?" she asked again, as her way of accepting the job.

"Time is of the essence on this one."

"Then we'd better get started," Kellan replied.

"Excellent," Midnight said with a smile. Suddenly, a waitress bearing a tray appeared, and set a glass of wine on the table in front of Kellan as Midnight lifted her own.

"Always happy to run with a talented coworker," she toasted. They clinked glasses and drank, and Midnight began filling Kellan in on the broad strokes of the run.

They had only three days to plan and carry out the assignment if they wanted to get paid, so as soon as they finished their wine, they adjourned from the Alabaster Maiden and went to Kellan's apartment to begin planning. Even though the basics of every B&E run were the same, every situation was unique, so they had a lot of work to do.

After hours of reviewing the initial data and planning their tasks for the next two days, both women were ready to crash. Midnight accepted Kellan's offer to stay at her place for the night rather than going home. That way they could resume work earlier in the morning. Midnight sacked out on the couch, and Kellan lay in bed, her brain repeatedly reviewing what they knew so far about the run, until she finally drifted off to sleep.

In her dreams, Kellan was running, running through dimly lit corridors at once familiar and strange. A reddish orange light was growing brighter behind her, and she ran faster, feeling heat against her back. She looked behind her again to see if it was gaining on her, and ran smack into a wall, falling to the floor as she rebounded.

But it wasn't a wall, it was a massive troll. Lothan glowered down at her, bushy white brows drawn together over dark eyes.

"What are you running from, Kellan?" he asked her.

"I don't know."

"Just turn around and look."

"I . . . I can't."

"Why not?"

"Lothan, I'm afraid."

"Fear doesn't make things go away, Kellan," he responded calmly. "Fear simply makes things."

"I don't know what it is. . . ."

"The only way you will know is to turn and look."

The light grew brighter, casting Lothan's craggy features in sharp relief, shedding a glow the color of blood over his rune-stitched coat and the gleaming stone in his staff. Kellan felt the amulet she wore at her throat growing hot. She slowly began to turn around.

A shadow flicked across the edge of her vision, silhouetted black against the light, and Kellan felt a stabbing pain in her back. She fell forward, clutching the lapels of Lothan's coat as he sadly shook his head. Her back felt hot and wet, and her vision swam, beginning to go dark.

"Too late," the old troll muttered. "Too late."

"Lothan!"

Kellan bolted awake, her hand clutching the sheets and blankets in an iron grip. Her breath came in ragged gasps as she blinked in the darkness of the room, lit only by the slivers of moonlight and neon that found a way around the edges of the shades.

"Kellan, are you all right?" Midnight said softly from the doorway. Kellan started; she hadn't heard Midnight approach, couldn't see her in the dark.

"Yeah . . . yeah, I'm fine. Just a dream."

"I heard you call out Lothan's name." Midnight stepped into the room and glided to the side of the bed as Kellan pulled up her knees and sat up.

"He was in the dream."

"I always suspected that having Lothan as a teacher would be a nightmare," Midnight quipped, and Kellan gave a soft, humorless snort.

"No, not like that," she said. "He was just there. It wasn't about him."

"I'm sure Lothan would be disappointed to hear it." Midnight sank gracefully onto the edge of the bed. Kellan could see her more clearly now, clad in a tank top and panties as pale as her skin, eyes and hair dark as her namesake.

"Do you want to talk about it?" Midnight asked gently, and Kellan shook her head.

"No, it's okay. It was just a dream."

"Okay. I'm sure it's just pre-run nerves," the elven woman replied. "But if you decide you do want to talk . . ." She let the offer hang in the air.

"Thanks," Kellan said.

"No worries." She patted Kellan's arm reassuringly. "You go back to sleep."

Kellan slid back under the covers and closed her eyes with a sigh, feeling Midnight stand up from the edge of the bed. She felt better knowing there was someone close by. Midnight was right, it was probably just stress—wondering about how things were going to go on the run. Kellan relaxed, and soon she was asleep again; and this time, no dreams came.

On her way to Lothan's the next day, Kellan again found herself wishing he had let her keep the summoning circle. She had decided to ask the troll mage if she could use the workshop to prepare and perform another summoning ritual.

"Another one?" he asked. "Well, I'm glad to see you're taking the need for practice seriously. Do you need—?"

"I've got everything I need," Kellan interjected. "Thanks!" she called, as she headed down into the basement.

As she began constructing the summoning circle, she realized it was just as well that she'd cleared away the previous one, since this time she wanted to summon a water elemental. From their analysis of the situation, she and Midnight had concluded that a water spirit would be the most useful for the run. She would have liked to summon a more powerful air elemental, too, but buying ingredients for the water-summoning ritual practically cleaned her out of nuyen, and the process took a whole day out of their preparations.

When Kellan emerged triumphantly from the workshop hours later, Lothan took only a casual interest in her efforts.

"I assume things went well," he commented, without looking up from the book he was reading when Kellan came into his study to say good-bye, "since nothing has floated away in a flood." He flipped a page. Lothan was the only person Kellan knew who read actual dead-tree books rather than using a data-pad, or just watching a sim, for that matter.

"It went fine," she said. "No problems."

"Good."

"Hey, I might be out of touch for a couple of days."

"Very well," Lothan glanced at her. "Contact me

when you're back in touch and we'll plan our next lesson."

"Great. Later, then."

Lothan didn't comment on the time it took to perform the ritual—far longer than if Kellan were simply practicing—or on her plans, whatever they might be. Lothan had been working the shadows for longer than Kellan had been alive, and she knew he subscribed to the idea that business was business, and, if it didn't affect him, it was none of his. At least, that's how he expected other people to treat him. Kellan felt sure that Lothan, in contrast, actively kept tabs on things he considered likely to affect him. In fact, she wondered as she rode away from the troll's house, how did Lothan know she was conjuring a water elemental?

4

The cyberclinic was called Nightengale's, and was located on John Street downtown. It was supposedly named for "Nurse Nightengale," the persona of a decker who worked the shadows in the 2030s. When she made the big score, she retired and used the money to open the clinic. That, and the fact that Nightengale's clients *really* valued their privacy, told Midnight the clinic's security would be up to date.

The corner of John Street and 2nd Avenue was practically in the shadow of the Space Needle, just across the street from Seattle Center. Their synchronized watches read 11:40 P.M. as they approached the target. Kellan could see the monorail gliding along its elevated track above them as she and Midnight headed down Broad Street.

Just the sight of the monorail made Kellan wince as she recalled her botched run that nearly turned it into an instrument of death. Her eagerness to set up her own jobs and make a big score had led Kellan to go looking for a chemical weapon left over from the days of the Ghost Dance War. Only it ended up in the hands of Zhade, a toxic shaman who wanted to use it to poison the whole metroplex. Stopping Zhade's scheme had cost Kellan, both personally and professionally. It had been a near disaster, and she was determined that something like that would never happen to her again. It was why she was working so hard on her lessons with Midnight and Lothan, and why she was concentrating on getting work; she knew it would be a while before she felt ready to step out on her own again.

The weather had turned cloudy and damp during the day. The streets were slick with water, the clouds blocked out all but the city lights, and the steady rain kept people off the streets this late at night. There was enough traffic to blend into, but not enough to get in their way. Stowing their bikes in a spot not far down the street, the two women dismounted and made their way to an alley, where Kellan went to work on the first part of their plan.

It was easy to recall the water elemental she'd summoned. The rain seemed to shimmer as the spirit appeared before Kellan in its immaterial, astral form. She could command it to take on physical form, but that wasn't necessary for her current purpose. Reviewing the words of the spell in her mind, Kellan drew on the elemental's energy for additional power, and began weaving magic around her and Midnight.

"It's a low-power spell," she warned.

"I know, you only mentioned it about six times," Midnight replied. "Don't worry, it'll be fine. I just need to pass casual inspection."

Kellan nodded and spoke the final words, setting the spell in place. Suddenly, the slim elf woman in sleek synthleather was replaced by a slightly shorter human woman with brown hair. She was wearing medical scrubs and a lab coat under a long synthleather

overcoat. The stranger standing in front of her looked
Kellan over and smiled widely.

"Good job," she said, and even her voice was different
from Midnight's rich tone. It was higher and
squeakier. "You look just like her. How do I look?"

"Just like the trids we got," Kellan said. Just a single
day's surveillance of the clinic had turned up some
employees who were close enough to her and Midnight's
size for a disguise spell to work. It was fairly
easy work to match the details once the computer created
3-D models from the trideo footage for Kellan
to study.

"Perfect," Midnight said, "let's go."

Kellan did her best to look casual as they walked
to the clinic. It was a three-story building of mirrored
glass and chrome, set on the corner. Half of the windows
on the first floor facing the street were transparent
and showed the lobby, lit dimly from the doorways
beyond it. They avoided the front doors and went
around to the side employees-only entrance.

Midnight took a credstick from the pocket of her
coat—one they'd lifted earlier from the Nightengale's
employee whose appearance Midnight now wore. She
slotted the stick in the reader beside the door and it
beeped as the door unlocked. She pulled it open and
stepped inside, holding it for Kellan to follow.

"Keep your eyes open," Midnight said quietly, and
Kellan concentrated for a moment, allowing her
awareness to expand to include the astral plane. She
could see the auras around herself and Midnight, and
see through the spell concealing them. So could any
magician or spirit they encountered, she knew, so they
needed to be cautious. Kellan glanced back, and could
also see the shimmering glow of a ward placed around

the building to ensure privacy from magical eaves-
droppers and to guard against noncorporeal intruders.

"It's clear," she whispered.

"This way," Midnight said, heading down the hall.
They avoided the main lobby, and went instead
toward one of the small offices on the first floor.

"Evenin', ladies," came a voice from down the hall.
Kellan forced herself to take a deep breath before
turning around. A man in a uniform bearing the logo
of Wolverine Security Services came toward them.
Midnight didn't hesitate before returning his greeting.

"Hey," she said, "sorry, I forgot a report that's due
in the morning. I just wanted to duck in and file it
quick, so I can still get it in on time."

"You're supposed to sign in, Carrie," the guard
replied.

"I know," Midnight smiled sweetly with her false
face. "But I didn't want anybody to know I'd forgotten, you know? Please? It'll only be a minute."

"Okay, but check in with me before you go, all
right?"

"You bet, thanks."

The guard sauntered back toward the lobby while
the women proceeded to the office. Kellan sighed in
relief.

"Nice job . . ." she started to say, but Midnight
silenced her with a look. They had to stay in character,
and they had to get the job done as quickly as possible. Kellan pulled her cyberdeck out of its carrying
case and set it on the desk. She plugged it into the
desktop terminal and powered it up.

Midnight stayed by the door and kept watch through
a tiny crack while Kellan worked. The deck quickly
interfaced with the terminal, and Kellan launched a

spoofing program to circumvent the system's normal password protection. She didn't use the electrode net that would allow her to experience the deck's inputs faster, because it would overwhelm her normal senses, and they might need to react quickly, even with Midnight on the lookout. Kellan was especially appreciative of the customized software Jackie Ozone had installed on her deck; most would-be deckers were forced to program all their own tools, or make do with utilities purchased from people they couldn't entirely trust.

Tense seconds ticked past as the software of the two machines wrangled, then the terminal's image changed to a welcome screen.

"We're in," Kellan said quietly.

Kellan's fingers quietly flew over the terminal's keyboard. She started up the search function and input the parameters.

AKIMURA, TOSHIRO, she typed into the search window. Another password box appeared, and Kellan sicced the spoof program on it. Alphanumerics flashed through the box faster than the eye could follow. Then the box turned red and flashed.

"Damn," Kellan muttered, drawing Midnight's glance from the door. "System's getting edgy." Kellan quickly launched additional programs. She quietly smothered the system's concerns in a layer of soothing code, diverting its inquiries, flattering it with rapid-fire responses to checks for authorization. The software did most of the work far faster than she could even think about it. In a few moments, the flashing red box disappeared, replaced by a virtual folder. It opened to reveal a series of files: medical charts, customer information and progress reports.

Kellan glanced over at Midnight and nodded. She returned the nod and kept watching the door while Kellan ordered the terminal to download the files to her cyberdeck's memory. The scrolling bar on-screen showed the transfer would take less than a minute. As soon as it was done, Kellan selected DELETE from the system's menu.

ARE YOU SURE YOU WANT TO DELETE THIS FILE? the system inquired. Kellan hit OK and the computer responded with PASSWORD REQUIRED.

"Carrie, are you—?" came a voice from the doorway. Kellan turned toward it just as the security guard who greeted them opened the door. Before either of them had a chance to react, Midnight went into action.

Grabbing the guard's arm, Midnight dragged him off-balance into the room and twisted his arm behind his back in a powerful lock, pushing his wrist toward his shoulder blade. The guard involuntarily cried out before Midnight pressed a drug patch against the side of his neck. He continued to struggle for a few moments, but his efforts rapidly got weaker until he slumped in the shadowrunner's grasp and Midnight lowered his limp form to the floor.

A hard glance from Midnight, entirely out of character with the appearance she wore, allowed Kellan to tear her eyes from the guard and turn back to the terminal. She tapped commands into the cyberdeck to give the appearance of the proper code to get the system to delete the files, and to overwrite the areas where they were stored, to make sure it wouldn't be easy to recover them.

Midnight dragged the guard to the side and quickly moved back to cover the door. Kellan noticed that she had drawn her slim automatic pistol and held it at the ready. The sound of the keys seemed incredibly loud as she strained her ears for signs of any other sound. There was no response to the guard's strangled cry, no sound of alarm, nobody rushing to check.

The terminal finally responded and deleted the selected files. Kellan double-checked to make sure they were wiped from the system before she disconnected her cyberdeck and powered it down.

"It's done," she said quietly, stowing the deck back in its carrying case.

Midnight nodded in response, indicating with one hand that Kellan should remain where she was as she opened the door and cautiously looked out into the hall.

The beep from the guard's commlink made Kellan jump.

"Station One," the voice over the link said. "What's your status? Over."

"Go . . . now!" Midnight hissed.

"Station One, do you copy?" the voice said. "Station One . . ."

Kellan bolted out the door headed for the exit, with Midnight close behind her. She could hear booted feet on the tile floor, and—just as she hit the crash bar on the door, sending it flying open—she heard a shout from behind them.

"Halt!"

The shadowrunners didn't even slow down, dashing out the door and into the steady rain, running out of the alley. Kellan nearly collided with a knot of people splashing through the rain, heads down, wearing disposable translucent slickers over their street clothes. They came up short, staring in surprise at the women running past them, then scattered at the banging of the metal door and the yells of the security guard, who was brandishing a heavy pistol.

Two shots rang out, sending the pedestrians scrambling for cover. Kellan heard one bullet ricochet too close for comfort. Cars blared their horns and squealed, slamming on their brakes as Kellan dashed across the street. She and Midnight reached their bikes at the same time, mounting up and kicking them to life. Midnight turned and fired a shot in the direction of the guard as he rushed toward them. It went wide, but forced him to seek cover against the corner of a building.

"Go!" Midnight said, and they roared away from the curb as two more shots from the security guard splashed in the street nearby, cars swerving out of the way as the motorcycles dodged around them. Kellan nearly lost control of the bike on the rain-slick pavement, but managed to right herself as they put on a burst of speed heading down John Street.

By the time they peeled around the corner to Western Avenue, Midnight gave Kellan the thumbs-up. There were no signs of pursuit, but still they kept their speed up, and an eye out for Lone Star patrols as they headed down the waterfront. When the sides of the massive reconstruction of the Renraku Arcology loomed high overhead in front of them, Midnight took a left turn into the heart of downtown Seattle, heading uphill away from the waterfront. Traffic thickened, and they merged into it as Kellan allowed herself to breathe a small sigh of relief. The run was done, and they'd gotten away clean.

5

They pulled up outside Dante's Inferno, just a few blocks from the arcology. As usual, the Inferno was packed with would-be club-goers. There was a line stretching down the block, under a temporary tarp tunnel bounded by porta-barriers. Midnight pulled her bike into the alley alongside the club, and Kellan followed. They parked their bikes in empty slots at the rack, which automatically locked them down when they inserted their credsticks in the slot at the top of the rack and keyed in their parking slot number. Kellan had dropped the disguise spell once they were out of sight of the clinic, and Midnight shook rainwater from her hair, grinning widely.

"How about I buy you a drink?" she asked Kellan, who smiled in response.

"Best idea I've heard all night."

The two of them headed past the line of hopefuls waiting to get into the club and right up to the massive troll barring their way at the door. He topped three meters, and the tailored tux barely contained his bulging muscles as he stood with arms folded across his massive chest, looking down from his post. Curling horns like a ram's swept back from a shaved pate that showed faint black stubble.

"Hoi, Newt," Kellan said, and the troll answered her smile with one of his own, showing his tusks.

"Hey, Kellan," he rumbled. "Midnight. Zappinin'?"

"Business is good," Midnight answered, brushing one hand along Newt's massive forearm. She rested her fingers near his wrist for a moment. "*Very* good, and we're looking to celebrate."

Newt smiled again, this time slow and sly. "Well, then, you came to the right place." He stood aside and lifted the velvet rope for the two of them to enter. "Right this way, ladies," he said with a bow. Midnight favored him with a dazzling smile and swept past like royalty given her rightful due. Kellan paused for a moment, as always, to savor the jealous looks from the wannabe clubbers, who must be wondering who these women were and how they rated.

"I might be meeting some friends . . ." she told Newt in a low voice.

"No problem," he said. "Just have 'em tell me you're expecting them."

Kellan nodded, doing her best to keep the swelling pride she felt from showing too much. She remembered when she couldn't get a bouncer at the Inferno or Underworld 93 to give her the time of day. Now her name was opening doors for other people. She really felt like *somebody,* like she was putting past mistakes behind her.

She caught up with Midnight in the foyer of the club, decorated in lush wine-dark velvet and gold, just as she hit the steps leading up to the main entrance. Reddish light pulsed from within, and the flaming letters over the doorway warned all who entered to abandon hope. Kellan found it ironic tonight, since she felt more hopeful than she had in a while.

Beyond the main entrance, Dante's Inferno was laid out as a showplace and spectacle for the in-crowd of Seattle. The central area was a giant cylinder, seven stories tall, with spiral ramps and floors made of transparex, so you could look up or down through them to see the whole of the club. Down the hollow core burned a column of holographic fire, where images of nude figures writhed—in pleasure or torment, it was difficult to tell. Surrounding the transparent dance floors were bars and seating for patrons to drink and people-watch.

There was plenty to watch, as usual. Dante's attracted a young crowd with money to burn. Corporate *sararimen* looking to ditch suits and ties and blow off some steam mixed with elves in the latest designer fashions; club-kids decked out in synthleather, body latex and holocloth; and exotic changelings, or maybe just humans with cosmetic modifications. Kellan spotted several unusual shades of hair and skin color, scales and horns, along with at least one dancer with a swaying furry tail.

Midnight led them up the ramps to the second level, which was decorated predominately in gold, with Roman-style statues set in alcoves in the walls, some of them bearing coffers and jars overflowing with golden coins that seemed to spill out endlessly—a clever holographic projection. This level was devoted to Greed, just as the first level of the Inferno was dedicated to Envy (for those waiting to get into the club surely envied those already inside). Each of the other levels reflected another of the seven deadly sins in an orgy of overindulgence.

They ordered drinks at the bar. When those arrived, Midnight lifted her glass and favored Kellan with a smile.

"Here's to a good night's work," she said. They clinked glasses, and Kellan relished her Forbidden Apple martini (one of Dante's specialties). Midnight took a sip of her own drink, then held up a hand to speak as she swallowed.

"Mmmm, speaking of which," she said. "We should make sure business is taken care of. Is the data all set?"

Kellan opened her cyberdeck's carrying case and popped the optical chip out of the deck's drive, holding it out to Midnight.

"Right here."

"Good," she said, plucking the chip from Kellan's fingers and turning it over in her own. She slipped it into one of the pockets of her jacket, producing a credstick in return. Kellan took out her own credstick and touched it to Midnight's. The sticks swapped bits, and funds were transferred into Kellan's account.

"Now I can buy the next round," Kellan said.

"Sorry," Midnight replied, taking another sip of her drink. "But I can't stay. We still have to conclude the deal."

Kellan looked crestfallen. She'd been looking forward to celebrating their good fortune. "I'll come with you," she said, but Midnight shook her head.

"Sorry, but this is a one-on-one meeting. It's what the Johnson wants. Maybe next time. You have fun and I'll let you know when everything is squared away. Maybe I can swing back afterward."

"Null sheen," Kellan replied. Midnight finished her

drink and stood to leave. As she stood, she leaned in to Kellan, resting a hand on her arm.

"You did a good job tonight," she said.

"Thanks," Kellan smiled. "You, too."

After Midnight left, Kellan thought briefly about calling it a night, but then reached for her phone. *Frag that,* she thought. *I don't get to celebrate a big payout that often.* She started calling around to see if some of her friends were available; after all, there was no point in having clout at a place like Dante's if you didn't use it.

Liada and Silver Max weren't around, but Kellan did get hold of Tamlin and invited him to meet her at the club.

"Hey, Tam, I've got another call, I'll see ya soon," she said as the call waiting on her phone beeped. She glanced at the ID on the screen before answering.

"G-Dogg," she said. "I was just about to call you."

"Kellan, where you at?" he asked.

"Dante's, you wanna come by for a drink? I'm buying. . . ."

"Hey, sounds good, and I've got some news."

"What's up?"

"Tell you when I get there. Later."

Kellan pressed the END button on her phone, wondering about G-Dogg's news.

Orion showed up at the club first, dressed for a night out, and Kellan's face lit up when she spied him down on the first floor of the club heading for the ramp.

Tamlin O'Ryan was an elf, like Midnight, and carried himself with a similar catlike grace. But where Midnight was a panther, disappearing into the shadows,

Tamlin was a lion, fierce and proud. He'd been a member of the Ancients, the biggest elven gang in Seattle, until Kellan discovered someone was using his gang as pawns, setting them up for a fall. She'd managed to convince Orion of the facts, but he couldn't convince the gang's leader, and got kicked out for his trouble. Even though Kellan was eventually proven right, Orion was through with the Ancients. He still carried himself like a street warrior, though, always ready for a fight.

He wore the same leather jacket he'd always worn, the Ancients emblem long ago removed from the back, but the ballistic cloth lining as serviceable as ever. Part of his dark hair was pulled back in a high tail like a samurai, the rest allowed to fall free to his shoulders, partly covering his pointed ears. Black jeans covered the tops of heavy motorcycle boots. The only real color was his forest green shirt, decorated with Celtic knot-work around the square collar.

"Hey, Kel," he said when he reached the bar. "What's going on?"

Kellan patted the stool next to her. "Pull up a seat and have a drink," she said. "Business was good tonight."

"Yeah?" he inquired as he sat down. "How good?"

"Good enough that I'm buying."

Orion grinned. "That's all I need to know."

As good as his word, Orion didn't ask Kellan about the details of the job she'd just pulled. It was better not to ask your friends questions they might not be able to answer.

"Glad biz is good for you at least," he said after the bartender took his order.

"Hey, things will pick up for you, too," she said, and Orion shrugged.

"Hope so. Too bad your job didn't need any more muscle along."

"You know . . ."

"Yeah, I do," he said. He knew if Kellan could have included him in the job, she would have. "I didn't mean anything by it."

"Null sheen."

"There's G-Dogg," Orion said with a nod, glancing down through the dance floor.

"Wizard. I called him, too."

G-Dogg was Orion's opposite in many ways. He was an ork, one of the metahuman races not blessed with grace or beauty. Instead, G-Dogg was more than two meters of muscle packed into a tee-shirt that stretched across his broad chest and over his bulging arms. The blue-gray shirt bore the logo of the Big Rhino, an ork restaurant downtown, and G-Dogg wore a black leather vest over it, along with a Native-style bone-and-rawhide collar. Black jeans, combat boots and leather wristbands completed the outfit.

If it were just his size and clothes, G-Dogg might be mistaken for a human biker who'd gotten muscle replacement surgery, but you only had to look at his face to see he wasn't human at all. He had the sloped forehead, beetled brow and pointed ears common to orks. His long black hair was a mass of dreadlocks, decorated with bits of metal and pulled back into a bunch at the nape of his neck. Metal gleamed from his ears as well. Small, yellowed tusks jutted up over his upper lip, giving him an underbite and a jutting jaw. Still, the dark eyes didn't miss a thing, and G-Dogg held that chin up with pride and attitude, as if he were the most glamorous simstar. He walked like he owned the place, and people treated him accordingly.

G-Dogg received waves, nods and shouted greetings from people as he passed. He spotted Kellan and Orion at the bar as soon as he hit the second floor, and headed right for them, nodding and acknowledging his other friends and acquaintances briefly. Though he seemed as friendly as always, Kellan didn't think he seemed in his usual high spirits, and she frowned in concern.

"Heya, Kel," the ork rumbled in his deep bass voice when he finally got over to them. "How's things?"

"Just celebratin' a job well done."

G-Dogg nodded. "Good for you. Let me give ya the news, then we'll get down to it." His eyes shifted to Orion for a moment.

"It's frosty," Kellan said, and G-Dogg shrugged slightly, as if saying it was Kellan's business whom she trusted.

"I got word there's somebody looking for you," he said.

"Who's that?"

"Guy named Toshi Akimura. He's been asking around real quietly, but the word came to me, just like it always does."

Kellan felt like G-Dogg had just reached into her chest and squeezed her heart. "What?" she said dumbly, unable to comprehend for a moment.

"Akimura," G-Dogg repeated slowly. "He's this big-time fixer, been round fer a while now."

"Akimura?" Kellan repeated, more to herself than anyone else. "That can't be."

"You know him?" G-Dogg asked.

"Do you?" Kellan countered. He shrugged.

"I've heard of him. Like I was sayin', Akimura is a big-time fixer—least he was a few years ago. Haven't heard much about him lately. He operated out of New Orleans for years, but I heard he has some old connections in Seattle."

Kellan swallowed, her mouth suddenly dry. "Must be why I've never heard of him," she said as casually as she could. "Did you hear anything about why he's looking?"

G-Dogg shook his head. "Nope, just that he's lookin' to talk."

"Did you . . ." Kellan began, her palms starting to sweat.

"Tell him anything?" G-Dogg asked. "C'mon, Kel. You know me better than that."

"Right, right, natch," she replied, wiping her palms surreptitiously on her jeans.

G-Dogg wasn't the type to give away information, especially on his friends. When Kellan first met him, she had been looking for him because she heard G-Dogg knew people in the shadows. He hadn't even admitted to knowing *himself* at first, since he didn't know who Kellan was. She had no reason to think he'd be any freer with information about her—at least not unless there was serious cred involved, and if that was the case, she didn't think G-Dogg would be at the Inferno telling her about it.

"Maybe he's looking to hire," Orion suggested helpfully. G-Dogg shrugged and cocked his head in a noncommittal gesture.

"Could be," he said. "Only way to find out is to talk to him. If he is hiring, it's probably pretty hot biz." He didn't indicate whether or not he thought Kellan could handle that.

"You know what he's doing in Seattle?" the elf asked, and G-Dogg shook his head again.

"Nope. Hadn't heard he was here until tonight."

Undergoing treatment at a top clinic, Kellan thought to herself. Akimura asking around for her *couldn't* be a coincidence, but how could he possibly know about the run on Nightengale's so quickly, and how could he know she was involved? Did someone spot them and see through her spell somehow? Did he know about Midnight, too? Could *she* have told him, sold Kellan out somehow? Why?

"Hey, Kellan."

G-Dogg's voice brought Kellan's glance up to meet the ork's, interrupting her out-of-control train of thought.

"What?"

"I said, do you want me to pass on a message to Akimura? Maybe put out some feelers and find out if he's hiring or something?"

"Yeah . . ." she said. "Yeah, sure, sounds like a good idea. Like you said, it's probably pretty big-time, right?"

He nodded. "Let me make some calls—"

"Hey, doesn't have to be right now. I invited you guys over for some fun. I just finished a job—I don't have to start looking for another one tonight."

"Never rains but it pours," Orion observed wryly.

G-Dogg regarded Kellan with an unreadable look for a moment before breaking into a wide grin.

"Hey, I'm always willing to help lighten yer credstick, kid," he said. "Let's get a new round. I've got some catching up to do!"

They got a table, and Kellan bought another round of drinks. As soon as they arrived, she excused herself to go to the bathroom. Once she was out of sight in the shadowy hall leading to the restrooms, she immediately took out her phone and dialed Midnight's number.

"Please leave a voice message at the tone," said a pleasant synthesized female voice. Fraggit, Midnight wasn't answering for some reason. Probably at the meeting with the Johnson.

"Hey, it's me," Kellan said curtly. "Hit me back." She hit the END button and jammed the phone back in her pocket. There was no way of knowing why Midnight wasn't answering. She could be handling a delicate meeting, off celebrating on her own, or just sleeping, for all Kellan knew. Or she could be in trouble. Kellan could do nothing but wait until Midnight contacted her.

Kellan went into the restroom and splashed some water on her face, taking a second to compose herself. G-Dogg was right about one thing: there was no way of knowing what Akimura wanted without talking to him. There was no point in panicking. She would wait until she heard from Midnight, and tell her what was going on; then they would decide what to do about it. Until then, Kellan was going to enjoy herself. *Live for tonight,* she told herself in the mirror. That's what she resolved to do.

Though she enjoyed Orion and G-Dogg's company, and even managed to dance like she meant it, G-Dogg's news nagged at Kellan, and the more time that passed without her hearing anything from Midnight, the more concerned she became, until she finally begged off the rest of the night a couple hours before the Inferno closed, proclaiming herself exhausted and in need of a few hours' sleep. Orion and G-Dogg offered to escort her home, but settled for getting her to her ride, once Kellan assured them she was more than sober enough to get to her doss on her own. She'd been pacing her drinking—easy, given her mood.

Orion picked up his katana from the weapons check, and as they left the club, they discovered the rain had stopped. The line of clubbers outside had thinned, but not disappeared entirely. It was more like the party inside had spilled out onto the sidewalk, with knots of people talking, laughing, dancing and drinking out of flasks and cheap plastic bottles. Music blared from cars parked with the windows rolled down or doors open, and even from the miniature speakers built into some people's jackets and clothes.

Newt gave them a wave as they headed out, and G-Dogg clapped the big troll on the arm. Kellan headed toward the bike rack, where Orion's ride would be parked as well. Weaving through the people on the sidewalk, Kellan heard someone yelling, but she didn't pay any attention until the voice said, "Hey, girly—you with the ork and the elf!"

She turned to look behind her as she walked into the alley, and the voice yelled, "Hey! Hey, I got a message for you!"

Kellan could see a dark figure momentarily silhouetted in the lights from the street. Then light flared red-orange in his hand, illuminating a ruddy face painted with upside-down black triangles over his eyes and a jagged black line across his mouth. She had a fleeting thought that he looked like a pumpkin carved for Halloween.

"Akimura says, 'See you in hell!' "

Then he drew his arm back and hurled a flaming bottle in a fiery arc.

"Look out!" Orion shouted, slamming into Kellan and pushing them both against the near wall just as the Molotov cocktail crashed to the ground where they had been standing, spreading ghostly blue alcohol flames edged in yellow.

G-Dogg cursed and slapped at where drops of burning liquid had splashed his arm and vest. That's when Kellan saw that the bottle-thrower had friends backing him up. Friends with faces made up like jack-o'-lanterns, wielding knives and clubs and, in one case, a burning torch. They charged.

Orion moved to meet them, ducking under a swinging club to punch its wielder in the solar plexus. The man doubled over, dropping his weapon. The elf followed through by bringing his knee up into the man's chin, snapping his head back and sending him sprawling. As he turned, Orion whipped the long carrying case off his back and into his hand.

G-Dogg stepped between the gang and Kellan, catching one knife-wielder's wrist in his massive hand. He twisted hard and the man—little more than a punk kid—yelled in pain before the ork punched him hard in the face, sending him tumbling back into one of his friends.

By this point, onlookers were rushing to the mouth of the alley and cheering for one side or the other. A woman with her head shaved and painted in red and black snarled and came at Kellan with a bowie knife. There was a loud *crack* as Orion hit the woman in the back of the head with the end of his sword's carrying case, sending her stumbling to the side.

Kellan seized the opening. Hunkering down next to a puddle collected in a depression along the side of the alley, she held out a hand and whispered the words of the binding ritual she had so recently performed, reaching out to and *through* the water, out into the depths of the astral plane, where her call was heard and answered.

The puddle suddenly roiled like a boiling pot, and a swirling column of water rose, the rainwater collected in the alley drawn to it like a magnet. Streamers of water split off from its sides, stretching out to form arms, and a mass of white foam capped its head like a crown. The spectacle of the manifesting water elemental brought the brawl to a sudden halt.

"Mage!" one of the gang called out, and several of them dropped their makeshift weapons as they turned and ran for the end of the alley. The spectators parted to let them through, and even moved back a couple of steps from the looming shape swaying near Kellan. Even in the Sixth World, it wasn't every day they saw a mage call up an elemental in an alley. G-Dogg grabbed Orion's arm to keep the elf from going after the fleeing gang members.

"Let 'em go," he growled, and Orion took one last glance at their backs before easing his arm from the ork's grasp and turning back toward Kellan.

She slumped against the wall until the gangers were out of sight. Then she raised her hand toward the elemental once again. *Return,* she commanded silently, *to where you came from, and wait until I call again.* She felt the spirit accede to her wishes, and the pillar of water collapsed back onto the pavement with a splash, spreading across the alley and extinguishing the last flickering remains of the burning alcohol.

The show obviously over, and faced with the glares of three angry shadowrunners, the crowd quickly dispersed, going back to whatever it was they were doing, or moving on to avoid trouble. Newt shouldered aside and scattered the few that remained as he approached.

"You guys okay?" the troll rumbled, looking them over for any signs of injury.

"Yeah, we're just wizard," Kellan said bitterly, dusting off the sleeve of her jacket.

"Well, I guess we know what Akimura wants," G-Dogg said just loud enough for Kellan to hear.

"Yeah." She had a sick feeling in the pit of her stomach. "I guess we do." The cyberdeck Kellan carried over her shoulder and the data it contained suddenly felt very heavy.

6

"Where are we going?" Kellan asked Lothan, as he guided her into the darkened alleyway. Strange shapes seemed to loom in the shadows, just out of sight.

"You'll see," he said quietly. "This way."

It got more difficult for Kellan to see where she was going. She didn't have troll night vision to rely upon. She reached out a hand for the wall to steady herself and to have a point of reference.

"Keep going!" Lothan growled, pushing her roughly from behind.

Kellan stumbled forward, then tripped over something, falling face-first into a puddle of cold, oily water. She sputtered and coughed, the wind knocked out of her, and rolled over on her side. Her foot was caught on something—whatever she'd tripped over. A sack or . . .

Light flared in the darkness as Kellan looked down to see Midnight's lifeless eyes looking back up at her. Some of the elf's long, dark hair was floating on the surface of the puddle. Her dark eyes were wide open and staring into nothing, a look of surprise frozen on her still, cold, pale features.

"Oh, God," Kellan moaned. "Midnight. Oh, God. . . ."

A massive pair of booted feet stood just on the other side of the prone corpse.

Kellan looked up to see Lothan standing over her. One hand clutched a ball of fire, but the flames didn't seem to affect him. He just smiled wickedly, showing his tusks, the flames illuminating his craggy features from below.

"Akimura says, 'See you in hell,' " he growled, and with a *whoosh*, his entire body was engulfed in flames, a dark, shadowy bulk surrounded by fire, eyes glowing, crooked fingers reaching out toward her. . . .

The shrill tone of Kellan's phone jolted her awake with a gasp. She gulped in air, surprised and grateful that it wasn't burning her eyes or lungs. Then she fumbled for the still whining phone, hauling it out of her pocket and flipping it open.

" 'Lo?" she mumbled, rubbing her eyes with her other hand and trying to clear her head.

"Kellan, it's me," Midnight said on the other end, causing her to sit bolt upright.

"Midnight!" she said. "Where have you been? Where are you? Frag, what time is it?"

"It's morning, Kellan," Midnight replied, her calm tone cutting through Kellan's confusion, and making it clear she had no idea why Kellan was so out of sorts. "I'm calling to let you know how things went. Is there something wrong?"

"You could fraggin' say that. I think this Akimura slag tried to have me killed last night."

"What? What happened?"

"A bunch of Halloweeners jumped us when we left the Inferno."

"Well, that is Halloweener territory . . ." Midnight began.

"Yeah, except one of them said, 'Akimura says, "See you in hell"' before he threw a Molotov, then they rushed us. Midnight, how could this slag know about the run?"

"I don't know," she replied.

"So you haven't heard anything about this?"

"No. I just called to let you know things went smoothly last night, and the Johnson was pleased with the results of the job."

"Was Akimura the Johnson?"

"I don't know," Midnight replied. "I met with a middleman, and he said the client was happy with the results."

"After they came after me," Kellan said, "I was worried something might have happened to you."

"Was anyone hurt?"

"No, Orion and G-Dogg cracked some heads, and I called up an elemental and scared them off. We took off before any more trouble showed up."

"Where are you now?"

"At Lothan's place. I didn't know if it was safe to go home, so I asked him if I could crash here."

"Did you tell him why?"

"Just that there was trouble at the Inferno. He didn't ask."

"All right," Midnight said firmly. "I'm going to see what I can find out. You should probably stay put for now, until I can get an idea of what's going on."

"I can help . . ." Kellan offered.

"I'll let you know when there's something you can do," came the reply. "Don't worry about it, Kellan. We'll figure it out. For now, just lay low. Odds are this will blow over."

"Okay," she sighed. "Let me know what you find out."

"I'll call you later. Keep your head down, *wakarimasuka*?"

Kellan nodded, even thought Midnight couldn't see her. "Yeah, yeah, you, too," she said, hitting the END button.

"Ah, Kellan," Lothan stuck his head into the room. "You're awake. I thought I heard your voice."

Kellan slipped her phone back into her pocket and stretched, hands balled up into fists, arms reaching up overhead. "Yeah," she said, "what time is it?"

"Almost time for practice," Lothan replied. When Kellan flashed him a sour look, the troll returned a crooked smile. "But first, I think some breakfast and perhaps a morning toilette are in order?"

Kellan stretched again and nodded. "Yeah, thanks," she said, throwing off the blanket and getting out of bed. She grabbed her bag and headed for the bathroom, trying not to think of the image of Lothan standing over her and Midnight's dead body in some dark alley. She knew Lothan and Midnight had some history, and weren't too fond of each other, but she told herself it was just her imagination getting out of control, the stress after the run-in with the Halloweeners. That had to be it.

The Jackal's Lantern was naturally closed during the daylight hours, its patrons and hangers-on usually staggering back home (or wherever it was they slept it off) in the early hours before dawn. The front door was locked, the shades drawn, the CLOSED sign flipped on in the window, and no doubt whatever passed for a security system in the place switched on to deal with the daytime predators of Redmond.

Midnight took only passing notice of these things, and made her way around to the alley entrance. The narrow passage was strewn with trash that had been ground down into the asphalt so many times it was practically part of the alley surface. The brick exterior of the rear of the bar was, if possible, even more layered with graffiti than the front, covering every centimeter of the metal door and the exposed pipes and wires. She was a little surprised it didn't cover the guy who was lounging against the wall in a metal folding chair. Though if you were willing to count his face paint as graffiti, she guessed it did.

The kid appeared to be of a mixed Hispanic heritage, with dark hair shaved down to little more than black stubble across his skull. Upside down black triangles were painted over his eyes, a jagged black grin across his mouth. A black tank top clung to his skinny torso, and loose-fitting black pants with orange trim and piping sagged from his waist, held up by a discarded seat belt turned into a fashion accessory.

He jumped to his feet when Midnight came into the alley; she gave him the barest nod of acknowledgment, feeling his eyes assessing her. He slotted a credstick in the door and pushed it open as she approached, and Midnight favored him with a brush of her fingers across his chin and a dazzling smile.

"Thanks," she said as she breezed past into the back of the bar, paying the sentry no further mind, and allowing the door to swing shut behind her. Midnight kept alert for any signs of trouble as she made her way past the storeroom and what passed for a kitchen, and out into the bar itself.

The Jackal's Lantern was decorated—if such a term applied—like some sort of demented concentration camp: coils of barbed wire running across the tops of the backs of the booths; mutilated dolls dressed in black dangling from nooses or shut into wire cages hanging from the ceiling; parts of mannequins festooned with bits of black and orange crepe paper, and rubber Halloween masks nailed to the walls, along with black-light posters, and light-up orange plastic jack-o'-lanterns on the tables. The shades were drawn so that only narrow, hot bands of light cut through the cool dimness of the place, painting stripes on the floor to match the very old-fashioned striped prison clothes of some of the dolls.

The gang members sitting at the tables and stools scattered throughout the bar were subdued. A few were idly playing pool, but most were just talking, drinking and smoking, creating a faint haze that hung near the ceiling. The quiet buzz of activity became complete silence the moment Midnight walked through the door. A dozen pairs of eyes focused on her.

She headed unerringly toward the one ganger sitting at the bar. He was wearing a rubber mask that was a poorly made imitation of a troll's face. The dark eyes behind the mask were surrounded by puckered scar tissue, and they narrowed as Midnight approached. A blunt-fingered hand stabbed out a cigarette in a cheap tin ashtray on the bar, then he leaned forward, elbow resting on one knee, his other hand on the bar, looking like he was ready to pounce.

"Do you have it?" he asked in a gravely voice. Midnight's expression didn't change.

"Ever consider the theater, Slash?" she asked, and

beneath the edge of the mask the gang leader's mouth twisted in a bitter smile.

"What the frag are you talkin' about?"

"The performance last night. I understand there was some improvisation. Was that your direction?"

"Hey, we got the job done, and nobody got hurt," he growled, "and nobody needs to, as long as we get what we were promised."

Midnight was well aware of the other Halloweeners on their feet, none of them more than three or four meters away from where she stood. In particular, she took note of the ork with the livid scar down one side of his face that gave him a kind of lopsided grin, standing quite close to Slash, black-gloved hands resting near the heavy knife sheathed at his belt.

"I expect to get what I pay for," Midnight replied coolly, not taking her eyes off of Slash.

"And you got it."

"Close enough, I suppose," she said. She reached into one of the pockets at her waist and produced a credstick, which she tossed into the air. Slash caught it with ease, turning it over in his fingers.

"It's all there," she said, "certified, but it's encoded. I'll transmit you the code on my way back downtown."

If the Halloweeners' leader was surprised or disappointed by Midnight's caution, the mask covered it. He set the credstick down on the bar, one hand covering it.

"You've got my number," was all he said, and Midnight nodded.

"I do, and I'll keep it in mind in the event that any further opportunities come up."

Midnight didn't look back when she walked away from Slash, deliberately didn't make eye contact with any of the Halloweeners, trusting to Slash's desire for the credit over any momentary fun he might get from causing her trouble. He might be crazy, but he wasn't stupid; the Halloweeners let Midnight walk out, and quietly resumed their conversations. The ganger at the back door watched Midnight go with another appraising leer.

She waited until she was a few kilometers from the Jackal's Lantern and just outside the edge of the Redmond Barrens before she pulled over and took out her phone, tapping a preset sequence. It would unlock the escrowed funds downloaded onto the certified credstick. She probably could have cheated the gangers and gotten away with it, but she couldn't afford trouble at this stage of the game, and if a little credit in the hands of the Halloweeners furthered her plans, then it was a small price to pay.

Tucking the phone away and kicking her bike back to life, Midnight smiled. "Well, Silk," she said quietly to herself as she lowered the faceplate of her helmet, "let's see you get Kellan to listen to you now." Everything was going according to plan.

Kellan allowed the hot spray of the shower to wash away the lingering images of her dream, along with the cobwebs in her head. By the time she got dressed again—in her fatigue pants and a clean shirt from her bag—and towel-dried her hair, Kellan could smell something cooking in the kitchen. Her stomach growled, and she realized she couldn't remember the last time she ate. When a run was going down, in the planning and preparation leading up to the action, she often skipped meals or forgot to eat altogether.

In the kitchen, Lothan handed her a steaming mug.

"Coffee?" he asked, and Kellan accepted it gratefully.

"Thanks," she said, sipping at the hot brew, savoring its taste and aroma. Kellan was incredibly grateful at that moment that Lothan was a connoisseur who hated soykaf. He was willing to spend the cred it took to get real coffee—which wasn't as expensive in coffee-obsessed Seattle as it was elsewhere, but it still wasn't cheap. Out of respect for the quality of the drink, she had learned to drink it black, rather than adding soymilk.

Kellan sat down at the kitchen table, sipping her coffee while Lothan busied himself at the stove. Watching him handle the pans and utensils was like seeing a big man use children's toys, but he had a deft hand nonetheless. Lothan poured eggs from a carton into a bowl, and whipped them with some soymilk and dried herbs.

"Are you planning on a lesson today?" he asked, keeping his eyes on his work.

"Yeah, if that's okay," Kellan replied.

"It's fine. I just didn't know if your other business was concluded or not."

Kellan took a gulp of coffee. "Not exactly. Well, I don't know," she said. Lothan still didn't look up from what he was doing.

"Oh?" was all he said.

"Just a few loose ends to wrap up."

"I see. Well, I assume none of these loose ends are going to show up on my doorstep like you did last night?" Lothan poured the eggs into a pan, to the accompaniment of a sizzling sound, and began stirring. Kellan stared into her coffee mug. He had a point: by coming to him, Kellan had involved him, which meant he had a right to know at least some of what was going on.

"We had a run-in with some Halloweeners," she began.

"I know that much from what G-Dogg told me," Lothan replied, tapping the spoon on the side of the pan, then tipping the skillet to allow the uncooked egg to run to the side. "What he didn't tell me is why the Halloweeners decided to cause trouble right in front of Dante's place. G-Dogg and Orion seemed to have no idea. Do you?"

"The Halloweeners wouldn't mess with you, Lothan—" Kellan began, but she was cut off when the troll moved the pan to a cold burner and set it down with a loud *clack*.

"I realize that," he said, turning to look at her for the first time. "I'm not worried about some gangers, even ones as psychotic as them. What I'm concerned about is trouble from whoever convinced the Halloweeners it was worth their while to risk pissing off Dante."

"It's not a problem," Kellan said firmly.

"Well, good, then," Lothan said, scooping the eggs onto a plate and setting them in front of Kellan. "Then why don't you eat and clean up the dishes, then meet me in the study when you're done?" The mage left the room without further comment. Kellan heard the door down the hall close behind him as she picked at the steaming scrambled eggs with a fork.

As always, she felt bad not telling Lothan more about her potential problem, but, frankly, the less he knew, the better for everyone, including him. He was a professional. He knew the score. She didn't want to cause trouble by getting the old mage any further involved than he was already—he couldn't reveal what he didn't know. That, and Kellan didn't know if she completely trusted Lothan.

Drek, Kellan didn't know if she completely trusted *anybody*. That was life in the shadows. Everybody looked out for number one, and half of them would frag you just for some extra spending cred. The trouble was telling which half. It was one of the first things Kellan learned in the shadows of Seattle, the most valuable lesson Lothan had taught her so far. On their first run together, Lothan chose not to tell Kellan that he had his own, separate deal going with an employer who was setting them up. She stumbled across this knowledge in the middle of a firefight, and, fortunately for her, Lothan switched sides for his own benefit. It was "just business," after all.

Still, Lothan was the most experienced mage and shadowrunner Kellan knew, and he was teaching her how to expand and control the magical talent she'd discovered she possessed. She'd learned plenty about the magical arts from him, and now could do a lot more than just throw fire around. Like Midnight said, in the Awakened world people with magic were a valuable commodity, and spell-slingers were in demand in the shadows as much as anywhere else. Kellan owed Lothan something, didn't she?

She glumly pushed the food away and admitted to herself that there was no way she was going to be able to concentrate on anything Lothan wanted to teach her today—not until she knew more about just what she had stepped into. It should have been easier to let Midnight take care of things, but Kellan just couldn't wait around for something to happen. She needed to find out more on her own. She needed to *do* something, and she knew just whom to talk to about it.

Kellan got up from the table, dumped the eggs in the garbage, rinsed her plate and fork and grabbed her gear. She pulled on her jacket and threw the strap of her bag over her shoulder as she headed down the hall to Lothan's study. She knocked, then waited for Lothan's response before opening the door to the dimly lit room. The troll mage was ensconced in his massive leather chair, scrolling through some document on the small fold-out computer screen on his desk. He swiveled the chair around to face the door.

"Lothan?" she said. "I've changed my mind and decided to pass on the lesson today. I've got some stuff I need to take care of."

There was a pause as he regarded her, his face unreadable.

"Very well," he said, turning back to his work. "Will this be another extended sojourn?"

"I don't know. I'll stay in touch." She turned to leave, but Lothan's voice stopped her just outside the door.

"Kellan? Don't do anything foolish, and be careful."

"Yeah," she replied, shifting the strap on her shoulder. "I will."

As she was heading out the door, Kellan hit a button on her phone and held it to her ear.

"Jackie?" she said after a moment. "It's Kellan. Are you busy? I need some information about somebody...."

Anyone who didn't know her might mistake Jackie Ozone for a corporate businesswoman, with her casually stylish clothes, carryall for the essentials of twenty-first-century electronica, and the sleek chrome datajack at her right temple. She looked like just another of Seattle's many corporate execs and employees taking advantage of a pleasant afternoon to get away from the fluorescent lights and recycled air of their offices for a few minutes. When Kellan approached the bench where Jackie sat, she looked up from her pocket secretary, stowing it away in her bag and favoring Kellan with a welcoming smile as she moved over to allow her to sit down.

"Long time no see," she told Kellan. "What've you been up to?"

With a shrug Kellan said, "I've been busy."

"Mmm-hmmm," Jackie said, taking a sip of whatever was in the paper cup sitting next to her on the bench. "Making friends all over the place." Kellan looked at her and saw a sly smile.

"You heard."

"Let's just say word is starting to get around."

"Then you know why I'm looking for more intel."

"About a gang?" Jackie asked innocently.

"About whoever is behind them."

"Then it wasn't just random."

Kellan shook her head. "No, it was personal."

"Personal? Or business?"

"That's what I need to find out."

Jackie nodded. "Done any digging yourself?"

Kellan shook her head again. "Not yet. First I want to find out more about what I might be digging up."

"How serious is this?"

"I don't know."

"Okay," Jackie said. "Why don't you tell me about it from the beginning."

So she did. Leaving out the details of the run and Midnight's involvement, Kellan related the incident outside Dante's Inferno—in particular what the Molotov-throwing Halloweener had to say.

"And you're sure that's what he said?" Jackie asked. When Kellan nodded, Jackie mused out loud. "Toshiro Akimura."

"Who is this guy, Jackie? G-Dogg said he was some big-time fixer or something."

"He is—or at least he was."

"Was?"

"Well, last I heard he had dropped out of sight for a while. There were rumors, but . . ."

"What kind of rumors?"

Jackie shrugged. "The usual—that he made a bad deal or crossed the wrong person—nothing definite."

Something that might have put him in a hospital? Kellan wondered.

"Why would Akimura want to sic a gang on you?" Jackie asked, and Kellan shrugged.

"I don't know."

"Kellan . . ."

"Jackie, it's business," Kellan said stubbornly. "I'm just trying to figure out where all this is going."

"Sounds to me like the question is what have you gotten into," Jackie replied wryly. "But okay. Akimura started making a name for himself maybe eight, nine years ago. He operated out of New Orleans, managed a pretty big operation there."

"Shadow biz?"

Jackie nodded. "But his real business was information."

"Decking?"

"Dealing. He had a huge intel-gathering network,

but he also seems to be one of those guys who has a knack for learning things and understanding their importance or potential value at the time he gains the knowledge—even when it's not obvious to anyone else. He earned a lot of favors and cred by passing information on to the right people at the right time. And, he worked for a dragon."

"What?" Kellan said, a bit loud in her surprise, and Jackie looked around to see if anyone noticed, giving Kellan a look that told her to keep her voice down.

"A dragon?" she whispered, and Jackie nodded.

"Yeah, and not just any dragon, the great dragon Dunkelzahn. After the Big D bought it, word got out that Akimura had been working for him, and people naturally assumed that the dragon had known everything Akimura had known—and that earned Akimura a lot of trouble. No matter how philanthropic Dunkelzahn turned out to be, people didn't like the idea of someone spying for a wizworm.

"But Akimura still had his greatest asset—information—so he stayed in business. But things happen."

"That's it?"

"Kellan, fixers know better than anyone that information is valuable. They keep a low profile. When they don't—well, anyway, that's all I know." At Kellan's crestfallen look, she added, "I'm guessing you want more."

Kellan smiled. "Thanks, Jackie. You're the best."

"I'm not promising anything," the decker replied. "There might not be anything else to find. You sure there's nothing else you can give me to go on?"

"I can't," the younger woman said. "I'm sorry, Jackie, but . . ."

"It's not just you involved in this, is it?"

Kellan bit her lower lip for a moment, then shook her head.

"Got it. I'll be in touch." They got up to leave, and Jackie let Kellan go first, as she got her things together. As the other woman slipped past her, the decker spoke quietly over her shoulder.

"Watch your back, okay?" she said.

"I will, and thanks."

Kellan had nearly reached her bike when her phone trilled.

"Yeah?" she said into it.

"Kellan," Midnight's voice replied. "I need you to meet me right away. We've got trouble."

7

They agreed to meet in the U-District, and Midnight refused to elaborate any further over the phone, so Kellan kept glancing over her shoulder all the way there, fighting the uncomfortable feeling that there was a target painted on her back. She fidgeted in the parking lot near the Chinese restaurant Midnight had named, waiting for her to arrive, and feeling increasingly exposed every minute she stood there. She took a little comfort in the fact that she looked very similar to the university students who apparently used the parking lot as a regular shortcut on their way to or from classes.

When Midnight pulled up, she parked her bike next to Kellan's, pulled off her helmet and shook out her hair, setting the sleek helmet with its mirrored face-plate in front of her without dismounting.

"What's going on?" Kellan asked. Midnight looked grim.

"Akimura's on to us," the elf said flatly. "A couple of orks tried to introduce my head to the pavement not too long after we talked this morning. They found out it was a bad idea, but one of them mentioned Akimura's name."

"How did he find out?"

Midnight shook her head. "I don't know, but I think our client might have sold us out, or simply got careless. It wasn't anything we did."

"And now he's coming after us?"

"It looks that way."

"But why? It was—"

"Just business," Midnight concluded. "I know, but for some reason Akimura is taking it personally."

"Because we erased some data?" Kellan asked.

"Maybe, or maybe because he thinks we *have* the data. Do you still have a copy?"

Kellan nodded. "Maybe we can make a deal with him for it," she began, but Midnight shook her head.

"No way. If it's the data he's worried about, there's no way for him to know we're not double-dealing, that we won't sell the data to someone else after we take his money."

"Frag," Kellan muttered. "What are we going to do?"

"I've got an idea," Midnight began, but Kellan's phone rang. When the elf nodded for her to take the call, Kellan pulled out her phone and checked the ID before answering. It was G-Dogg.

"Kel," he said.

"Hey, G-Dogg," she interjected, "I'm kinda busy . . ."

"Null sheen. I just wanted to tell you, Akimura reached out directly to me to say he's looking to set up a meeting with you."

"What?" The look on Kellan's face made Midnight cock her head in curiosity.

"He wants a meeting."

"G-Dogg, he got the Halloweeners to try and burn me and now he wants to meet? Forget it!" Midnight's eyes narrowed a bit as she realized who and what Kellan was talking about.

"Yeah, it has ambush written all over it," G-Dogg said, "but I figured you should know. Funny thing is, Akimura pretended not to know anything about that biz with the Halloweeners."

"Did you believe him?"

"Nah. But I don't know what his game is. You in over your head, kid?"

Kellan thought about how to answer that, but realized she really wasn't sure. She looked at Midnight for a moment.

"Thanks, G," she said. "It's frosty. Let me know if you hear anything else, 'kay?"

"You bet," he said, and Kellan hung up.

"Akimura wants a meeting," she told Midnight quietly. "He contacted G-Dogg."

"And what does G-Dogg think?"

"That it's a setup."

Midnight's mouth quirked in a hint of a smile. "No kidding."

"You said you had an idea?"

Midnight nodded. "Yeah. Let's get the frag out of town for a while."

"Run?"

"Hell, yeah!" Midnight said. "Do you want to wait around while somebody lines up another shot?" When Kellan shook her head, Midnight continued, "While I was trying to find out more about Akimura, I ran across another job I think we'd be perfect for—one that gets us out of the metroplex for a while, maybe long enough for things to cool down and for Akimura to give up and head back to New Orleans."

"Where and for how long?"

"Tir Tairngire," the elf said with a smile, "for at least a few days, maybe longer. What do you think? Feel like a visit to elf-land?"

Jackie Ozone settled comfortably into her reclining chair and pressed the connector cable into the jack at her temple. It slid easily into place with a faint click, and she rested her cyberdeck on her lap, within easy reach of her fingertips. Already she could feel an electric tingle of anticipation, as well as the initial synching of her nervous system with the simsense interface.

She tapped the GO key, and a wall of silver-gray static momentarily engulfed her senses. She felt weightless, formless in a mysterious void. Then, just as suddenly, the world came back into focus, even sharper and clearer than usual—more real than mere reality.

In Jackie Ozone's place stood the cartoon image of a young girl of Japanese heritage with large, liquid eyes and dark flowing hair held back by a headband etched with circuit diagrams. Her flowing white dress fluttered and shimmered in a nonexistent wind.

She stood under an ebony sky crisscrossed with neon lines, and spangled with lights like stars. High overhead orbited pyramids, pagodas and whirling satellites. The land to the horizon was like smooth black glass, etched with glowing lines and circuit patterns. Cubes and polygons of pure white and in a rainbow of colors hovered just above the ground. They represented the myriad host systems of the Seattle Matrix, familiar territory to Jackie. The virtual reality of the Matrix was the decker's playground, battleground and home. With the cyberdeck's systems interpreting computer inputs as sensory data, a decker could interact with the virtual world as if it were real, but without the limitations of the real world.

Jackie stepped onto a dataline and, in a rush of movement, zoomed at the speed of pulses of light through endless kilometers of spun fiber-optic cable. In seconds, the vista of the Matrix shifted and she found herself elsewhere, standing beside a small, spinning white pyramid. There was nothing to distinguish it from any of the endless other systems, which was just as it was supposed to be. Jackie's virtual persona brushed a hand across the pyramid's smooth surface, her cyberdeck communicating a complex encrypted key to the host system. The pyramid opened, unfolding into a doorway, and she stepped through.

The Shadowland system was one of several pirate and underground data havens catering to the needs of those specializing in information: finding it, acquiring it and, most importantly, selling it to those willing to meet their price.

Beyond the doorway was a virtual representation of a bar, its surfaces all polished black marble highlighted by veins of white and silver, tables of gleaming chrome and smoked glass, and booths of dark, polished wood and soft black leather. It was filled with a menagerie of characters drawn from history and fiction, dream and nightmare. They chatted in an unintelligible buzz of conversation as ice clinked in thick glasses. Privacy protocols made it impossible to hear any conversation but your own.

Jackie spotted her contact immediately. Even though some patrons of the bar sat alone, as if waiting to meet someone, every persona was unique, custom-crafted and coded by deckers who made their own rules. Except one. This individual's persona didn't prove a reckless disregard for programming protocols, or show off an individual flair and attitude. This persona was a standard, realistic representation of a woman hidden behind a nondescript dark suit and stylish sunglasses—the very image of corporate conformity. The perfect mask of her face didn't betray the annoyance in her tone as Jackie slid into the booth opposite her.

"I hope this is important," she said tartly. "I don't like meeting here."

"Only you can be the judge of that," Jackie replied, "but I think you'll find that it's worth your trouble."

"If this information is so important, then we should meet someplace more secure."

"Trust me, Eve, there is no place more secure than Shadowland."

Jackie's contact considered that for a moment. Then she nodded curtly.

"All right, what have you got?"

"A name. Toshiro Akimura."

Although the features of Eve's persona lacked the refinement necessary to make her thoughts visible on her face, Jackie was an expert at reading reactions during conversations in the Matrix. The pause before Eve replied, and the way she steadied her voice when she did, told Jackie a great deal.

"What about him?"

Jackie shook her head. "No free samples."

"Just a name isn't worth much," Eve scoffed.

"Well, I guess I could find out if anyone else in the company is interested . . ." Jackie replied.

There was barely a pause before Eve responded. "What do you want?"

Jackie's persona beamed an impossibly wide smile.

"Twice the usual finder's fee, plus first shot at any follow-up work based on this."

"The usual fee plus twenty-five percent, plus a bonus, if what you've got is worth it."

"Done."

Eve's persona reached into her suit jacket and withdrew a small card, which she slid across the table. When Jackie's persona picked it up, her cyberdeck accepted a download of data from Eve's system, which contained the requisite codes to access the funds she had just unlocked as part of their deal. Eve waited while Jackie checked to make sure the data was correct.

"So?" she asked.

"Akimura is in Seattle."

"Why?"

"I don't know that yet, but I know it has something to do with Kellan Colt. He's been trying to set up a meeting with her. He also apparently paid one of the downtown gangs to cause her trouble—either a genuine hit that failed or a successful attempt to scare her."

"Colt? The girl from that cargo acquisition?" Eve asked. "What would Akimura want with some punk-kid shadowrunner? Did she do something to cross him?"

"I don't know yet."

"You don't know much, do you?"

"I know you lost track of Akimura and that you didn't know he was in Seattle, and I know that I can find out more, if you're interested."

"I'm interested," Eve said, "but I need all the details next time we meet. I want proof Akimura is here. I want to know why he's here, what he's doing, and the name of everyone involved in his biz, and I want to know if it gives us a shot at him."

Jackie nodded. "No worries. I'll come up with the data."

"I'm glad you brought this one to me, Jackie. I won't forget this. If it pans out, I'll see to it you're properly rewarded."

"Always a pleasure doing business with you," Jackie said, as their personas both slid out of the booth and stood. "I'll have more soon."

"Good hunting," Eve said, then turned and walked out of the bar. Jackie did the same before logging off the system and the Matrix.

She felt heavy as the sensation of her real body returned. She slowly opened her eyes, blinking against the perceived brightness of her room's subdued lighting as her pupils adjusted.

She checked her cred balance again just to make sure everything was in order. It would be even fatter after she tracked down more information for Eve. The company woman played it cool, but Jackie could tell she was actually excited about this intel. It was a pretty rare event for one of Cross Applied Technologies' top agents to go rogue. It was even rarer that he lived to enjoy his freedom, and the company had to be very interested in finding out if the apparently untouchable Toshiro Akimura was potentially vulnerable. So would Akimura's other enemies, for that matter.

Yes, this promised to be a profitable operation. She would pass on some of what she found out to Kellan, so that her friend could keep her head down and stay out of the line of fire. Kellan was a good kid, but she just hadn't developed the chops yet for facing off against a fixer of Akimura's caliber—not face him and hope to survive the encounter. Jackie didn't want to see her get hurt, and this way it seemed like she could protect her friend and rake in the nuyen at the same time.

Settling the cyberdeck comfortably in her lap once more, Jackie called up the system's display mode, overlaying floating screens of data on her vision, and began figuring out sources to track down why a shadow fixer who operated mostly in New Orleans was in Seattle, and what his interest might be in a young shadowrunner like Kellan Colt.

Icarus Ascending sustained its reputation as one of Seattle's trendiest restaurants because it served what it classified as elven cuisine: a northwestern fusion of traditional Asian, vegan and Irish/Celtic dishes with some creative reinterpretation. Most of Icarus' patrons chose not to question how a traditional cuisine could exist for a people who'd only been around for fifty years or so. If they thought about it, they usually chose to ignore the question and just enjoy the illusion Icarus created—an opportunity to step out of the mundane world for an hour or two and indulge in something exotic and magical. Naturally, a great many of the restaurant's patrons were humans.

Midnight hated the place. It was designed to appeal to faerieland wannabes and tradfant elves and dwarfs who wished they came from someplace magical and special. It was a childish fantasy of dashing and beautiful elves playing Celtic harps and living in tree houses, dwarfs in their stout stone halls drinking hearty ales and singing rousing songs. Given the choice, she wouldn't be caught dead in the place, but it didn't surprise her in the slightest that her contact wanted to meet there. And if that was what she needed to do to get the biz, then she could stand it.

She waited at the bar. It would have been easy to pick him out when he arrived even if she hadn't memorized recent holos of him. He was escorted to his table as if he were visiting royalty, the staff's deference so sickeningly overdone that you'd think they'd never seen an actual elf before—despite the fact that they themselves were elves. Midnight allowed him to settle into his seat and acknowledge the liveried waiter before she picked up her drink, slipped from the bar stool and strolled over.

She'd chosen her outfit for maximum effect. Rather than her usual close-fitting synthleathers and vest with numerous pockets, she wore a dark Ultrasuede skirt, slit up the side to show a generous amount of leg clad in dark, sheer stockings, and black suede boots with silver toe caps and heel accents. She had left her smooth raven hair down, so that it flowed freely over the shoulders of the deep blue blouse, which was unbuttoned to show some décolletage. A silver necklace with a Celtic knot-work pendant completed the outfit and sent a subtle message of their common heritage. The black synthleather handbag she carried concealed just enough of her usual equipment to make her feel not entirely naked. She didn't expect to need any of it, but she believed in being prepared, especially when walking into an unfamiliar situation.

"May the shadows fall lightly across your path," she said in greeting. The translation wasn't exact. She spoke in Sperethiel, the elven language, and every word carried multiple layers of meaning. A more traditional greeting would have been to wish the man a bright and joyous day; Midnight's implied a measure of daring and risk, and his answer made it clear he understood her perfectly.

"May you carry your light with you," he replied in the same language, suggesting the importance of honesty and cooperation among those who walked the dark path together. Midnight nodded her understanding.

"Won't you please sit?" he asked, switching to slightly accented English, and gesturing to the empty chair across the table from him. Midnight slid into it gracefully, setting her drink on the edge of the table. The man opposite her gave her a long, appraising look.

"Your facility with our language is quite good for someone who has been away from the Land of Promise for so long," he said. Midnight inclined her head gracefully, refusing to rise to the bait of his implication. She was not interested in playing his little games.

"Thank you," she said. "I do not have as many opportunities to exercise it as I would like."

"I can imagine."

She doubted that. "I'm pleased you agreed to this meeting, Mr. Telestrian. It wasn't necessary for you to come to Seattle."

"It seemed the most efficient approach," Telestrian said. "How could I refuse such an opportunity? Especially since the invitation came from someone I've heard so much about."

"Have you? I'm surprised. I would suspect it is forbidden to speak my name."

"It is," he replied, "but just because something isn't supposed to be done . . ."

"Doesn't mean that it isn't done," Midnight concluded, and he smiled faintly.

"Exactly."

"Which is precisely why we are here," Midnight said, and the man's attitude immediately became more serious.

"I found your offer . . . intriguing," he said, leaning forward slightly.

"I thought you might."

The exceptionally discreet waiter reappeared, and they put their conversation on hold while they ordered. If the waiter took any special notice of the woman dining with the wealthy and influential Timothy Telestrian, he didn't show it. After he withdrew, Telestrian returned his attention to Midnight.

"I'd like more details on the information you're offering," he said. "I need to know if it will be worth my while."

"I'll leave that for you to judge," she replied, "once I've placed it in your hands."

"I would be willing to provide you with a finder's fee," he began, "and have someone else retrieve the information. . . ." Midnight shook her head.

"I'd rather do this job myself," she said. "And if you want the information, then you need to go through me."

"A chance to visit home?" he inquired.

"To take care of some unfinished business," Midnight replied, and Telestrian arched a delicate eyebrow in response.

"I need to at least know the general nature of this information," he countered.

"Notes on a research project that was supposed to have been terminated by order of the Council of

Princes, and evidence that it was not, in direct violation of their edict."

A slow smile spread across Telestrian's handsome face. "Clear proof of defiance of a Council edict?"

Midnight nodded. "Plus possible links to similar instances. Certainly enough to start a comprehensive investigation."

"Possibly implicating others . . . ?"

Midnight smiled widely. "Possibly."

"And you're certain you can acquire the information?"

"I'm sure I can, with your help," Midnight assured him.

"I cannot be connected with this in any way."

"Naturally. There will be no reason for your involvement to be revealed."

"How will you—?" he began, but Midnight gently covered his hand with hers.

"It's better you don't know," she replied, and he nodded in understanding. "I'll only need a few things that shouldn't be a problem for you to provide, assuming that we have a deal."

Telestrian looked from Midnight's hand over his to her smiling face, and smiled in return. "I believe that we do," he said. "Shall we toast to the enterprise?"

"By all means," Midnight said, lifting her glass. "Here's to the resolution of old business . . ."

". . . and the creation of new opportunities," Telestrian concluded.

"I couldn't have put it better myself."

Glasses clinked, and Midnight threw Timothy Telestrian a smoldering glance over the rim of hers as she sipped her drink. If things went well, the new opportunities would be considerable; far more than just settling some family infighting—but there was no reason he needed to know that.

Now only one element remained to be put into place.

8

The gleaming sword slashed through the air, keeping a steady beat: one, two, three, turn, one, two, three, spin. Tamlin O'Ryan, dressed only in a loose-fitting pair of jeans, performed a deadly dance of flashing steel as he moved up and down the floor of his converted loft, in a warehouse in the district of Seattle called Tarislar, elven for "remembrance."

The dying rays of the sun gleamed on the sword's razor-sharp edge as it twisted and turned, as Tamlin hacked at imaginary foes on all sides, moving through the steps of the set with the ease of constant practice and the power of the magic flowing through his body.

Not all of the Awakened cast spells and summoned spirits. Some, adepts like Tamlin, focused their magical talents inward, on the improvement of body and mind. They gained preternatural strength and speed, sharper senses, amazingly quick reaction times. What other street warriors accomplished using cybernetic implants, adepts achieved with magical power, dedication to their art and training. Some said it made them something other than human, but Tamlin, an elf, had little concern for his "humanity" and little love for humans.

After all, Tarislar earned its name in memorial of events that took place many years ago, when the "human" government of Seattle rounded up metahumans in the dead of night and forced them into "relocation centers," intending to deport them elsewhere, claiming they were diseased, a threat to public health and safety.

Tamlin's father was among the first elves born in the world, right around the time of the Awakening. His son knew very little about him. Tom O'Ryan had been a student of history at the University of California—Berkeley, which was where he developed his great love of swords. When he learned he was going to have a son, he bought the unborn baby a toy sword. Tamlin remembered playing with that sword, but the Night of Rage took his father before he was born.

His mother was human. He remembered in vivid detail what she told him about the armed men coming to their door late at night. He remembered how she and her husband were led away to join the stream of displaced metahumans being herded down to the docks—the crude jokes about her being a "faerie fragger," unclean because she was carrying a metahuman's child. He remembered what she told him about the big warehouse, stinking from so many bodies packed together in one place, the sudden explosions, the screaming—

Tamlin's blade slashed down when the door buzzer sounded. He grabbed the sword's scabbard, sliding the blade back into place with a click, and grabbing the small green towel from the back of the beat-up chair to mop his forehead and neck as he headed for the door. The buzzer sounded again.

"Yeah, yeah," he muttered, "I'm coming." He draped

the towel around his neck and peered through the peephole to see who was there, hand near the hilt of his sword, just in case. After a quick glance, he rolled the door open.

"Hey, Kellan," he said with a note of surprise.

"Hey," she said, standing in the doorway. "Can I come in?"

"Sure," Orion stepped aside. The loft space wasn't very big, but it was almost palatial compared to the standard living space in the run-down elven neighborhood. The high ceilings and skylights made it look bigger, and the space was open enough for Orion to work out. Most of the furniture was secondhand, but a few personal items gave it character here and there: a Celtic-style wall hanging, the place where a spare sword hung from a peg, the blend of neo-Celtic elven and Japanese furniture and decorations.

Closing the door, Orion asked, "You want anything? Water or something?"

"Yeah, thanks," she said, and Orion walked the few steps over to the small kitchen, pulling two bottles of water from the fridge. He passed one to Kellan before opening the other one and taking a long gulp.

"So what's going on?" he asked. He set down the water, threw the towel back over the chair and picked up the tee-shirt draped over the back of his ancient sofa, pulling it on and tugging his ponytail out of the collar.

"Came to see if you were interested in a job."

"Yeah? What's cooking?"

"Data extraction . . . in Portland."

Orion nearly spit out a mouthful of water. He paused and forced himself to swallow, taking a gasping breath.

"You serious?"

"Yup," Kellan said. "Midnight has—"

"Wait a minute, this is Midnight's run?"

"She's setting it up. Look, I know you're not Midnight's biggest fan . . ." That earned her an incredulous look.

"You could say that," Orion snorted.

"But this is business. It's not personal."

"Does Midnight know you're talking to me?"

"Yes, of course she does," Kellan said.

"But she didn't want you to, did she?" There was enough of a pause before Kellan could formulate a response for Orion to pounce. "No, I didn't think so," he concluded.

"That doesn't matter," Kellan replied, shaking her head. It had taken some convincing to get Midnight to agree to include Orion in the run, but ultimately Kellan had won out.

"I only go where I'm wanted, Kellan."

"And *I* want you on this job. I convinced Midnight you had to come with us."

"Because I'll blend in?"

"Because you're the best one for the job," she said firmly. "And because I trust you to have my back."

Orion regarded her steadily for a moment before his expression softened.

"Okay," he said, "what's the job?"

"We go to Portland, do a datasteal, turn over the goods and get out. It'll be for a few days, maybe longer."

"Midnight tell you who it was for?"

Kellan shook her head. "Of course not. I'm not even sure she knows."

"Oh, I'll bet she does. I don't think she would be leaving town for a trip into the Tir without knowing."

Kellan shrugged. "Hey, it's a good opportunity and—"

"And I need the work," Orion concluded.

"Actually, I was going to say, 'And I've always wanted to see Tir Tairngire,' " Kellan replied, "but, yeah, that, too."

"You might find out Tir Tairngire isn't all it's cracked up to be," Orion said.

"Have you ever been there?"

Orion shook his head. "No."

"Have you ever wanted to go?"

"I could have lived there if I wanted to. My mom applied for citizenship for me as soon as I was born, and they granted it for me, but they wouldn't grant it for her."

"Because she was human?" Kellan guessed.

"Yeah."

"But there are humans living in Tir Tairngire, aren't there?"

"Sure, as second-class citizens so the elven nobility have 'peasants' to push around, but they make sure to give priority to their own kind."

"Okay, so I guess I won't be retiring there," Kellan said. "But it's still a good opportunity and . . ." She shrugged and looked away.

"And what?"

"And it's a chance to get out of town for a few days."

"Because of what happened last night?"

"Yeah. I think I need to let things cool off for a while."

"Who is this Akimura slag the Halloweeners were talking about? He must have some pull if he got them to jump."

"I guess he does," Kellan said. "Jackie says he used to work for a dragon."

"A dra—are you fragging serious?"

Kellan nodded.

"Wait, 'worked' for a dragon?" Orion asked. "What happened?"

"It was Dunkelzahn."

"Damn," the elf said. "So after the dragon got killed?"

"I dunno. I guess he was still in the game, but who knows?"

"And you really don't know how you might have crossed him, why he's after you?" Kellan just shrugged, and Orion arched his eyebrows.

"It was just a job," she said defensively. "We erased some data about him at a cyberclinic."

"We? As in Midnight?"

Kellan nodded.

"Great," Orion muttered.

"It was a job," Kellan repeated, and he sighed.

"Okay, you're right, it's probably a good idea for you to get out of town for a while. And if you're going to go to Tir Tairngire with Midnight, you *are* going to need somebody watching your back. So I'm in."

Kellan called Midnight to let her know Orion was in, and they agreed to meet early the next morning. Midnight needed to make some arrangements, and Kellan needed to get more of her gear and some rest before they headed out on another run.

Orion insisted on going home with her, and they rode in close formation down the highway.

"Akimura might be having your place watched,"

he cautioned. "It's the first place anyone would look for you."

"Assuming they know where I live."

"Kel, this Akimura slag knew you were at Dante's last night. He gathered intel for a *dragon*. If he's as hot a fixer as you say, there's probably not a whole lot he doesn't know about you."

Kellan wondered if Orion was right. How much *did* Akimura know about her? Was it even safe to go back to her place? She carried most of her essential running gear with her at all times, but she wanted to get more clothes, a spare sidearm, and a few other essentials. That's what she said to Orion, but secretly, she also wanted to find out if her home was still there. She'd worked hard to carve out her own small piece of success, to make a home for herself in Seattle, and the idea of it being violated made her angry.

Why was this drekhead making this into a vendetta anyway? Anyone working the shadows knew you didn't make business personal. She didn't have anything against him. Hell, she didn't even know who he was, even after the run, until G-Dogg told her. She would have been just as happy working for him protecting that data, if he'd been willing to pay. It wasn't personal until someone made it that way.

They pulled up outside Kellan's place in Puyallup. It was getting dark, so the streets were rapidly emptying, the daytime inhabitants of the area retreating behind locked doors as the nighttime populace of the Barrens stirred. Soon there would be fires burning on street corners to illuminate the night, and shouts, laughter and gunfire interrupting the residents' sleep. Even the edge of the Barrens, where Kellan lived, was mostly lawless. The police weren't paid to patrol or respond to calls in the area, so nothing short of a full-scale riot would get any official response.

They stowed and locked up their bikes before heading upstairs. Orion wore his sword and pistol openly, and Kellan found her hand straying close to her own gun as they entered the lobby of the run-down building and she keyed open the cheap maglock with her credstick. Her apartment was a third-floor walk-up, as the elevator in the building had long since broken down and nobody bothered to fix it.

The ork couple on the second floor was having dinner, or arguing, or both. One of their several children was wailing loudly, and Kellan winced at the deep voice yelling for the kid to shut up. She wondered for a moment if it was the mother or the father. Probably the mother, but she had a hard time telling the deep, accented voices apart.

She and Orion kept their eyes peeled for any signs of trouble, but there were none in the stairway, or in the hall outside her apartment. A quick glance showed no signs of entry: the door and its sturdy maglock were both intact. Kellan keyed it open, noting that the lock hadn't been scrambled. She turned the handle softly and pushed the door open as she drew her gun. Orion did the same behind her.

They went in high-low, covering the inside of the main room of the apartment. There was no one there, and everything looked exactly as Kellan had left it. She stepped inside quickly, and Orion followed, closing the door behind him. A quick check of the bathroom and bedroom revealed nothing, and Kellan allowed herself to breath a sigh of relief, holstering her gun.

"Okay," Orion said. "Get what you need and let's go."

"Go where?" Kellan asked.

"Back to my place. You can crash there for the night."

"I . . . thanks," Kellan said. She'd been going to object, then realized there was no good reason for her to refuse Orion's offer. Staying at her own place any longer than necessary when somebody was looking for her was foolish, and she didn't want to crash at Lothan's place again and further pique the troll's curiosity.

It didn't take long for Kellan to gather up what she needed, stowing it in a carryall slung over her shoulder. As she reached for the doorknob, a loud bang made her jump and reach for her gun instead. Orion grabbed her arm to steady her.

"It's okay!" he said. "It came from downstairs, probably just something thrown against the wall." They paused and listened and, sure enough, a fresh bout of yelling came from the apartment a floor below. Kellan dropped her hand to her side, letting out a sigh.

"Sorry, I'm feeling kind of jumpy."

"No wonder," the elf replied. "C'mon, let's get out of here."

It was fully dark by the time they got back to Orion's place, having stopped off along the way to pick up some food. Soon they were sitting on the floor of the loft sharing Chinese food out of folded paper cartons and covered tins. Orion was very proficient with chopsticks, but Kellan used a plastic fork to spear another piece of soy-based "chicken" covered in orange sauce.

"Not exactly what I figured life in Seattle would be like," Kellan said abruptly, her voice glum. Orion gave a short, humorless laugh.

"Why, what did you think it would be like? Glamorous?"

She shrugged, chewing before she answered. "I don't know. The shadow-biz in Kansas was strictly small-time, so I figured Seattle would be . . . *it,* you know? The big time."

"You haven't done so bad," Orion said, scooping up a mouthful of lo mein. Kellan shrugged again, picking at her food.

"Yeah, I guess. I just wish . . ."

"What?" the elf asked, cocking his head in a way that reminded Kellan of a curious cat.

"I just wish I had the kind of confidence Midnight has, or Lothan."

"If you ask me, you pick the wrong role models," Orion said, wrangling another bite of noodles.

Kellan gave him a hard look. "What do you mean?"

"You know what I mean," Orion mumbled with his mouth full. He stabbed the chopsticks into the carton and put it down next to him, chewing and swallowing as he did so. "What Midnight and Lothan have isn't confidence, it's arrogance. They're so full of themselves they can hardly get out of their own way."

There was a moment of silence as Kellan and Orion looked at each other across the short space separating them. Then Kellan burst out laughing. She leaned back against the side of the couch, holding her sides and laughing so hard tears started streaming down her cheeks. Orion looked at her with a puzzled expression.

"What's so fraggin' funny?" he demanded.

"Arrogant?" Kellan said, gasping for breath. "Midnight and Lothan are arrogant? Have you looked in a mirror lately, elf-boy?"

"Wait," Orion said, eyes narrowing, "are you saying . . . ? I am *not* arrogant!" As he said it, Orion drew up to his full height, proudly raising his chin. It was too much for Kellan and she collapsed into a fresh gale of laughter.

"Oh, oh, my God," she gasped, her sides starting to ache.

"I'm not," Orion repeated, less forcefully. "I mean . . . it's not arrogance, when, well"—his scowl began to twitch and split into a smile—"not when you're as good as I am."

He almost managed to keep a straight face, but Kellan's laugh was infectious, and a guffaw escaped Orion's lips. Then his haughty composure cracked completely and he started laughing right along with her. He lunged forward on his knees, covering the distance between them, and brushed his fingers along Kellan's sides.

"Arrogant, am I?" he said. "Who's the greatest swordsman you know?"

"No!" Kellan shrieked as the elf tickled her sides, doubling over as she squirmed and tried to escape. She was still pressed against the couch, and there was no room to maneuver.

"Say it!" Orion demanded. "Say, 'You are the greatest warrior in the world, Orion.' "

"Frag you!" Kellan gasped defiantly, then she shrieked again with laughter as he renewed his onslaught. She tried to fight back, but she couldn't catch her breath.

"Okay, okay!" she yelled. "You are—you're the

greatest, most amazing warrior in the world." Orion let up on her and sat up with a triumphant grin.

"See? Now was that so—*oof*!" Kellan bowled the elf over as she surged up from the floor. In an instant, Orion was flat on his back, with Kellan sitting on top of him, straddling his hips to pin him down. She grinned maniacally.

"The 'great warrior' should do a better job watching his back," she jibed. But Orion just lay there, looking up at her with an odd expression of surprise and wonder. Kellan's breath came in gasps after their struggle. He was suddenly aware of Kellan's closeness, her scent, the flattering flush the sudden exertion gave to her cheeks and lips.

"You always told me to watch out for the unexpected," she said to him, leaning down into his face.

"You're right," he replied quietly. "I did. You're a good student."

"You're a pretty good teacher." She slid her hands off his shoulders and onto the floor next to his head, bringing her face even closer. He could feel her chest brush against his with every breath.

"You're teaching me a few things yourself."

Their lips touched gently, then Kellan's hand slid along his neck, fingers tangled in his long, silky hair. She felt Orion's strong hands sliding up her back, pressing her to him, and she sank to meet him in a fierce and passionate kiss.

9

The woods where Kellan wandered were dark, lit solely by the waning moon and the few stars visible through the tattered clouds overhead. A mournful wind moaned among the trees, making them sway and whisper all around her. She was lost, with no idea where she was or how she got there.

"Hello?" she called out, her voice swallowed up by the darkness. "Is anyone there? Anyone?" The wind was cold, and she hugged her jacket close, shivering. The cold of the wind was nothing compared to the chill that ran down her spine when a familiar voice howled out of the wilderness.

"Kellaaaaaaaaan," came the bloodcurdling cry, carried on the wind.

"Orion," she whispered. Then she bolted toward the source of the voice. Branches whipped her face in the darkness, and she threw one arm over her eyes as she clawed her way forward. She staggered up a slope, weaving in and around the dark trunks looming up all around.

"Orion!" she called out, but there was no response, nothing but the cry of the wind.

The trees thinned and Kellan could see a rocky crag

looming ahead, deep shadows in the creases and cracks of the stone. Nestled at its base, in a narrow crack in the dark stone, came a fiery golden glow, like a false sunrise. Kellan put her head down and charged up the ridge toward the light. She paused for a moment at the entrance, resting a hand against the cold rock wall, her breath coming in ragged gasps.

"Orion? Tam?" she called out again, but there was no answer. The glow within the cave flickered, like a dancing flame.

Kellan ducked her head and went inside, then bolted to the side of the figure lying on the dark stone floor of the narrow cave.

"Tam!" she cried. Blood was pooling around him, glistening wet against the thirsty black stone. She felt it, hot and sticky on her hands, but ignored it as she tried to turn him over. He was still warm, but when she pressed a hand against his neck she felt no pulse, and his head lolled limp, his long hair matted with blood.

"No . . ." Kellan whispered, "please, no. . . . Tam . . ." She brushed aside some damp locks of hair, hoping for him to stir, for some sign of life. There was nothing. Light spilled out across the motionless face, relaxed, as if he were only asleep.

"Kellan," a voice whispered, and she turned to see the light glowing brightly behind her, so bright she had to throw up a hand to shield her eyes. Squinting into the light, she thought she could almost see someone, or something, there.

"Kellan," the voice called again, stronger this time, like someone welcoming a long-lost friend or loved one.

"Who is it?" she asked. "Who's there? I need help, he's hurt!"

"He's dead, Kellan, you can't help him."

"No!"

"You can't help him, Kellan. Let go . . ."

The light grew brighter and Kellan bowed her head over Orion, holding his body close.

"Kellan . . . Kellaaaaan," the voice called. A hand reached out to her, glowing like the sun. "Kellan!"

She started awake with a gasp, shaking off the hand on her shoulder and fumbling for the gun that should be holstered under her arm.

"Easy, easy!" Orion said quietly. "It's frosty. You were just having a dream."

Kellan took a deep breath, looking up into Orion's deep green eyes, wide with concern, his brow furrowed.

"Oh, God, just a dream . . ." she breathed. "What time is it?"

"Almost time to get going," Orion replied.

The abandoned car dealership was full of shadows and the smell of dust, ash and old grease. The windows were long since covered with panels of wood and plastic, the cracked glass alternately taped up or left hanging, with fragments of glass scattered and crushed on the floor. Since the building was dry inside and structurally sound, it likely had served as shelter for others before them, but it was empty when the shadowrunners arrived.

Kellan brushed dirt off her fatigue pants and shook out her jacket before pulling it on, trying to get rid of the dust it had picked up when she'd used it as a pillow in an effort to catch a little sleep on the floor. There was no knowing when they would get the chance to sleep again, and she hadn't felt well-rested since the run on the clinic. She nodded gratefully as Orion handed her a self-heating meal pack. Steam rose from it as she unzipped the metalized plastic. She snapped off the spoon and scooped out a mouthful of the flavored soy. It was fairly bland, but at least it was hot. As she ate, she glanced around the room.

"Where's Midnight?" she asked.

"Said she needed to get things ready," Orion said with a shrug. He was sitting on a discarded barrel, one booted foot raised, the other dangling near the floor, idly stirring his food. It was the first time they'd been alone since the previous night. Midnight had arrived at Orion's place early to make preparations for their departure, and they'd been working hard all day.

"Hey," he said hesitantly, "about last night . . ."

"It's fine," Kellan said quickly. "I mean . . . it's fine."

"I didn't mean—" he began again, but Kellan cut him off.

"Don't worry about it. It's no big deal. You're not looking for anything serious, and gods know *I'm* not looking for anything serious. I mean, look at how we live," she nodded to the dingy surroundings, sighing and stabbing her spoon into the meal pack. "What happened, happened, but it doesn't have to be a thing. It doesn't have to affect our professional relationship, right?"

Orion's eyes came up to meet hers, then he slowly drew in a breath and nodded.

"Yeah, of course," he said. "It's frosty."

"Great," Kellan said. "Good." She took another bite of food, but she'd lost her appetite and the processed soy protein tasted even more bland than before.

"Yeah," Orion replied, settling back to eat in silence. He hadn't taken more than a few bites when the side door of the building opened quietly. Both of them set down the meal packs and rested their hands on their weapons. As the slim form of Midnight appeared, shadowed in the doorway, they relaxed.

"We're all set," Midnight announced. She was dressed in her working clothes of close-fitting synth-leather, including a vest with numerous pockets for tools and other gadgets, under which she wore a holster rig. Another gun was strapped to her thigh, and her long hair was pulled back and coiled at the nape of her neck to keep it out of the way. "You almost ready to go?" she asked them, jerking her chin in their direction.

"Yeah," Orion said, picking up his food. They ate quickly, gathered their gear, and hit the road.

Midnight had picked up a midsized van, which was parked outside. They'd stashed their bikes in a safe location nearby, from which they could reclaim them when they got back to Seattle. At least Kellan hoped they'd remain undiscovered, since she really didn't want to have to replace her ride with part of the profits from this run. The van was nondescript and in good shape, though probably at least five or six years old; the height of anonymity. They loaded their gear in the back, and Midnight slid into the driver's seat.

Night had settled fully over the metroplex. In the distance to the north, Kellan could see the glittering lights and corporate towers of downtown. The Barrens neighborhood around them was lit only by a few scattered and sputtering lights, and a fire burning in a barrel a few blocks away. They watched carefully for any signs they were being followed and saw none, and

Kellan hoped that meant Akimura would lose their trail once they left the metroplex. If they stayed out of sight for a while, perhaps his attention would shift elsewhere.

They drove south out of the metroplex and into Salish-Shidhe Council territory. The border guards at the checkpoint took little interest in their passing, and, despite Kellan's worries, didn't check their identification too closely—probably a direct result of Midnight setting up her credstick to pass the guards a little something as soon as they slotted it. Soon they were on the road through Council territory, headed for the border of Tir Tairngire. Traffic was relatively light, and they made good time. After a couple of hours, they found themselves on a deserted stretch of road. Midnight abruptly pulled the van off the highway, killing the headlights but continuing to drive.

They drove for ten minutes, then Midnight put the van into PARK and consulted a portable GPS unit to determine their position, leaning back over the seat to show Orion.

"From here we go off-road," she said. "We don't want to go through the checkpoints required to enter Tir Tairngire officially, and this route"—she pointed to the map display—"will still take us to the border. You're certain about your contacts?" she asked Orion, who nodded.

"Somebody will meet us on the north side of the river and help get us across."

Midnight nodded, but Kellan could see a hint of doubt in her face. Quite frankly, Kellan was surprised to learn that Midnight had relied on Orion's connections in Tir Tairngire for help. He still knew some people from his days with the Ancients, an elf gang with ties to the elven homeland, and those must be the contacts he used to set up this arrangement. Kellan assumed Midnight must have contacts of her own in the Tir, but she apparently chose not to use them, despite her general dislike and distrust of Orion. Kellan was curious, but as long as Midnight didn't volunteer any information, she wasn't going to ask.

They continued off-road with the headlights off. The moon shed very little light on their path, but Midnight maneuvered the van deftly, her elven eyes piercing the pitch-blackness to pick out a safe route. Still, their progress was much slower than it had been on the highway. It took them longer to cover the remaining distance to the border than it had taken to drive the previous leg, which was most of the total distance of the trip. It was nearly midnight by the time the van came to a stop. Kellan collected her gear as they climbed out, and Midnight locked the van.

"Okay, it shouldn't be far," she said, again studying the GPS. "Let's go, and keep an eye out."

They hiked the rest of the way to the river, which ran north and west of the city. Kellan tried to watch for any signs of trouble as they went, but she had a hard time even seeing where she was going, and generally found the wilderness unnerving. She was a child of the urban environment, and the Awakened wilderness made her jumpy—a feeling reinforced by her last trip out of Seattle, when several things had tried to kill her. On that last trip, she'd had the magical safety net of a skilled and experienced shaman to rely on for help in dealing with the scary things that went bump in the Awakened night. This time, she was the only magician on the team, the only one with the skills to deal with hostile spirits or other Awakened creatures, aside from the magic of Orion's blade.

Kellan's hand strayed repeatedly to the amulet around her neck, her fingers brushing its warm surface for reassurance. Night birds and insects sang in the forest as they made their way toward the river and the city lying on the far side of it. Their progress was almost painfully slow, and they maintained silence as they walked.

After a while, Kellan's thoughts began to drift. She'd assured Orion that last night was no big deal to her, but was that really true? Kellan considered herself to be experienced; she'd had to grow up quickly on the streets, and she'd had her share of fun, but never a serious boyfriend, and certainly not a relationship. She felt there wasn't much room for that in the life she'd chosen. *Listen to me,* she thought. *Like one night makes this a relationship.* The whole idea was ridiculous, to even—

"Down!" Midnight hissed, snapping Kellan's attention suddenly back to the present. She and the others dropped into a crouch near the trunk of a huge tree. "Don't move!"

Suddenly, Kellan heard a thumping sound. It took her a moment to figure out it was coming from above them, and she was shocked when she identified it as the sound of heavy leather wings beating the air. Her breath caught in her throat and she froze, like a mouse suddenly trapped in the open as a dark shadow passes overhead.

The sound got louder. Orion's hand wrapped slowly and deliberately around the exposed hilt of his sword, but he didn't draw it. Midnight pressed herself against the tree trunk, GPS monitor held against her stomach to smother any light, head tilted back to catch every sound.

A wind stirred the branches overhead and a shadow blotted out the light of the stars and the moon. Leaves rustled and Kellan had the impression of a powerful bulk flying just above the treetops. Moments after it passed, a piercing cry split the night—the high-pitched call of a hunter. It sent shivers down her spine as it echoed in the dark.

It seemed like forever before the sound of the wing beats faded away, before Midnight signaled they could move, before Kellan felt like she could breathe once more. She stood, a bit stiffly, as Midnight took up the lead again. Kellan skipped a few steps ahead to catch up with her.

"What the hell was that?" she asked, her voice barely above a whisper. "A dragon?"

Midnight shook her head. "Too small to be a dragon," she replied matter-of-factly. "Probably a wyvern. This area is full of them."

Full of them? Kellan thought, glancing in the direction she thought the creature had flown. Frag, what the hell had she gotten herself into?

They reached the shores of the Columbia River a few hours before dawn. On the far side of the river, they could see the lights of the city of Portland and, only meters from the south bank of the river, the Portland Wall.

It rose some ten meters high, formed out of gray ferrocrete and topped with coils of razor wire. It ran along the river as far as Kellan could see in either direction, surrounding the city that stood on the very edge of the elven nation. On the other side of the river was Tir Tairngire, the Land of Promise, the secure homeland established by elves, where they could live by their own rules. It was clear they didn't like uninvited visitors.

Midnight stowed the GPS and they stood in the cover of the trees along the bank. Kellan turned to Orion, who had his head cocked to one side, his eyes with a distant look, as if listening for something.

"When do these contacts of yours get here?" she asked. Orion's eyes shifted over to her, then down from her face toward her chest.

"They're here already," he said quietly, and Kellan looked down to see a small red dot of laser light painted in the middle of her chest. Reflexively, her hand went toward her gun.

"Telego carronasto!" a voice spoke quietly but commandingly from the shadows. "Do not move!" Orion caught Kellan's eye and nodded slightly, but she didn't feel all that reassured.

"We've brought the payment we agreed on," Orion said. *"Delarosa."*

A tall, slim figure stepped from the shadows of a tree only a few meters away. She was dressed in black and dark forest green, a commando-style pullover with pads of reinforced material at the shoulders and elbows, fatigue pants and laced-up boots. The hands holding the pistol trained at Kellan didn't waver, nor did her dark eyes. Her hair was cut short, such that Kellan took her for a man at first.

"I hope your credit is better than your Sperethiel," the woman said with a lilting accent.

"It's good," Orion affirmed. "Haven't we always dealt fairly with you?"

A tight mockery of a smile tugged at the corners of

the elf woman's mouth. "You Ancients aren't interested in things like fairness, or responsibility."

"Some of us are."

"You usually don't last long. Still," she slowly lowered the pistol and Kellan allowed herself to breathe again. "A deal is a deal, and we don't reject anyone's credit."

Orion nodded, his hand slowly reaching inside his jacket. He withdrew a credstick and held it out to the woman, who approached and plucked it from his hand.

"Half now, half on the other side," he said, "as agreed. You can check it, if you want."

"No need," she replied, stowing the credstick in one of the pockets on her belt. "Since I assume you also intend to leave the city at some point, and will need our assistance in doing so. If things aren't in order . . ." she shrugged, leaving the threat unfinished. "This way," she told them. Midnight followed the woman without comment, with Orion and Kellan walking close behind. Kellan became aware of the feeling of being watched, and wondered how many associates the elven woman had close at hand, in case there was trouble. Her eyes swept the trees, but she could see nothing in the dark shadows around them.

"Who is she?" she whispered to Orion. "A smuggler? Shadowrunner?"

He shook his head slightly. *"Rinelle,"* he said quietly. "A rebel. The Rinelle ke'Tesrae group sometimes cut deals with the Ancients." Kellan wanted to ask more, but thought better of it while the woman was still leading them.

She brought them to a spot on the riverbank where a small boat was concealed. When they arrived, a male elf, dressed in the same fashion as the woman, emerged from the shadows and silently began helping remove the camo netting over the small craft, balling it up and stowing it under the bench seats.

"Get in," the woman said, and the shadowrunners climbed on board. "Stay down and stay quiet," she told them, and she and the man took oars from the bottom of the boat. Kellan could see the craft was fitted with an outboard motor, but they made no move to start it. Instead, they paddled slowly and quietly. Kellan crouched in the seat in the prow of the boat, glancing at the dark waters of the river and the wall looming higher as they approached. They were committed. There was no going back now.

10

Lothan closed the book with a sigh after reading the same paragraph for what was probably the tenth time. Though the new text on enchanting he'd acquired was interesting, there were other things occupying his mind, despite his best efforts to banish those thoughts.

Standards, he chided himself silently, *standards.* After all, he didn't like it when others paid too much attention to his business, and he tried to offer them the same professional courtesy, so long as it didn't cost him anything, but Kellan . . .

Lothan snorted quietly in the dimness of his study. Kellan. She was an oddity in his life, to say the least. Lothan had been working in the shadows of Seattle longer than many of his fellow shadowrunners had been alive. He'd earned an enviable reputation as a master of the arcane arts, and also as a shrewd professional, who knew his business and delivered on his promises. He took reasonable pride in that reputation, and made it a point never to let personal feelings interfere with business.

Kellan was not Lothan's first student. *Though she may well be my last,* the troll thought soberly. She was certainly not the first young shadowrunner he'd taken under his wing. What was it about her that held his attention so? She was talented, but not the most gifted magician Lothan had ever encountered. She had spirit, an inner drive to succeed, that reminded him of his younger days, even if she was almost completely lacking in the foresight and discretion Lothan cultivated, and had from his earliest days in the business. No, there was something more to Kellan Colt, much as the old mage didn't like to admit it.

Perhaps it was the mystery surrounding her, a mystery even Kellan didn't understand. She had been told that the amulet she wore came from her mother, about whom she knew very little. It was a unique item of power, unlike anything Lothan had seen before. How did Kellan's mother come to have it, and why did she entrust it to a daughter who didn't even know her?

Lothan idly flipped through pages of the book, no longer looking at the words and diagrams, lost in thought. The amulet was certainly a curiosity, and he would have wanted to know more about it under any circumstances. But the amulet itself wasn't the real mystery, in his opinion. The thing nagging at his mind wasn't the amulet, it was who was interested in it, and why.

As a shadowrunner, Lothan was used to doing things without knowing why his employer wanted them done. But he also knew from bitter experience the importance of not running entirely blind. He always did his best to maintain a balance between professional discretion and necessary caution, and it was that foresight that had kept him from running into a number of pitfalls over the years.

Still, he saw no downside to things when Midnight had contacted him years ago and asked him to keep an eye out for a particular *objet d'arcane,* some trinket she was interested in. He didn't ask why or what it was, since he knew she wouldn't tell him, anyway. Instead, he did as he said he would and kept the item's description in mind in case it should happen to cross his path—which it did the night G-Dogg first brought Kellan to see him.

The old troll sighed heavily, snapping the book shut. He had misplayed the whole matter with the amulet by not telling Kellan of Midnight's interest sooner. Instead, Midnight had been the one to tell Kellan, and to tell her how she knew Kellan's mother, a shadowrunner who went by the street name Mustang. Her disclosure made it seem that he, and not Midnight, was keeping things from Kellan—that he, and not Midnight, was untrustworthy, when Lothan knew there had to be some ulterior motive for Midnight's interest—an interest beyond curiosity regarding the fate of a former business associate or her offspring. That was the mystery nagging at Lothan, the question to which he felt he must find the answer. What was Midnight's angle? It wasn't sentiment, he knew that for certain.

He told himself it was none of his business. Kellan was a big girl and a professional. She chose to work the shadows and she chose her own associates. Lothan was her instructor in the magical arts, not her guru, her mentor, and certainly not her surrogate parent. It wasn't his job to—

"Oh, fraggit," Lothan sighed. He took his pocket secretary from the pouch on his belt. The flatscreen sprang to life at his touch.

"Call Jackie," he told it, and the numbers flashed across the screen as it connected to the local telecom grid address. The WAITING light flashed for a moment, then the image on the screen changed to that of a cartoon girl, dark hair held back by a circuit diagram headband, tiny mouth curled up in a smile when she saw him.

"Hello, Lothan."

"Jackie, I need you to find some information."

"Sure thing," she chirped. "Usual rates?"

"Of course."

"What do you want to know?"

"I'd like you to find out more about Toshiro Akimura's recent activities, in particular, his apparent interest in Kellan."

There was no change in the icon's expression, but Lothan imagined he could hear a note of curiosity in Jackie's voice. "Kellan bring you in on it?" she asked.

"Of course," he replied, without missing a beat. "She was in need of some guidance."

The decker nodded. "Well, I told her I would find out more if I could, but Akimura is actually covering his tracks pretty well. I suspect that's why he hired Kellan to delete the information about him in the cyberclinic's records."

Lothan nodded sagely, since Jackie could see him through the comm unit's tiny camera—or by any number of other means, if she chose. "Hmmm, no doubt," he said. "Well, whatever else you can find would be appreciated."

"Null sheen," she said. "Hey, how's Kellan doing?"

"Oh, fine," Lothan replied. "She's just a bit concerned. I suspect even she wonders if she might be in over her head."

Jackie nodded knowingly. "I'll let you know anything I find out."

"Many thanks," he said, hitting the END button to terminate the call.

So, Kellan had already gone to Jackie about Akimura. He wondered what Jackie had told her, but he didn't want the decker to know that he was making inquiries without Kellan's knowledge—not just yet, anyway. He had another way of finding out more about Kellan's newly acquired trouble.

"Call G-Dogg," he told the pocket secretary.

Portland was nothing like Kellan expected. After everything she'd heard about the fantastic elven nation of Tir Tairngire, an Awakened land of metahumans and magic, she'd expected . . . well, she wasn't sure, maybe tall spires, pennant flags snapping in the breeze, enchanted woodland glades, griffins soaring between the towers like you saw on the trid programs like *Tales of Atlantis*.

She, Midnight and Orion were blindfolded by their "hosts" after crossing the river. Kellan bristled at the idea, but the Rinelle made it clear that it was the only way they would be escorted through one of the secret passages through the Portland Wall. What followed was a confusing series of twists and turns, such that Kellan wondered if they were being led into a trap. Then they were allowed to remove the blindfolds, and Kellan got her first look at the city the elves called Cara'Sir, the City of Rivers.

It was so . . . mundane. The city looming up beyond the Portland Wall was little different from Seattle. Sure, the buildings differed, and some of the neon and flatscreen signs Kellan could see were written in graceful elvish runes rather than English, Spanish or Japanese, but the city had the same sorts of roads, the same towers of steel and mirrored glass. Cars moved along those roads instead of horse-drawn carriages, and helicopters and tilt-rotor aircraft buzzed among the buildings rather than proud griffins or mighty dragons. It was a city like any other: big, sprawling, glowing, dark and dirty. Kellan quashed a surge of disappointment.

"Remember, the same amount when you want to leave," the female Rinelle member said curtly, "assuming you ever do." Then she and the other elf withdrew, leaving the three shadowrunners by themselves in a darkened parking lot.

"Nice," Kellan muttered, watching them go. When she turned back, Midnight was crouched alongside one of the cars parked in the lot.

"Keep an eye out," she said, taking some tools from her vest. Kellan and Orion kept watch while she worked, but there was little traffic so early in the morning on the outskirts of the city.

In a matter of minutes, Midnight disabled the lock on the car door, opened up a panel under the dash and hotwired the ignition system. The hybrid engine hummed to life, and Midnight gave a satisfied smile as she snapped the panel closed and slid into the driver's seat.

"Let's go," she said, and Kellan and Orion climbed in. Within moments, they were on the road headed toward the heart of the city.

"We'll need to ditch this when we get into the city proper," Midnight said, keeping her eyes on the road. "I've taken out the transponder, so it'll take the Tir cops a while to locate the car, but it's still a potential liability. Make sure not to touch anything bare-handed," she glanced over at Kellan, who jammed her hands in her pockets and slouched in the seat, doing her best to become inconspicuous.

"Where are we going?" Orion asked from the back seat.

"Safe house," Midnight explained. "A place I set up for while we're in town. Then we can get to work."

As they drove through the outskirts of Portland, Kellan watched the buildings, signs and people they passed. They were an odd mixture of the familiar and the exotic. Now that she had time to really take in the details, she saw that Portland was different from the metroplex she knew. Most obviously, there were far more elves than any place Kellan had ever been, other than the few elven neighborhoods of Seattle. Even on the outskirts, closer to the wall, the majority of people she saw were metahumans—dwarfs, orks and even the occasional troll—mixed in with a few humans and the expected elves. The further they went into the city, the more elves she saw, and the fewer of everyone else.

Kellan was also surprised by the state of some of the buildings they passed. There was one burned-out shell, surrounded by warning signs and yellow tape. She looked at the half-covered remains of a sign near the street, but it was written in elvish.

"What does it say?" she asked.

"It was a Peace Force station," Orion answered. "Tir police."

"What happened?"

"Probably the Rinelle, a terrorist bombing or protest." When Kellan turned toward Orion with a look of surprise, he shrugged. "The Council of Princes keeps a tight lid on the news from inside the country, but some of it gets out to people in places like Tarislar. Tir Tairngire has had a lot of political problems lately, and it's not likely to get any better. They might want the rest of the world to think they're one big happy faerieland, but the truth is it's probably only a matter of time before there's a civil war."

Kellan slumped back into her seat and thought about that as they traveled. Though downtown Portland was even cleaner and more orderly than the business district of Seattle, she thought she could see some of what Orion was talking about. Even in broad daylight, uniformed officers of the Tir Peace Force had an unusually strong presence on the streets. People went from place to place quickly, without lingering, and there was a sense of tension that seemed out of character in the gleaming plazas.

Midnight found a space along a side street to park the car. Before getting out, she turned to Kellan and Orion.

"Just act casual, don't make direct eye contact, and let me do the talking," she instructed them. They climbed out of the car and Midnight led the way down the street, cutting through an alley, and then walking a few more blocks. Kellan looked steadfastly straight ahead, working hard to not acknowledge anyone passing them on the street. They stopped in front of a small Thai restaurant on the ground floor of one of a row of converted brownstones. Midnight held open the door and waved them inside before following close behind.

The inside was cozy, with only a dozen or so small tables set with burning candles. The air was warm and smelled of spices. Only a single table was occupied, and the young elf couple there seemed to take no notice of the newcomers entering the restaurant.

The elf woman who greeted them had an exotic mix of elven and Asian features, her long, dark hair done up in braids coiled at the nape of her neck, decorated with beads and held in place with lacquered hair ornaments. She wore a colorful sari and moved gracefully as she smiled and bowed slightly upon seeing Midnight.

"Your reservation is ready," she said quietly, guiding the three of them to the back of the restaurant. They passed the table tucked away there and went through the doors into the kitchen, where the woman turned and brought them up a set of stairs to the second floor. They passed one closed door before the woman stopped at another and opened it.

The room beyond probably took up a good part of the back half of the building's second floor. It contained a small bed along with a couple of folding cots, an old table and some chairs. The wallpaper was probably older than Tir Tairngire itself, and the floor was hardwood that had seen better days. Blinds covered the two windows looking out into the alley behind the building, closed to block out most of the daylight. Midnight took in the room with a sweeping glance before turning back to the woman.

"Good," she said, handing her a credstick. The woman bowed again slightly, palming the payment, and withdrew. Midnight ushered Kellan and Orion inside and closed the door behind them.

"You know her?" Kellan asked and Midnight nodded.

"Well enough. The owners will provide the space and won't ask any questions, as long as we're discreet."

Kellan dropped her bag on one of the cots as Midnight moved a chair against the side wall of the room, with a view of the door and windows.

"Now," she said, "have a seat, and I'll tell you what we're doing." Orion grabbed the other chair, and Kellan sat down on the edge of the cot. Midnight crossed one leg over the other and clasped her hands in her lap, reminding Kellan of a teacher about to begin a lesson.

"Telestrian Industries is the largest corporation in Tir Tairngire," she began. "They have interests in biotech, computers, entertainment, data processing—you name it. They've got an arcology habitat here in Portland, and, of course, they've got close ties with the Tir Council of Princes.

"Until recently, James Telestrian III ran the company. It's privately held by his family, which is one of the most influential families in the Tir. Recently, James announced his intention to seek an appointment to the Council of Princes, and needed to turn control of the company over to someone else due to the requirements of Tir law. He picked his younger sister, Marie-Louise, for the job."

"And somebody is pretty hacked off about it," Kellan interjected.

"Got it in one," Midnight said with a sly smile. "James' son Timothy is an MBA graduate with ambition and sufficient talent, from what I've heard, and he's none too happy about being passed over for an opportunity to run the family business. He's looking for an opportunity to leverage control of Telestrian Industries away from his aunt, which is where we come in.

"Our job is to get inside the Telestrian Habitat and acquire a certain top-secret file, which our employer can use as leverage against his aunt, particularly if his father wants to avoid an embarrassing family squabble while he's trying to win the favor of the Council of Princes. Timothy Telestrian is willing to pay handsomely for the information, and, in addition, he can provide us credentials to get us inside the habitat and some of the codes we'll need to retrieve the data."

"Some?" Orion asked.

"Obviously, he can't give us anything that would implicate him, but what he can give us will make the job a lot easier."

Kellan nodded. "When do we go?"

"Well, time is of the essence," Midnight said. "Once James Telestrian is on the Council of Princes, Timothy loses most of his bargaining power, since his father's position will be established. I need to set up a meeting with a contact to get the information Timothy said he'd provide. Then we can review it, figure out our plan of attack, and get the job done. We'll be here for a few days at most. Then we're out, with enough cred to take it easy for a while."

Kellan couldn't help but smile at the prospect of the easy life for a little while. "Let's do it."

11

"You know, Lothan," the ork said, staring straight ahead, "this isn't exactly the smartest thing you've ever done."

"Yes, G-Dogg," he replied with a sigh, "I do believe you mentioned that, oh, half a dozen or so times already."

"I'm just sayin'," G-Dogg continued, his hands leaving the steering wheel for a moment to make a pacifying gesture. "It could be a lot of trouble for nothing."

"Perhaps," Lothan said, nodding his head slowly, "perhaps, but some things need to be done."

G-Dogg looked at the troll, and Lothan shook his head. "Don't read anything into this," he warned. "It is what it is."

He turned back to the road. "Well, if you're going to do this, then I'm coming with you."

It was Lothan's turn to look at G-Dogg, and the ork gave him a sidelong glance before returning his gaze to the road, shaggy dreadlocks bobbing.

"Hey, she's my friend, too," he muttered.

"I'll be glad for the company, then," Lothan said, a smile tugging at one side of his mouth.

G-Dogg drove them down Pike Street in Lothan's van. Traffic was fairly heavy, so things were stop-and-go as they headed downhill toward the waterfront. Lothan maintained an air of calm detachment, though he fought the urge to strike the car ahead of them with a fireball and blast it from the road. He didn't want to be late. Cursed traffic.

"Remember—" he began.

"Yeah, yeah," G-Dogg interrupted, "I know, street parking if at all possible. You've mentioned *that* a few times. If you know some magic for that, now would be a good time, cuz street parking's not lookin' too likely at the moment."

He's probably right, Lothan thought glumly. He didn't care for the idea of putting the van in a garage, since it limited their options if a quick departure was called for. Not that he was planning on one, but it paid to be prepared.

"Let me see what I can do about that," he said. If nothing else, it would take his mind off the traffic.

Lothan settled back in his seat, despite the somewhat cramped space. Though the Awakened world had included orks and trolls for decades, car manufacturers were only beginning to catch on to the idea that the bucket seat wasn't made with three-meter-tall metahumans in mind.

Lothan calmed his mind. One hand cupped near his solar plexus, he lifted the other over it, palm down, as if holding a small ball near his stomach. He breathed out, feeling the flow of mana, magical energy, in the ether around him. With the smallest effort of will, he took a portion of that energy and drew it in as easily as drawing a deep breath, channeling it into the space between his hands. He focused on his intent, and molded and shaped the energy in accordance with it. The air shimmered between his cupped hands, and it was to G-Dogg's credit that he gave what Lothan was doing no more than a cursory glance.

The troll mage breathed out one more time, quickly, almost explosively, and the shimmer between his palms took shape, becoming a ghostly outline of a bird, visible only as a distortion in the air. Lothan spread his hands in a gesture of release, and the shape flew, passing through the windshield in front of him and zipping away.

"That going to get us a parking spot?" G-Dogg asked, as if he saw wizards conjuring spirits all the time.

"If there's one to be had," Lothan said.

"Wizard."

There was a spot, and Lothan's watcher spirit guided them to it just in time to pull in as the other car exited. G-Dogg neatly maneuvered the van into the space, then killed the engine and hopped out to slot his credstick into the parking meter. It would deduct the cost of the space minute by minute from his account until they left.

The Hotel Nikko was at the corner of Pike Street and Third Avenue, west of the looming bulk of the Renraku Arcology and beyond the long shadow it cast over the downtown area in the late afternoon hours. The parking space they had found was only a few blocks down Pike Street, and although Lothan wasn't happy about walking uphill toward the hotel, he preferred knowing the trip back would be downhill. G-Dogg walked a step or two behind him, the ork's powerful legs keeping up easily with Lothan's longer stride. People on the sidewalk quickly gave way to the mas-

sive troll in the flowing coat and the dark-skinned ork
following close behind him.

Lothan didn't pause to admire the traditional
Japanese-style decor of the hotel's lobby, or to appreciate the aromas wafting from the attached restaurant as its staff prepared for dinner. He went directly
to the bank of elevators, punching the button for the
ninth floor with one blunt finger. With a sidelong
glance, he made sure the watcher he had summoned
still hovered close by his left shoulder. He hadn't
called the spirit merely for parking, after all. It would
serve as a watchdog for any signs of mystical trouble,
allowing Lothan to focus on more mundane concerns.

Once the elevator doors closed, G-Dogg shrugged,
adjusting the harness he wore under his vest, twisting
his neck in a stretch. Lothan likewise rested one hand
close to the pistol worn underneath his overcoat. It
was a familiar and reassuring weight, though it was
really the least of the weapons at his disposal. When
the doors opened, G-Dogg went out first, quickly scanning the hall before motioning for Lothan to follow.
Counting off the room numbers, Lothan stopped at
937 and rapped firmly on the door three times. There
was only a brief pause before it opened.

The figure standing about a meter back from the
door held a sleek pistol in a gleaming metallic, skeletal
hand. It matched the white face paint emphasizing his
sunken cheeks, narrow chin and long jaw, which made
his head look like a skull underneath the dark glasses
and the wide-brimmed hat. No emotion showed on
that face, as still, steady and mechanical as the hand
holding the gun.

"Lothan," the dark-clad gunman said quietly.

"Deacon," the mage replied in a cool tone, ducking

his head to step into the room. G-Dogg followed. The Street Deacon stepped aside to allow them to enter the hotel suite, but as Lothan passed, he held out his free hand, also made of metal.

Lothan sighed and reached slowly under his coat to produce his own weapon, handing it over to the Deacon butt first. He took the gun and set it on the nearby vanity before holding out his hand for G-Dogg's weapons. After the ork handed over his gun and his backup, the Deacon waved them on into the room, following just behind them.

On the far side of the suite's main room, windows looked out over the street below and toward the shadowy hulk of the arcology. The man sitting in one of the chairs by the window set his drink aside and stood to face them as they entered.

"Lothan," he said, "I'm glad you could make it."

"Akimura-san, this is not a meeting I would miss."

"I believe you're already acquainted with the Street Deacon."

Lothan nodded. "We've met," he said vaguely.

"Then I'm sure you've had the opportunity to appreciate his skill—as well as why I need someone like him on hand, given recent events."

"Of course."

Akimura smiled. "I'm glad we understand each other. Please, have a seat, I think we have a great deal to discuss."

"He's dead. There's nothing you can do."

The voice was soft, warm, even sympathetic, but also utterly without mercy, saying what Kellan feared, what she did not want to accept. She cradled Orion's limp, bloody body in her arms, rocking him gently as if he were only asleep, as if she could brush the hair away from his face and awaken him with a kiss.

"Let him go, Kellan," the voice said.

"No."

"You have no choice. You have to let him go."

She squeezed her eyes shut against the brightly shining light, pressing her face down against Orion's hair. It still smelled of him, mixed with the ever-present scent of blood.

"Come to me, Kellan." The voice was insistant. "I will make everything better for you. You will see. Come to me. I can help."

"No," Kellan whispered, "no." She wanted to scream, to shout it, but she couldn't seem to make her voice function properly. She couldn't move. It was like there was a great weight around her neck, dragging her down.

"It will all be over very soon now, Kellan, very soon. Don't be afraid."

"Kellan . . . Kellan."

"Orion!"

Kellan bolted awake to find Orion practically face-to-face with her. He grabbed her arms to steady her as she got her bearings. Then she threw herself against his chest and hugged him just to make sure he was real, tears welling up at the memory of holding his unmoving body.

"Hey, it's okay," he said soothingly. "It's okay." Kellan suddenly felt awkward, and pulled back, wiping her eyes with the back of her sleeve. "Another dream?" Orion asked.

Kellan nodded mutely.

"You want to talk about it?" She shook her head.

"It's okay," she began, but Orion cut her off with a wave of his hand.

"No, it's not. Kellan, there's obviously something going on, something that's bothering you. I'll admit I don't know drek about what dreams mean, but I do know that having nightmares all the time means something is wrong."

She didn't argue the point, and that seemed to deflate Orion's anger. "Look," he said gently, "it might help to talk to someone about it."

"I don't know what they mean," Kellan said, hugging her arms to her chest, hunched on the edge of the cot. "They're just these images . . ."

"Images of what?"

"Death," she said, glancing up to meet Orion's eyes. "Images of death, betrayal, and I don't know what to do about it, and I feel so . . . helpless." She shook her head slowly.

"Kel, they're just dreams."

"No," she said. "No, I don't think they are. I think they're more than that, but I just don't know what."

"Magic?" Orion asked, and Kellan nodded. "Have you asked Lothan about it? Or maybe Liada?"

Kellan shook her head again. "When I first started having them, I didn't want to talk to anybody about them because I didn't know what to say. Now I wish I had."

"Don't you think it could just be, you know, the stress of the run and everything else that's going on?"

"Maybe," but she didn't sound convinced. Looking around the room, she asked, "Midnight's not back?"

"She should be soon."

"Okay." Kellan sat up and took a deep breath. "There anything to eat?"

"Midnight said she'd bring something back with her."

Kellan nodded again, then stood and stretched, working the kinks out from sleeping badly on the hard cot.

"Did you get any sleep?" she asked.

"Enough. If you want to try to go back to sleep . . ."

"No, that's okay. I'm up now."

Kellan went to her bag and pulled out her cyberdeck. Setting it on her lap, she switched it on in "tortoise" mode, allowing her to access the grid without jacking directly into the Matrix, which wasn't necessary for the simple stuff she had in mind. She checked to see if she had any new e-mail or messages, but there was nothing—not that she'd been expecting anything, but it was something to do while they waited for Midnight to return.

"Kellan," Orion began behind her, "about the other night . . ."

"I told you," she said, without looking at him. "It's frosty, no problem."

"Well, I think I've got a problem," Orion said, and Kellan paused, fingers poised over the keyboard. "I think . . ." He paused, sighing.

"What?" She half turned to see Orion standing where she'd left him, eyes downcast. She'd never seen her friend look so uncomfortable. Even when he'd been called to account by the leader of the Ancients, he'd retained his usual proud bearing and defiant attitude.

"I don't want you think what happened, our being together, was just a casual thing," Orion said. He lifted his eyes to meet hers, and Kellan felt her pulse race. "It wasn't to me, anyway, and I don't think it was to you, either."

"Tam—"

"No, let me finish. I like you, Kel. I like you more than I ever thought I would like anyone ever again in my life. I . . . have feelings for you, and I understand if you don't feel the same way, but if I didn't tell you, I would always wonder. . . ."

Kellan got to her feet, setting the cyberdeck aside, and went to him. She rested her hands lightly on his chest, feeling the taut muscles under his shirt.

"I . . . I do feel the same way," she said hesitantly. "I just didn't . . . I didn't want it to be . . ."

"Unprofessional?" Orion suggested, and Kellan flushed and ducked her head, resting it for a moment against his chest.

"Yeah. Dumb, huh?"

Orion smiled and shook his head. "No, not really. We're both still feeling our way through life in the shadows, and reputation is important."

"I just didn't know what to say . . . what to do."

"Well, there's this for starters. . . ." Orion said softly, tipping her face up to his and leaning toward her.

Kellan felt the warm press of his lips, and melted against him as Orion's arms surrounded her and pulled her closer. Neither of them noticed the door to the room quietly open, or the dark-clad figure standing there.

Lothan took the seat Akimura offered him, pleased the fixer didn't subscribe to Japanese custom and have them all sitting on the floor. The padded hotel chair was comfortable, and even large enough to accommodate his size.

Toshiro Akimura was of somewhat less than average height, yet carried a commanding presence. He

was clearly used to receiving a certain measure of respect from the people around him. If he was at all
nervous about meeting with Lothan and G-Dogg, he
didn't show it. He was dressed fairly casually in a dark
sport coat and slacks with a cream-colored V-neck
shirt, though Lothan recognized the design as one of
Vashon Islands' lines of secure clothing for executives.
The coat was lined with ballistic cloth, and an en-
hancement to the weave of the shirt provided an additional layer of protection.

Akimura's dark hair was cut conservatively short,
revealing the gleam of the datajack at his right temple,
and his dark eyes were like shuttered windows, impossible to read. Lothan suppressed the automatic urge
to scan the fixer astrally; it would hardly be polite,
and, more importantly, if Akimura had arranged for
magical protection, it might be taken as a threat.

"I'm glad you contacted me to set up this meeting,"
Akimura began.

"And why is that?"

"Because I need to get in touch with Kellan Colt,
and I understand you know her quite well."

"Well enough."

"Then you can pass on a message for me. She's
in danger."

"Indeed?" Lothan raised one eyebrow. "I was
under the impression she was in danger from you."

"She's not," the fixer answered. "I don't mean Kellan any harm. On the contrary, I've been trying to
protect her, but I haven't been able to reach her."

"You have an odd idea of protection, Mr. Akimura.
Does it include sending a gang after the person you
are trying to shield?"

The other man shook his head impatiently. "I have

already answered this accusation. I didn't send the Halloweeners after Kellan. I only heard about it after the fact."

"If you didn't employ the Halloweeners, then who did?"

"I have my suspicions."

"But you choose not to share them?"

"Forgive my saying so, Lothan, but I don't know you, and you don't know me. I don't know where your loyalties lie, and you have no reason to trust me."

"That's quite true. So why should I believe any of what you're telling me now?"

"Because I know that Kellan is in very grave danger," Akimura said, fixing Lothan with a level stare, "and I doubt she is aware that someone close to her is planning to betray her."

Absorbed in their embrace, Kellan and Orion sprang apart when a synthleather satchel thudded to the floor of the small room. They turned toward the door where Midnight stood, holding a plastic bag that smelled of Asian take-out, and wearing a barely controlled smirk.

"I'm sorry," she said in a mocking tone, "I didn't mean to interrupt. Should I come back a little later . . . or maybe much later?"

Kellan looked at Orion, blushed furiously, and wiped her mouth with the back of her hand.

"No!" she said. "I mean . . . um . . ."

"It's fine," Orion interjected flatly. Midnight didn't say anything else, but the look on her face spoke volumes.

"I brought dinner," she said, carrying the food over to the table, "and information." She produced a datachip from her pocket, holding it up for them to see. "We've got what we need to get down to work, so let's do it . . . if that's all right with you two."

When they nodded agreement, Midnight passed the chip to Kellan, asking her to slot it into her cyberdeck so that they could look at the information while they ate. Kellan kept busy at the computer for a moment, but risked a sidelong glance at Orion. He looked up from pulling food cartons out of the plastic bag, caught Kellan's eye, and then glanced away as she did the same, both obviously wondering for the first time about the future after this run was finished.

12

"Someone is planning to betray Kellan?" Lothan asked. "I think I can guess who."

"I'm afraid I won't be able to confirm your suspicions at this time," Akimura replied softly.

"You don't offer much information, Akimura-san."

"I cannot. Not until I can better comprehend where things stand."

"Why are you so concerned with Kellan's welfare? She doesn't even know you."

"That is true, but I nonetheless owe her a debt," the fixer said, "and I always make good on my debts."

"You knew Kellan's mother," Lothan said. It wasn't a question.

Akimura paused for only a moment. "Yes, I did," he said, his expression unreadable.

"Well?"

"Very well."

"You're not Kellan's—" Lothan began, but the other man shook his head.

"No, I'm not, but I owe it to Kellan's mother to look out for her daughter. I owe her my life, many times over. We worked together once, quite closely."

"Then you know what happened to her."

For the first time since he'd sat down, Lothan saw the faintest crack in Akimura's emotional mask. A flicker of pain crossed the dark eyes, a grimace tugged at the corner of his mouth.

"She's dead, and I feel confident that her killer is after Kellan now. So once again: I need to know if you can get a message to her. We need to talk."

"Why haven't you contacted Kellan before now? If you had this information about her mother, and felt you owed her a debt . . ."

"I couldn't," Akimura replied. "I was . . . indisposed. If I could have gotten in touch with Kellan sooner I would have."

"The clinic," Lothan mused out loud. "You were at Nightengale's."

Akimura didn't flinch. "You have done your research, I see."

Lothan shook his head. "Not me, Kellan. She was hired to erase your records at the clinic—she assumed by you. That's why she thinks you're out to get her now."

"Was she working alone?"

"No, she was working with someone—someone else who says she knew Kellan's mother."

"Lothan, where is Kellan now?"

"As you can see," Midnight said, leaning over the diagram on the display of Kellan's deck, "the Telestrian Habitat isn't quite as big as the old Renraku Arcology, but it's still a huge area to safeguard. Even the best security measures cannot fully accommodate the sheer number of people who move in and out of the facility on a daily basis, and that's how we're going to get in."

"Huh?" Kellan asked.

"Blend in with the on-site personnel," Midnight prompted, "disappear into the crowd and let the daily routine get us closer to the goal."

"Won't it be that much harder carrying out the run with the place full of people?" Orion asked, emphasizing his question with a wave of his chopsticks.

"Not if we do it right," said Midnight. "If we try to get inside the habitat after hours, we'll need to get past the sorts of security measures intended to keep people out. If we go in as part of the regular traffic, security will be lighter because it has to be, and we've got a better chance of passing unnoticed, as long as we plan carefully and don't make any mistakes."

"That's likely," Kellan heard Orion mutter under his breath.

Midnight reached into her bag and produced a flat plastic badge. "These will get us past most of the security," she said. "They're keyed to the habitat's systems, and broadcast an ID code that will identify us as authorized employees, giving us access. We won't set off any alarms, so security will have no reason to question us."

"And if they do?" Kellan asked, recalling their brush with the guard at the cyberclinic.

"Then we improvise," Midnight said with a smile. "We set up a cover story and stick to it. We're out-of-town consultants, troubleshooters, brought in to handle a system-processing problem and we answer directly to Timothy Telestrian, who's the head of the NeuroTech Computing division."

"Won't somebody check?"

"Trust me, no one in Tir Tairngire wants to get a higher-up annoyed with them, and people learn not to question authority. As long as we play it like we're important enough not to be bothered, no one will bother us. They won't contact NeuroTech because they don't want to get on Telestrian's bad side. As long as it isn't any trouble for them, they're not going to worry about it."

"What about getting the data?" Kellan asked.

"That's going to be the harder part," Midnight said. "Once we're on the inside, we'll have access to a terminal, but our contact can't provide us with all the codes we need to get access to the files, so we're going to have to do some of it the old-fashioned way."

"Hacking into the files?"

"Right. And we'll need to be careful, since an external system alert can blow our cover."

"Kellan," Orion asked, "can you handle that?"

"Of course she can," Midnight offered supportively. Kellan seemed a little less certain.

"Well, Jackie has set me up with some good software," she began, "but hacking into a corporate main host—"

"We'll be inside the primary intrusion countermeasures of the habitat's system," Midnight pointed out. "All you'll need to worry about is the ice protecting the actual files. Even the encryption we can deal with once we're out."

Kellan nodded. "That's true."

"I wouldn't ask you if I didn't think you could handle it, Kellan."

Kellan glanced from Orion to Midnight, then nodded firmly. "Okay, then. No problem."

"Good," Midnight said. "Okay, this is what we need

to work on tomorrow, and we ought to get an early start. . . ."

"Where is Kellan?" Akimura asked again.

Lothan slowly stood, towering over the man sitting in front of him. "I'll pass on your message, Akimura-san," he said. "After that, it's up to Kellan."

For a moment, the fixer looked like he was about to say something more, but he simply nodded. "Very well," he said. "Please tell her that she can set up the meeting, and I'll agree to any terms she wants to place on our rendezvous. I need her to understand she can trust me."

"I'll tell her," Lothan repeated.

With a nod to G-Dogg, Lothan walked toward the door. The Street Deacon handed them their weapons, then stepped aside to allow the pair to pass. Lothan heard the door close softly behind them, but didn't look back or say anything until they reached the elevator.

"Lothan—" G-Dogg began, but the mage held up a hand for silence. Only once they stepped inside the elevator car and the doors closed behind them did he lower his hand, indicating that his companion was allowed to speak.

"What the frag is going on?" G-Dogg asked, his voice low.

"That's what I intend to find out," Lothan replied. "If any of what we've been told is true, then Akimura is right about one thing: Kellan is in danger."

"So shouldn't we warn her?"

"My very thought," Lothan replied, "but I want to use a means that's a bit more secure than a cell call. Akimura has resources enough to tap into that."

"Magic," G-Dogg said, and Lothan nodded. The elevator doors opened onto the lobby, and they made their way out to the street and headed back to the van.

"Yes," the troll mage said, "and while I'm making preparations, I want to try to get some confirmation of Mr. Akimura's story." He took his phone from his coat pocket and, as he opened the passenger-side door of the van, spoke into it.

"Call Jackie Ozone," he said, and the phone complied. It rang only twice before the decker answered.

"Jackie," Lothan said as G-Dogg started up the engine. "I may have some additional leads for you to follow, but I'm going to need that information a little faster than expected."

When they returned to his home, Lothan went directly to his basement workshop, instructing G-Dogg to keep in touch with Jackie and to discreetly find out what he could about Kellan's current whereabouts.

"Meet me back here in two hours," the troll said, and G-Dogg set off, leaving Lothan to get to work.

The mage began sketching a diagram on the floor of the workshop. It rapidly took shape as two concentric circles, the space between the circles filled with mystical symbols. Within the middle circle was a five-pointed star, with sigils at each of the points. Lothan's big hands moved quickly through the familiar patterns of the design. In the center of the star he drew the symbol of the all-seeing eye.

Sitting back on his haunches, Lothan appraised his work and decided it was sufficient. He set candles at the points of the star and, with a pass of his hand, kindled them into flame. Turning the lights off in the room, the mage sat in the center of the circle he'd

created, took a deep breath, and reached into the
pouch at his belt to withdraw a tiny plastic bag. With
another sigh, Lothan cleared his mind and began
working.

It was a fairly simple ritual. Centering himself, Lothan withdrew a two flaxen hairs from the plastic bag.
They were Kellan's hairs, gathered after one of her
many lessons. Lothan looked at them and thought
about why he had kept them. He had always told himself it was for an occasion like this. If Kellan got into
trouble, and it was difficult or dangerous to contact
her any other way, then he would have another means
at his disposal.

And if Kellan ever became a problem . . . Lothan
didn't allow himself to complete the thought. It was a
fact of life in the shadows. Never trust anyone completely, or you were setting yourself up for a fall. Lothan found it hard to believe that Kellan would betray
him, but how many betrayals were expected?

Lothan set charcoal burning in the tiny portable
brazier and sprinkled a few grains of incense on it.
Sweet, pungent smoke circled up around him, sym-
bolic of the element of air, the element suited to the
work he had in mind. Speaking the initial words of
the spell, Lothan cast the hairs onto the burning coals,
adding an acrid scent to the rising smoke. Inhaling
deeply of the scent, he chanted in a low and sono-
rous tone.

The repetition of the spell began to induce a trance,
and Lothan focused on Kellan: the image of her face,
the sound of her voice, the impression of her presence,
strengthening his connection to her into a bond that
transcended space and time. To his astral senses, a

faint silvery thread spun outward from his circle, drifting and floating in the ether, reaching out farther and farther.

Then, like a fisherman sensing a tug on the line, Lothan felt it. There was a faint psychic vibration, a shiver across his skin. He grabbed hold of it with his thoughts, anchored it with his will. Taking a deep breath, he let it out slowly and, like a swimmer slipping silently into a pool, the mage's spirit slid into the astral plane.

First came the feeling of weightlessness, of freedom from the bonds of the mundane world. Though it was something Lothan had experienced countless times, it was still a heady feeling, this power to fly free of flesh and blood. The troll's unbound spirit rose up from where his body sat, composed in meditation, and he fixed upon the shimmering thread, stretching off into the distance.

"Now then," Lothan murmured. "Let's see where you go." Up he rose, through the ceiling of the basement, through the walls of the building, out into the air. Arcing high over the Seattle metroplex, Lothan followed the astral thread—his connection to Kellan Colt—as it led him south.

When G-Dogg returned to Lothan's place, he found Jackie Ozone already waiting there. The decker acknowledged him with a nod as the ork came into the kitchen. G-Dogg wasn't too surprised to see Jackie in the flesh; few people got to meet Jackie face-to-face, but he knew Lothan and Jackie went back quite a ways. When the old mage needed her, Jackie was there.

"He still working?" G-Dogg asked with a glance toward the basement door, and Jackie nodded.

"Looks like," she said. "You find out anything more?"

"Just that Akimura's story checks out as far as I can follow it, but nobody really knows much. He's good at covering his tracks, so he might have been telling the truth, or he might still be trying to set Kellan up."

"Long way to go to set up a small-time shadowrunner, don't you think?" Jackie asked, and G-Dogg shrugged.

"How the frag do I know why people do anything? Did you find out anything?"

"I'd rather just tell it once," Jackie said with a glance toward the door.

G-Dogg went to the fridge to grab himself a drink as the basement door opened and a somewhat weary-looking Lothan emerged. G-Dogg could hardly remember a time when he'd seen the mage look so grim.

"Tir Tairngire," Lothan said with a note of resignation in his voice. "She's gone to Tir Tairngire. G-Dogg, we need to arrange another meeting. This time, I think Kellan has gotten in well and truly over her head."

Eve proved less reluctant to meet Jackie in the virtual bar at Shadowland when the decker contacted her and said she had additional information about Toshi Akimura. In fact, Eve was already there waiting when Jackie arrived for the meeting, which told her what she already suspected. Whatever Cross Corp's interest in Akimura, it was worthwhile for a corporate ladder-climber like Eve to drop everything to meet with her about it.

Jackie's persona slid into the booth opposite Eve's more photorealistic one. Privacy and encryption soft-

ware ran automatically on the deck sitting in Jackie's
lap in the real world, helping to safeguard their conversation and protect their identities from anyone who
might take undue interest.

"What do you have?" the company woman asked
without preamble. The impatience in her voice was
noticeable, even if it didn't show in her persona's
presentation.

Jackie settled into the seat, feeling the sensation of
the leather cool against her skin. It wasn't real, of
course, but it felt real, and it was soothing nonetheless.

"Akimura underwent long-term treatment at a cyberclinic called Nightengale's in downtown Seattle, not
far from the Space Needle," she began. "Someone
hired somebody to delete his records from the clinic's
files, but I managed to obtain a copy."

"From where?"

"An outside source," she supplied. "It's reliable."
The company woman nodded for her to continue.

"The records show that Akimura underwent some
pretty major treatment for a series of injuries that
should have killed him—did kill him, technically.
There was some reconstructive work, replacement organs, gene therapy, the works."

"Someone tried to kill him," Eve observed and
Jackie nodded.

"Looks like, and they came damn close to succeed-
ing."

"Do you know who arranged to have the records
wiped? Was it him?"

"I don't know yet, but I don't think it was."

"Why?"

"That's where it gets interesting. Akimura is definitely out of the clinic and back on the streets, and

none the worse for wear from what I've been able to find out. He arranged his release from the clinic a little while before the records were wiped. As I told you last time, he's looking for the shadowrunner named Kellan Colt."

"Have you figured out why he's looking for her?"

"Well, she's the one who wiped the records. She obviously believed that Akimura had hired her, but he claims he didn't."

Eve shrugged. "So? Maybe he's just tying up loose ends."

"Maybe," Jackie mused, "but I don't think so. For one thing, it doesn't fit Akimura's rep at all. From everything I've heard, he deals fairly with any shadow talent. A hire-and-burn arrangement doesn't sound like him."

"Or he's good enough that nobody ever found that out before."

"Like I said, that may be, but there's more to it. He's interested in this girl."

"Do you know why?"

Jackie paused. The question struck her as particularly . . . eager, like Eve was expecting a particular answer. She shook her head.

"No, not yet, but he's convinced some local talent to help him find her."

"Has she gone into hiding?"

"That," the decker said, "or she simply left town for a while when things got hot. But she's not in the metroplex any more."

"Where, then?"

"Tir Tairngire," Jackie said. Eve's persona leaned forward slightly, tense with a decidedly unvirtual excitement.

"Akimura is going after her, isn't he?"

"It looks that way," Jackie replied.

When the slow smile spread across the prefab face of the fixer's persona, Jackie knew it was in response to a deeply satisfied smile in the real world.

"Tell me everything," the company woman purred, "starting with who Akimura is taking with him, and I'll see that it's *well* worth your while . . ."

13

They went into the Telestrian Habitat late in the afternoon, when most employees would be looking forward to finishing up their work day and returning to their homes in the upper levels of the complex.

Kellan was concerned that, as a human, she would draw undue attention. However, despite Orion's statements condemning the exclusivity of Tir Tairngire's immigration policy, there were plenty of humans on the streets of Portland, and even within the habitat. Though elves were certainly in the majority, they were by no means the only citizens of the Land of Promise.

This must be what it's like to be a metahuman in a place like Seattle, Kellan thought. She felt as if she should offer some explanation for her presence. She felt distinctly out of place and edgy, and did her best to remember that no one they passed even suspected that she or her companions were anything other than what they appeared: corporate employees on their way to do a job.

Her clothes didn't really help Kellan's comfort level. They had picked up what Midnight considered a suitable wardrobe for each of them that fit their cover story of being troubleshooters from NeuroTech. Kellan wore a light sweater that succeeded in concealing the slight bulk of the ballistic cloth tee-shirt she layered underneath it. Her dark jeans had several pockets, and she wore her own boots, now polished to a dull glow. An artificially distressed synthleather shoulder bag held her cyberdeck and other essential equipment—it even featured a NeuroTech logo subtly stamped into the strap.

Orion looked equally uncomfortable in a pullover and sport coat combination, his long hair pulled back in the ponytail favored by most young elven corporate types, bound with a Celtic knot-work clasp. He wore dark sunglasses, which had the added bonus of allowing him to easily avoid eye contact with anyone.

Midnight looked every inch the confident corporate businesswoman in a charcoal pantsuit and low-cut black pullover that showed just the right amount of cleavage when she buttoned her blazer. Her black hair was likewise pulled back, giving her features a chilly severity that should make anyone think twice before questioning her. Like Orion, she wore dark glasses with fashionable frames. She carried a shoulder bag much like Kellan's that contained a pocket secretary and some office props along with her real gear. Kellan also knew Midnight wore a form-fitting layer of body armor, just in case.

While Midnight wore corporate drag like she was born to it, Kellan just did her best not to look out of place, wishing they could have taken Orion's suggestion and gone in after hours. At least then she'd know how to act. Fortunately, she also understood that people were *supposed* to feel a little uncomfortable approaching the Telestrian Habitat, so her reaction would seem pretty normal.

The only other arcology Kellan had ever seen was the Renraku Arcology in downtown Seattle, which was older and had been severely damaged by the actions of a rogue artificial intelligence in 2059. The Telestrian Habitat wasn't quite as large, but it was still impressive. The complex covered seven city blocks and soared upward, level upon level. Unlike the near-perfect geometry of the Renraku Arcology, however, this one was designed with an eye toward nature. The rising levels of the habitat were terraced with broad stretches of greenery: grass, flowers and even neatly manicured trees. The walls weren't cold steel and glass; they were warm adobe and woodland colors, with a texture almost like natural stone. It was like the habitat had been carved from a mountain, retaining some of its native life in the bargain.

It also retained the awe-inspiring quality of a mountain. Kellan couldn't help but gape a bit at the size and presence of it. The schematics Midnight had made them memorize didn't do it justice close up, and Kellan thought about the thousands of people who called this place home, all employees or dependents of Telestrian Industries, living together in one big, happy corporate community, with high, thick walls to protect them from the outside world. Did that make them feel safer, being apart from the rest of the world's problems? She wondered what it would be like.

Kellan stopped wondering as they approached one of the habitat's entrances and she saw the armed guards on duty. They looked smart in their crisp, dark green uniforms, but Kellan's eyes were drawn to the machine pistols they carried. They affected a bored air as Midnight slotted a credstick into the reader by the door and they checked her identification. They were all right, so long as the intel their employer provided was legit.

The guard nodded, Midnight removed her credstick, and he waved Kellan to approach. She slotted her credstick, then Orion did the same. The guards passed them through the doors with a wave and a slight nod of acknowledgment.

Midnight led the way into the habitat. Kellan glanced sidelong at the entryway, fully aware from the plans they'd studied of the kinds of scanners that were no doubt checking them out down to their fillings. Fortunately, none of them had any enhancements likely to trip alarms. Kellan and Orion, both Awakened, had no cyberware or other implants, and Midnight's were commonplace for a corporate troubleshooter, especially one working with computer systems.

Orion complained bitterly about having to leave his sword and other weapons behind, but Midnight said there was no way around it.

"Any weapons will set off the scanners, and there will be a dozen guards on us before we can blink," she said. "We'd never get inside, and even if we did, we wouldn't get far."

"What if something goes wrong?" Orion countered.

"If it does," Midnight replied, "we'll be inside a corporate habitat that has a huge, well-trained security staff. Do you really think a couple of guns and a sword will make any difference at all if we screw this up?"

Kellan thought about that as they made their way through one of the main lobbies of the complex. From the entrance, the Telestrian Habitat certainly didn't look dangerous, but she knew that looks were often deceiving—especially in Tir Tairngire.

The lower levels of the habitat were semipublic, de-

signed for shopping and recreation for the inhabitants
and any visitors, thus laid out like a sprawling mall.
The two floors above had numerous balconies over-
looking the public spaces, where a riot of greenery
grew in flagstone-bordered beds. Entire trees reached
to the upper floors, while flowers bloomed underneath
them. Many of the doorways were framed in broad
timbers, carved with designs that seemed vaguely Native American, Celtic and something else all at once.

Midnight led them past the shopping areas toward
a bank of elevators. Telestrian employees moved past
and around them, hardly giving them a glance. Kellan
noticed there were fewer humans inside the habitat
than out on the streets, and virtually no other metahumans in sight, but there were still enough humans to
keep her from standing out. She even spotted a couple
of dwarf technicians ambling off an elevator, chatting
about some technical problem they were trying to
solve.

They were alone in the elevator car. As the doors
closed, Midnight threw a glance at Kellan and Orion,
and then at the corner of the ceiling before looking
back at the doors.

Cameras, Kellan thought. It wasn't safe here for
them to speak openly, just in case someone was watching and listening. The same was probably true of most
of the complex, at least in the public areas. Kellan
leaned against the back wall and tried to look bored.

They exited the elevator on the fourth floor, and
Midnight led them down the hall like she had walked
the route many times before. Windows on one side
looked out over the street below and the vista of the
city of Portland beyond. People were just getting out
of work and the streets were filled with traffic and

pedestrians, either headed home or on their way out for the evening.

The guard sitting in front of the double doors at the foyer where the hall ended glanced up as they approached. Midnight produced her credstick once again with a smile.

"We've got a work order," she said casually, and the guard took the stick and slotted it into the reader on the desk.

"I don't have anything scheduled," he said, looking at the display.

"Last-minute call," Midnight replied. "A problem with one of the intranet hubs. Mr. Telestrian wanted it looked at on the off-shift so it would be up and running again for tomorrow."

The guard's eye flicked down to the display once again, reading the confirmation code, then back up at Midnight, who stood, cool and confident, like a loyal company employee without a concern in the world, certain of her place and her duty.

"Okay," he said, removing the stick and handing it back to her. "You know the drill: if you need to leave the floor for any reason, you need to check out and check back in at this station." He glanced at his desktop. "I'm going off duty in a few minutes, but somebody will still be here."

"Lucky you," Midnight replied lightly. "Hopefully we won't be here all night."

"Good luck," the guard told them, and Midnight led them through the doors and into the corridor beyond. She gave Kellan a brief glance and a nod to say things were going according to plan, and then glanced around to get her bearings before leading them down the hall toward one of the offices. Once they were inside, Midnight closed the door behind them and locked it.

"All right, kids," she said, unslinging her bag. "Let's get to work."

"Is it just me," Orion asked, "or was that way too easy?"

Midnight shrugged. "It helps when you have the boss countersigning your permission to get inside," she said. "Would you prefer it to be a little harder?" The elf shook his head. "Good. Then watch the door."

Orion stayed by the door, flattened against the wall, while Midnight and Kellan went over to the desk and examined the workstation there. It was the standard setup: a flatscreen display with a manual keyboard and jacks for direct neural access, all connected to the complex's main host system. Midnight slipped under the desk and pulled the plug on the terminal's connector, while Kellan took out her cyberdeck and sat down in the chair behind the desk.

She unreeled the deck's connector cable, passing it to Midnight, who plugged it into the system. Kellan took the electrode net and settled it across her forehead, making sure the connections were in place. She did an initial power-up on the deck, feeling the familiar tingle of the trodes that told her everything was functioning correctly. Midnight slipped out from under the desk and crouched next to Kellan's chair.

"The file we're looking for is named Morningstar," she said. "Don't worry about decoding it; we can take care of that once we're out of here. Just find the file and copy it . . . and keep it quiet. If there's any noise or any trouble, get out of the system and we'll clear out of here, okay?"

Kellan nodded, and Midnight gave her a smile that

spoke of complete confidence in her abilities. "Okay then," she said. "Get to it. We'll keep watch."

Taking a deep breath, Kellan tapped the GO button on her deck, and the real world faded away in a shower of gray static, replaced by the sleek digital virtual reality of the Matrix. She was inside the representation of her deck, an almost featureless white room. The Telestrian terminal port looked like a stone gateway, carved with curving runes and covered in creeping ivy, in stark contrast to the sterile surroundings. Beyond it was a path deep into a primeval forest, a virtual representation of the Telestrian host system.

Kellan stepped onto the path that would allow her to access the system. Once she stepped across the threshold of the gateway, the way she came faded into the background of greenery. Though Kellan was sure she could find her way "back," the effect was disconcerting. It was like stepping into another world, somewhat like what she felt in the forest along the border when the wyvern flew overhead. She was in unfamiliar territory, but she had ways of navigating it.

With a thought, Kellan activated a search program on her deck. Instantly, a glowing form shimmered into existence in the air in front of her—a tiny sprite with silvery, shimmering wings. They buzzed, blurring in the air as she hovered close to Kellan's face.

"Find Morningstar," she ordered the search program, and the sprite bobbed for a moment before zipping off into the shadows of the forest. Everything was silent once more, and Kellan waited.

The moments seemed to crawl past, and Kellan was sure she could hear things moving out in the darkness of the woods. *Security programs,* she thought. They were sweeping the system, sniffing out the spoor of unauthorized users. She hoped her deck's masking programs were enough to keep her hidden, but she knew that the longer she spent in the system, the greater the chance the sentinel programs would detect something amiss and—

Suddenly her sprite reappeared, hovering and bobbing in the air in front of her. Kellan reached out and brushed her hand across the glowing sphere of light around the tiny figure, and the clearing shifted around her. One path became softly illuminated, and Kellan moved toward it, toward the part of the host system isolated by her search. The branches and leaves closed in overhead, creating a kind of natural tunnel layered in shadows, lit only by the glow of her sprite.

The clearing she stepped out into appeared small, surrounded on all sides by the towering trees, and Kellan suddenly noticed it was night, despite the fact that sunlight had been filtering through the trees when she'd entered the system. Now the circle of sky in the midst of the trees was black, spangled with stars and lit by the glow of a crescent moon. From what she'd learned about Telestrian Matrix iconography, the nighttime setting suggested a higher-security node within the system.

Lush grass covered the surface of the clearing, along with a scattering of fallen leaves. In the middle of the clearing stood a low pillar supporting a carved stone bowl about a meter across. The pillar rested in the intersection of four large flagstones set into the ground. At the corner of each stone sat a statue of a wolfhound, pale gray stone gleaming almost silver in the moonlight.

With a thought and a flick of her wrist, Kellan dismissed the glowing sprite. From a pocket, she withdrew a filmy length of black cloth, like a shadow you could hold in your hand. She flung the shadow cloak around her shoulders, activating the stealth program to conceal her from any guardians of the forbidden glade. Then she approached the stone bowl.

When Kellan set foot on the flagstones, the eyes of the statues flared with greenish light. Her breath caught in her throat and she paused in midstep, ready to flee or to fight if she had to, but the stone hounds did not move. The light died as quickly as it had appeared, fading until it was gone. Kellan allowed herself to breathe once more. She said a quiet and fervent thanks to Jackie Ozone for setting her up with custom software.

She stepped up to the pillar and looked into the bowl. It was nearly filled with clear, shimmering water. The inside surface of the bowl was intricately carved with a design that reminded Kellan of a complex printed electronic circuit. She bent her head close to the surface of the water, observing the reflected glimmer of the stars and the moon, and for a moment marveling at the programming skill that went into creating it. Hidden inside her shadow cloak, she herself cast no reflection.

"Morningstar," she breathed, setting up faint ripples across the surface of the water. The system responded to her invocation of the file name, and the ripples set the reflections of the stars swirling in the depths of the water. The reflections coalesced, becoming a bright point of light concentrated in the center that sent out ripples of its own as it broke the surface, floating as light as a cork. Kellan reached out to take it.

Her fingers stopped scant centimeters away and she

pulled back her hand. This was too easy. There had
to be more security protecting the file. Even if the file
was encrypted, it should be harder to take in the first
place. Kellan looked around the glade, but saw nothing. She looked down into the water, and there still
was nothing there but the glimmering light of the
Morningstar file she'd called up. There was no sign
that anything had detected her presence or alerted
the system. She reached out once again, and saw the
reflection of her hand, reaching from below to take
the file as her real hand reached from above.

Kellan stopped again and drew back her hand. She
looked at the hound statues, standing silent and still.
She could feel something, a sensation of being watched.
Even though their hardware and software did much
of the work, deckers like Jackie Ozone claimed they
developed a sixth sense for what was happening in the
virtual world. For the first time, Kellan really understood what they meant. She knew that the system suspected her; she didn't have much time.

Wrapping her hand inside her shadow cloak, Kellan
reached out a third time. This time, there was no reflection in the now-still waters, no sign she was there
at all. She gently plucked the glowing light from the
surface of the pool, sending out the slightest of ripples.
Quickly, she tucked the file away in a pocket, and her
cyberdeck downloaded it to its storage memory. The
file was fairly small, and was hidden away in a moment. Kellan turned and slipped away from the glade
and past the hounds as quickly as she dared.

Through the darkened woods, this time without the
light of her sprite to guide her, she found her way
back to where she'd entered the system. Her persona
waved a hand as Kellan commanded the cyberdeck to

log off. A doorway, framed in ancient carved stone and covered with clinging ivy, appeared out of the shadows. Kellan breathed a sigh of relief and stepped through the doorway to complete the log-off function. She was on her way back to the real world and safety.

Leafy tendrils shot out across the exit, and Kellan ran into them. They flexed like steel wire and she felt them grab at her arms and legs, wrapping tighter and tighter and as she struggled. Kellan heard a sound behind her. She whipped her head around toward the dark woods and saw the two hounds emerge from the shadows of the trees, their eyes burning with a greenish light.

14

Kellan struggled against the grip of the tightening vines as the stone hounds stalked closer. She knew that what was happening wasn't real, just simsense piped into her brain to interpret the actions of the software in the system, but it *felt* real. If the hounds got their teeth around her throat, it would be as real as it needed to be.

She had to get loose, to get out of the system before the guardian ice programs reached her. They had to be scanning her now, double-checking her credentials. She fought, her cyberdeck translating her struggles to be free into commands to the system to unlock the log-off protocols. But the vines held fast, the system didn't respond: it was suspicious, it wanted confirmation first, and if it didn't like what it found . . .

The hounds crept closer. Kellan thought she could hear them panting, but could no longer distinguish between her imagination and what was really happening to her. She managed to pull one arm free of the vines: the system was having trouble penetrating her deck's masking routines. It didn't quite know what to do with her. Kellan braced her free arm against the stone framework of the doorway, leveraging the system's momentary weakness in the hope of breaking loose. The vines held tight as she pulled, then a couple of them tore free of the doorway. She wasn't sure what to do; she wasn't sure that any of the software Jackie had loaded onto her deck could help her with this. Kellan probably had an option at this point—she just didn't know what it might be.

One of the stone hounds growled, and she turned to see it standing close, eyes still burning. It bared sharp fangs, lips curling impossibly back. Her struggles were making it clear that Kellan didn't belong here, and the system was responding. She struggled harder, but still couldn't pull free, still mired in the security of the log-off protocols. The hound barked, a sharp sound, then it gathered itself and leapt at her.

Suddenly the world dissolved into a chaos of gray static and noise. Kellan thrashed, hands flailing to ward off the leaping hound, senses reeling, her arms still held in a tight grip.

"Kellan, Kellan!" a voice said. "Shhh, it's okay, it's okay, you're out."

"Orion?" she mumbled. Her vision began to clear, dark blurs resolving themselves into recognizable shapes.

"It's okay," came the reply again, "you're all right."

"You've just got a little dumpshock," Midnight said. "It'll pass in a minute, but we need to get out of here. Can you stand?"

Kellan could see her two companions crouching next to where she sat. Orion loosened his grip on her wrists and Kellan massaged them, trying to get her bearings.

"I think so," she said. Carefully, she pushed up from the chair, wobbling a bit as she stood. Her own body felt foreign to her, but the sensation was passing quickly.

Midnight gathered up the discarded electrode net and Kellan's cyberdeck, slipping them into the bag resting beside the chair.

"Did you get it?" she asked, and Kellan gave her a blank look.

"The file," Midnight said, more insistently. "Did you get it?"

"Give her a minute to get her bearings," Orion said hotly, but Midnight kept Kellan pinned with her gaze.

"Yeah, yeah, I got it," Kellan muttered, nodding her head, which was starting to ache. "What happened?"

"You were thrashing around," Orion replied, "like something was attacking you. We decided to get you out of there and pulled the plug." Midnight's expression told Kellan it had been Orion who made the decision.

"Thanks," she said. "There was some ice. . . ."

"Just forget it for now," Midnight said crisply. "The ice probably triggered a security alert. We need to clear out."

"But if the system is on alert—" Orion began, but Midnight silenced him with a look.

"I've got it covered," she said. "Now let's go. Kellan?"

"Yeah, I'm ready," she said, steadying herself against the desk.

Midnight took a palm-sized device from her shoulder bag and tapped a control. Putting it away, she moved toward the door.

"All right. Walk away like we finished the job and are going home," she instructed them. "You'll recognize the signal when it comes; then clear out as quickly as possible." She led them out of the office back toward the guard station. There was no one at the desk when they got there.

"Where's—?" Kellan began, but before she could finish her question a dull boom echoed in the distance, and a vibration shook the building.

"What the frag?" Orion exclaimed as a high, whining alarm sounded in the hallway.

"That's the signal," Midnight said. "Let's go."

In the main corridors of the complex, uniformed guards were quick-timing it toward the exit doors, and Telestrian employees were scrambling to get out of their way. To Kellan's surprise, rather than trying to get out of the way, Midnight grabbed a passing guard by the arm.

"What's happening?" she asked with a note of real concern in her voice. "Was it a bomb?"

"Miss, you must clear the area *immediately*," the hard-faced elf replied curtly. "Clear the area for your own safety." Then he turned and hurried to catch up with his unit.

"You heard the man," Midnight told Kellan and Orion with a sly smile. "We should clear the area, right now."

No one stopped them from leaving the building in a group with a number of other visitors and employees, joining the milling crowd outside. Telestrian guards kept people back from the building and Kellan heard sirens as Tir Peace Force vehicles closed in on the habitat. On the far side of the complex, a dark column of smoke rose into the sky.

"Keep walking," Midnight told Kellan when she looked back, and they headed away from the habitat at a brisk pace. It seemed to take them no time at all to reach their car, parked several blocks away, and Midnight pulled out onto the street, cruising away from the habitat back toward their safe house.

"What was that all about?" Orion asked, once they were in the car and on their way.

"A fail-safe," Midnight replied. "A small remote explosive and a prerecorded threat call to Telestrian. The company has had occasional trouble from the Rinelle, after all, so they have to take every threat seriously."

"They'll assume there's a second bomb," Orion said, and Midnight nodded.

"Or several more. They'll continue to evacuate the facility as they search, and no one is going to be paying attention to a low-level alert from the computer system. If we're lucky, the high alert will override the lower-priority alert we set off, and it'll be at least a couple of hours before they even notice it."

"Nice," he said with a satisfied nod. "Looks like we're in the clear."

"Kellan, once we get back to the safe house, I want to check the file and make sure it's all there before we set up the meeting with our principal to conclude our business," Midnight said. Kellan nodded.

"No problem. So . . . that's it?"

"Just about. We just need to close the deal and turn over the goods," Midnight said. "Why, looking to spend some more time enjoying the sights of Tir Tairngire?"

Kellan shook her head. "Not so much," she said. "I'm just wondering if things have cooled off back home."

"I'm sure you have nothing to worry about," Midnight replied.

Business was business, Jackie Ozone believed. She didn't double-cross a client who didn't cross her first. She had no ties to Toshiro Akimura, and didn't care one way or another about the relationship between him and Cross Applied Technologies. Whatever beef Cross had with Akimura, or vice versa, Jackie's only concern was how she could profit from it. And at the moment, it looked like she stood a good chance to make a very handsome profit off the information she passed along to Cross. So why did she have a bad feeling about the whole thing?

Because Akimura's not the only one involved, she told herself, drumming her fingers nervously on her desk. Whatever was going on, whatever the fixer wanted, it involved Kellan, and now it involved Lothan, too. It was one thing if Cross decided to have it out with Akimura, but the chances were now increasing that someone else—someone else she knew—would get caught in the cross fire.

What if this turns out to be another Zhade? Jackie wondered. She had provided information to Eve on a previous job that had brought Kellan into conflict with a toxic shaman who wanted to poison the whole Seattle Metroplex. Given the dangerousness of the circumstances and the difficulty of regaining control over the situation, Jackie would have cut her losses. But not Kellan. She chose to go after a shaman who was armed with a deadly toxin in an attempt to correct her own mistake.

Jackie chewed her lower lip nervously as she

thought. Her dealings with Eve had always been fair, but she knew the Cross company woman had ambitions. Everyone in the corporate world did, especially in positions like hers, or they didn't *get* into jobs like hers. Eve definitely saw the information about Akimura as an opportunity—but an opportunity for what?

Akimura appeared to have it in for Kellan, so Kellan would probably be glad if Cross decided to take him out; theoretically, problem solved. But from what Lothan had told her, there was more going on here. Akimura claimed he wasn't after Kellan, but that someone else was. Akimura could be lying, but what if he wasn't? What if a third party, like Cross, upset a delicate situation? It shouldn't matter, Jackie told herself. It was only business, but . . .

"Oh, fraggit," Jackie muttered. She flopped down into the padded swivel chair and picked up her cyberdeck, settling it on her lap. There was only one way to figure this out. Taking the optical cable from the deck's spool, she plugged it into the jack at her temple and powered up the deck.

Ready or not, here I come, she thought, and hit the GO button.

By the time they got back to the safe house, Kellan had shaken off the worst of the dumpshock, but a mild headache and a lingering feeling of unease still nagged at her. Despite her frightening brush with the security software, the whole run just seemed too easy. She supposed she could credit Midnight's skill for pre-planning, and the help of her contacts inside Telestrian for the low level of challenge, but Kellan's gut instinct told her something was off. Unfortunately, she had no access to additional information to help pinpoint the source of her worries, and so she had no choice but to push her concerns to the back burner.

She turned her thoughts to the file she had saved to her cyberdeck. She'd been told it was important in a power struggle within Telestrian Industries. What could be so valuable about it? If it was the key to someone's downfall, why wasn't it better protected, instead of being tucked away in an obscure part of the system?

Kellan slumped gratefully onto a cot once they got inside their room. Orion grabbed a bottle of water for himself and one for Kellan, and Midnight began changing out of her corporate clothes and into her working gear.

"Burn that data onto a chip," she said briskly to Kellan. "I'm going to let the client know that we're ready to meet and hand over the goods."

"Hey," Orion said, "give her a minute to rest, will ya?"

Midnight shot him a hard look. "Every minute we delay is another minute closer to Telestrian taking action. Whatever they do will almost certainly knock down the value of what we've got. The sooner we hand off the goods and get paid, the sooner we can drop out of sight. We can rest when we've got the cred, but the job isn't over until then."

"She's right. It's okay," Kellan said. She sighed and pushed herself up off the cot, pulling off her sweater and tossing it on the floor. Orion gave her a concerned glance.

"You all right?" he asked in a low voice.

"Yeah, just tired. I just want to get this over with."

He nodded and went to gather his own gear as Kellan sat down at the table, got out her deck, slipped on the trode net and pulled up the Morningstar file. She glanced over the file information floating on the virtual screen supcrimposed over her vision. As she had suspected, it was a pretty small file, probably text-only, maybe a few graphics; certainly no video, sim-sense or other complicated data. Maybe it was e-mail or some other kind of correspondence. Kellan looked over at Midnight, getting suited up to go out again, and commanded her deck to run a decryption program on the file.

It only took a few moments. Apparently the data encryption was old. So was the file, in fact. Kellan noted the date stamp and realized the file was last modified nearly twenty years ago! With another glance at Midnight's back, Kellan opened the file, and the first page scrolled up in the air in front of her. She'd guessed right—it was a text file.

Project Morningstar, Kellan read, *Dr. Marc Thierault, ThD, Supervisor. A study on advanced applications in conjuring for—*

"How's that file coming?" Midnight asked from behind Kellan's chair. Kellan nearly jumped to her feet, her head turning so fast that she almost dislodged the trode net.

"Fine! Um, fine," she replied, fumbling to slot a blank optical chip into the deck's port. She closed the file with a blink, then ordered the deck to burn a copy to the chip.

"Good. I'm going to make a call. I'll be back in a minute." Midnight stepped out of the room, phone in hand, and Kellan pulled the chip from the deck. As the door closed, she stared at it for a moment, then slotted another chip into the port. Orion came over and sat opposite her.

"So?" he asked quietly, one eyebrow raised.

"So what?" Kellan replied, not looking away from the virtual display.

"So what's in the file?"

Kellan didn't bother to deny opening it. "I didn't get much of a look," she said in a low voice. "Something about advanced applications in conjuring."

"So, spirits and stuff?"

Kellan pulled the second chip from the port, took off the trode net, and powered down her deck. "Yeah. I don't know how advanced it can really be, though, since the file is twenty years old. Anything in it has got to be pretty out-of-date by now."

Orion's eyebrows shot up. "Doesn't sound to me like dirt to embarrass a company rival."

Kellan shrugged, running a hand through her hair. She stashed her cyberdeck back in her bag, grabbed her armor-lined jacket and pulled it on over her tee-shirt. "Maybe it has some skeletons in it that Daddy Telestrian wants covered up from back in the day. Who knows?"

Orion shook his head slowly. "I can't wait to get out of here," he muttered.

"Yeah, me, too." She glanced down at the chip she was still holding in her hand, then took Orion's hand and pressed the chip into it.

"What's this for?"

"Insurance," she said simply. "I don't know what it is about this place, but it gives me the creeps. I've been on edge ever since we left Seattle."

"I don't think it's Tir Tairngire," the elf replied. "I think it's—"

Midnight opened the door and stepped back into the room, tucking her phone away. Her glance at their clasped hands and the faintest hint of a smile said she was surprised not to have caught Kellan and Orion in an embrace like before. Orion slipped the hand holding the datachip into his pocket.

"It's on," she said. "Let's go, Kellan."

"I'm ready," Orion replied, but Midnight shook her head.

"They wanted me to come alone. I was able to talk them into two of us, but no more."

"Then you should take Orion," Kellan said. "He'll watch your back."

"It's much more important to have magical backup," Midnight countered.

"Kel, go," Orion said as Kellan started to protest. "Let's just get this over with."

Midnight nodded in agreement. "Listen to him. We don't have time to argue."

Hacking into Eve's e-mail was the easy part. Jackie knew some of the system's vulnerabilities—she'd made a point of studying the Cross system when it became clear that her relationship to Eve was going to develop beyond a casual one. But she'd had no need to exploit those weaknesses until now. Decrypting the correspondence took a bit more work, but it turned out to be well worth the effort.

"Drek," the decker muttered as she finished reading the e-mail. This didn't look good at all. Not only had Eve been in contact with Cross' head office more times in the past couple of days than most employees at her level were in the average month, she'd also made arrangements to fly to Québec immediately for a high-level meeting, promising to present an extremely important document upon her arrival.

Jackie had poked around in Eve's e-mail before, and she knew that Eve invariably created a draft file of information she planned to present to any level of management. The draft and the final file she created resided together on her personal node at the Cross branch office in Seattle, and Eve would also carry a copy of the file on her pocket secretary. Jackie had no trouble finding the file she wanted. Eve had done a serviceable job of protecting the file, but her efforts were no match for Jackie's skill and determination.

What Jackie found in the file made her very glad she'd decided to ignore her reservations against crossing her client. The file contained all the intelligence Jackie had provided to Eve, linked to company information identifying Akimura as a former agent of the Seraphim. Jackie had only heard rumors of the top-secret division of Cross corporate security; professional black ops, full-time shadowrunners working for the company, so she didn't recognize a lot of the organization Eve was outlining. One thing was certain, though: megacorps like Cross didn't let go of their agents easily, if at all.

Eve's file laid out a plan for sanctioning Akimura in such a way as to neatly tie up any loose ends involving him and some "unfinished project" in Tir Tairngire. *So there is a connection,* Jackie thought, continuing to read. Eve planned to present the whole package to her superiors as a fait accompli, probably working under the assumption that it was easier to ask forgiveness than wait for permission, and possibly lose the credit to some other corporate climber.

No wonder Eve was acting like I'd just handed her

the find of the year, Jackie thought. She had underestimated the fixer's reaction. She thought Eve had tried and failed to cover some small excitement over the intel about Akimura. Now it looked more like she had done well not doing cartwheels. This could be a coup to make her career: bringing down a rogue company agent who'd managed to avoid retribution for years, and fixing whatever dust-up he'd been involved with all those years ago.

Apart from feeling like she should have asked for more money, Jackie wouldn't normally have cared one way or the other about Eve's plans, or about being outmaneuvered. If Akimura slipped up and Cross was going to come down on him like an orbital mass driver, well, that was life in the shadows. The problem was in the implications Jackie saw in the file, the timetable and the end point for what was clearly planned as a dramatic presentation to the company.

Company assets already in place, said the concluding bullet point, *to ensure immediate sanction and to sanitize the scene.* Eve meant to hand her bosses a gun, pointed at Akimura's head, so that they could pull the trigger or authorize her to do it. Corporate assets set up to close in when the order came down, everything neatly in place. They would also make sure there were no witnesses or loose ends, which meant . . .

"Anyone with Akimura will be taken out, too," Jackie muttered. "Damn." The Cross agents would try and minimize what they'd call "collateral damage," but they wouldn't discriminate, and any eyewitnesses to the operation would be killed as a matter of security.

"Damn," Jackie repeated. Akimura was a walking target, and anyone with him was going to get caught in the cross fire. That included Lothan and G-Dogg and, if they found her, Kellan and anyone with her. Jackie couldn't get in touch to warn any of them. Any Matrix communication could be intercepted, especially if they were already under surveillance. If Cross decided she was a loose end instead of a valuable asset, Jackie could count herself right alongside any other "collateral damage" of the operation. For all she knew, things were already underway, just awaiting a final order from the home office to execute, literally, the final stages. There was nothing in Eve's notes on the actual timing or just how far she planned to reach out, but that didn't mean these other assets weren't part of the plan.

"So," she wondered out loud, staring at the text on the virtual display, "the question is, what do I do about it?"

It was getting dark as Kellan and Midnight got into the car and pulled out onto the street. She didn't ask Midnight where they were going; odds were she wouldn't say, and Kellan didn't really know Portland well enough for the answer to mean much, anyway. She just had to trust that Midnight knew where she was going and what she was doing, and that the run would soon be over.

"When we get there—" Midnight began.

"Yeah, I know, you'll do the talking," Kellan replied.

"I was going to say, I'm counting on you to keep an eye out for any magical trouble," the elf said.

"That's not one of my talents."

"Sorry."

Midnight shrugged. "Don't worry about it. This'll all be over soon."

They turned smoothly and accelerated onto a main street. The traffic was heavier, but still light compared to Seattle at the same time of day. *Probably more traffic and emissions restrictions here,* Kellan thought idly.

A faint pop from the tiny commlink in her ear caught Kellan's attention, and she sat up in her seat.

"I think I might have some company here," Orion said, "and it doesn't sound like the usual dinnertime rush."

"Get out of there," Midnight said, indicating she'd heard the broadcast, too. "Get out right now."

"No drek," Orion replied, "I'm—" a dull *whump* interrupted the transmission, and then all they heard over the link was the sound of a hacking cough.

"Orion? Orion!" Kellan said. There was no reply except for a loud thud, followed by silence.

"Orion!" Kellan repeated.

"Kellan, stop," Midnight said. "Turn off your link. We don't want anyone else to pick up on the signal."

Kellan turned to look at the other woman in shock and horror. "What are you talking about?" she cried. "Orion is in trouble. We have to go back!"

Midnight only raised an eyebrow and gave Kellan a look of pity. "We can't go back," she said like she was explaining to a child. "We couldn't possibly get back there in time to do any good."

"I could astrally project—" Kellan began, but Midnight shook her head, changing lanes and heading for an upcoming exit.

"And do what once you got there?" she asked.

"You wouldn't be able to affect anyone. All you could do is watch, and there's a good chance they brought along magical backup."

"They . . . Telestrian?"

"Odds are. You'd just get fragged yourself."

"But how did they find us so fast?"

Midnight shrugged.

"You said it was taken care of!"

"It appears I was wrong," she said with an air of icy calm, turning off the main road.

"Where are we going?" Kellan asked.

"We need to get out of the city, then out of Tir Tairngire," Midnight answered. "This deal is blown. Our meeting could be compromised, too."

"But we can't just leave! Orion—"

"Orion is on his own!" Midnight snapped. "There's nothing you can do for him! Going back now would be suicide and you know it, Kellan! He knew the risks, and I don't think he'd want you throwing your life away to come after him."

"But . . ." Kellan began, then the words died in her throat. Midnight was right. The one thing Orion wouldn't want was her doing something stupid to help him. She would never hear the end of it.

"He's dead, Kellan, you can't help him." The image from her dream came rushing back: Orion's limp, bloody body, lying in her arms.

"No!"

"You can't help him, Kellan. Let go . . ." Her dream was true. It had come to pass.

"I still have some contacts," Midnight was saying. "They should be able to supply us with a safe way out, though it can't be the way we came in." Kellan wasn't really listening. She looked at the buildings and streets of the city flashing past, painted purple and red by the last rays of the setting sun, and blurring as she blinked back the tears at the thought of all the things left unsaid and undone because of the reality of life in the shadows.

15

Orion wanted to put his fist through the wall in frustration, but he knew it wouldn't do any good. He wished he'd had just a few more minutes to talk with Kellan, to tell her . . . Well, a lot of things, but he'd been about to tell her that he didn't think it was Tir Tairngire or the run that was giving her the creeps—it was Midnight.

Orion didn't trust Midnight at all, and he didn't know why Kellan trusted her so much. Well, that wasn't quite true. It was obvious Kellan admired Midnight's experience and her style. She wanted Midnight's approval; she wanted someone who knew the shadows to tell her she was doing a good job. She certainly didn't get that approval from anyone else, especially not Lothan.

Kellan told him once that she never really knew her mother. He figured that in some ways, Midnight must be like the mother she never had, and Kellan wanted to live up to her example.

Orion blew out an exasperated breath. Some example, he thought. Though if he was honest with himself, he would admit that he'd felt the same way when he first joined the Ancients. He remembered how he had admired guys like Green Lucifer, *omaes* who seemed to *own* a room when they walked into it. He had wanted to be just like them, to have respect—their respect. Now, more than anything, he wanted Kellan's respect. He wanted . . .

With an explosive sigh, Orion got up and started pacing the confines of the small room like a caged animal, running a hand through his hair and pulling it out of the ponytail. He just wanted this run to be over! He wanted to get ten minutes alone with Kellan so they could talk—really talk—about what had happened between them. He wanted to get her away from Midnight's constant supervision, just for a little while.

He picked up his commlink and fit it over his ear, thinking that he would call Kellan—to tell her what, though? To be careful? She already knew that. He turned and picked up his sword from where he had laid it on the table. Maybe cleaning and checking his weapons would take his mind off of—

A noise caught Orion's attention—more precisely, a *lack* of noise. The continuous hum of activity from downstairs had died away, and now the building was unusually quiet. Odd, since the restaurant was still open, and he should have been able to hear the murmur of customer conversations and the sounds of the employees working in the kitchen. Orion cocked his head and listened carefully.

For a moment there was nothing. Then he caught the sound of shuffling, brief movement—difficult to place. He drew his sword from its sheath, reached for his pistol, and keyed his commlink.

"I think I might have some company here," he said, "and it doesn't sound like the usual dinnertime rush." There was a crackle and a pause on the other end.

"Get out of there," Midnight replied curtly. "Get out right now."

"No drek," Orion said, "I'm—"

He didn't get to finish the sentence. Something came crashing through the window to hit the floor of the room, trailing a cloud of white smoke. Gas! Orion turned his head, coughing as the acrid vapors stung his eyes and made his throat and lungs burn. The broken window was out as an escape route, so he headed for the door.

A booted foot kicked in the door as thin red beams of laser light swept the gas-filled room. Dark figures, their faces obscured by the insectlike features of gas masks, leveled rifles high and low.

"Drop your weapons!" an electronically muffled and modulated voice shouted from behind a mask. "Down on the floor! Now!"

Coughing and choking on the gas, Orion hesitated for only a second before letting sword and gun slip from his fingers to clatter to the floor. He fell to his knees as the dark-clad figures approached, methodically sweeping around the room.

"Orion? Orion!" came Kellan's voice over the commlink.

He tried to say something, to warn her, to tell her what was happening—anything—but coughing was consuming all his oxygen. He looked up just in time to see the butt of a rifle as it connected with the side of his head, and everything went black.

Rough hands slapped Orion awake, and he was aware of voices growling at him as his head swam.

"Avano! Avano, versoniel!" someone said, and Orion opened his eyes. The hard-eyed elf looked at him with

contempt, letting him slump back onto the hard cot once it was clear he was awake. It took a moment for Orion's vision to clear. His throat felt like someone had scrubbed it with steel wool.

"Ni . . . ni hengar Sperethiel," he managed to croak. *I do not speak Elvish.*

"Humph," the elf snorted derisively, as if to say, "Of course not."

"Get up," he said.

"Who are you—?" Orion began, but the elf lunged forward, grabbing his shirt in both hands and hauling Orion to his feet.

"I said *get up, makkanagee!* You will stand respectfully when you address your betters, gutter trash."

"That's enough, Javin," said another voice, and Orion turned to see the only door in the room open to admit two others. They were both elves, but quite different in dress and manner from the elf called Javin. He wore military-style fatigues matching those of the men who broke into the safe house.

The newcomers were a man and a woman. He wore a tailor-made suit with a silk tie and a forest green shirt. The tie's neo-Celtic pattern was popular in Tir Tairngire. Everything about him, from his clothes to his neatly trimmed and styled blond hair to his controlled smile said he was a man of power and influence.

The woman wore a crisp, tailored skirt and blouse, but instead of a blazer she sported a deep blue robe, its edges and hem stitched with complex, intertwining elven script. *A magician,* Orion thought, a corporate wagemage.

Orion felt a chill come over him. The run was compromised, and he was a prisoner. All shadowrunners knew they risked death, but that was the least of the things that could go wrong. The worst nightmare for a shadowrunner was capture, because shadowrunners were nonentities. Their employers wouldn't acknowledge their existence, and society didn't care what happened to them. A captured shadowrunner could be interrogated, killed or worse, and there would be no hope of respite or rescue, unless he had friends who were willing to put their own lives on the line, or who were in high enough places. *Please,* Orion thought, *please don't let Kellan be foolish enough to come after me.*

"There's no need to make our guest uncomfortable," the other man said to Javin, "unless he proves uncooperative. Please"—he gestured to a table in the midst of the room, flanked by two chairs—"sit down."

Javin practically tossed Orion into the chair, but he slumped there gratefully as he tried to get his bearings. The other man sat across the table from him, like they were meeting for an ordinary business discussion.

"Do you know who I am?" he asked, and Orion looked closer at him, thinking back on the briefing documents he'd gone over with Kellan and Midnight, the background data on the run.

"Telestrian," he muttered. "James Telestrian."

"Very good," the elf answered with a slight nod. "So if you know that, you also know why you are here. Who hired you?"

"I don't know what you're talking about," Orion replied.

When Javin jammed the stun baton into his ribs, he was caught completely by surprise. Orion involuntarily cried out and fell off the chair, doubling up on the floor as the electrical charge burned through his nerves, setting them on fire with pain. He gasped for air as the initial surge of pain passed, leaving a dull, burning ache in its place.

Telestrian shook his head sadly. "I told you," he said, "there's no need for you to be uncomfortable, unless you choose to remain uncooperative." He nodded toward Javin, and the elf grabbed Orion and roughly hauled him up, dropping him back in the chair.

Telestrian glanced at the bored-looking elf woman standing behind him, nearer to the door.

"Well?" he asked, and she shrugged.

"He's an adept," she pronounced, "but I don't see any etheric connections to anything apart from that sword, or any significant mystic defenses."

Telestrian turned back to Orion. "Do you understand what that means?" he asked, and Orion mutely shook his head.

"Ms. Othorien here is a mage of no small skill. If I ask her to, she can take what I want to know directly from your mind." Orion felt a cramp of fear that dampened the aftershock of the stun baton, but he forced himself to remain outwardly calm.

"Why don't you, then?" he asked.

"Because the process is . . . not pleasant," Telestrian replied. "In fact, it's difficult, and can do some permanent damage. I also needed Ms. Othorien to evaluate you and make sure you didn't have any magical defenses that would complicate things. I'd prefer to handle this the easy way, but it's up to you."

Orion's head slumped forward, his arms hugged across his chest. He bit his lower lip. He didn't know much about magic, but he figured Telestrian was telling the truth. Even he couldn't hold out against a mage forever; sooner or later, she would break down his defenses, and just take whatever she needed to know. There would be nothing Orion could do about it. He slowly raised his eyes to meet Telestrian's cool, even gaze.

"Go to hell," he said.

Javin stepped in with the stun baton again and Orion tensed, ready to move. If he put up a fight, maybe Telestrian's hired muscle would be forced to kill him, or would at least do enough damage that the wagemage wouldn't be able to get anything out of him.

Before Javin could bring the stun baton into contact with Orion a second time, a trilling musical tone sounded from the inside of Telestrian's jacket, and he held up a hand to stall Javin's attack. Orion remained poised, watching for a better opening. Telestrian took a phone from his pocket and answered it, eyes narrowing in annoyance.

"What is it? I said no interruptions." He listened for a moment. Orion couldn't make out what the other party was saying, but it seemed to catch the elf's interest.

"Does he, indeed?" Telestrian replied, sounding bemused. "All right, arrange it. I'll be there in a moment." He put the phone away and stood, straightening his jacket and glancing at Orion.

"I'm afraid we'll need to postpone our chat for a little while," he said. "But it will give you time to consider your answers, and your attitude, for when we resume." He turned, closely followed by Ms. Othorien, then Javin. The elven bodyguard gave Orion a backward glance as he headed out the door, and his lips curled into a predatory smile. Orion had no doubt that Javin would kill him at the earliest opportunity, and enjoy it, which actually gave him a strange measure of hope. If he could provoke Javin, he had a chance to end his captivity. The door closed and locked behind them, and Orion was left alone.

He returned to the cot and collapsed, his side still aching from the stun baton hit. He did his best to try to rest, since he would need his strength to deal with what came next.

Please, he thought again, *please just let Midnight get Kellan out of here and back to Seattle.*

"What if they don't come?" Kellan asked.

"They will," Midnight replied calmly. "Don't worry."

Kellan lapsed back into silence. The comment struck her as funny in a horrible way. Don't worry? Of course not, what was there to worry about? They were only stuck in a foreign country with one of the most powerful local corporations on their tails and no sure way of getting out of the city and back to Seattle, where they might still have to deal with an angry fixer, and Orion . . .

Kellan took a deep, shuddery breath. *Not now,* she thought. *No crying.* She couldn't start thinking about Orion or she wasn't going to be of any use to anyone. But her mind and her heart refused to cooperate. Midnight had been right—they had to leave him behind. If Telestrian Industries had raided their safe house, there was nothing they could have done to help him by going back. Even though their decision made good, logical sense, she still felt like they'd abandoned him, left him to his fate so that they could get away. Now he was in the corp's hands, assuming they didn't just . . .

Stop it, Kellan told herself again. *Just stop it.* She blinked and wiped her eyes with her sleeve. Midnight kept her gaze focused out the window of the small, abandoned Soya-King where they waited.

"They're here," she said quietly, tapping Kellan on the arm. Kellan quickly gathered her composure and her belongings as Midnight slipped out of the booth, Kellan following close behind.

The woman who'd met them north of the river was waiting in the parking lot, apparently making a call from a public Matrix terminal. She glanced up as Midnight and Kellan passed by, but didn't acknowledge them in any way. Midnight led Kellan away from the pools of light around the parking lot to the darkened corner of a building down the street. It wasn't long before the elven woman followed them.

"I see our cred was good," Midnight observed quietly, and the woman smiled, though the expression didn't touch her eyes.

"Good enough," she said.

"There's more where that came from."

"This way," the Rinelle said, and she started walking down the street. Midnight followed without comment, Kellan at her side.

"Where will you get us out?" Midnight asked. "I just need to know the drop-off outside."

"Near 84. We have made all the arrangements," the woman replied, and Midnight nodded, apparently satisfied.

Kellan glanced up at the wall, which was looming closer as they headed east, and was now only a few short blocks away. The rebel brought them to an abandoned lot between two darkened buildings. It looked to Kellan like whatever had been there had been demolished fairly recently, leaving only a scattering of brick and broken glass. Two dark figures stepped from the deeper shadows.

"You know the routine," the woman said, holding out a strip of dark cloth to Kellan, who took·it and began tying it over her eyes. There was nothing to do now but trust her fate to strangers, and hope to make it through the night.

Orion sat up quickly at the sound of someone outside the door, the twinge in his side making him regret it. The lock clicked and the door swung open to admit Javin the leg-breaker, who gave him the same contemptuous sneer as before. Orion expected Telestrian's pet wagemage to be with him, but Javin was alone. He was also leveling a snub-nosed automatic pistol in Orion's direction.

"Get up," he said flatly, and Orion slowly rose to his feet. Javin sidestepped out of the doorway and gestured toward it with his gun, never taking his eyes off Orion, who hesitated for a moment. Was Telestrian's muscle here to escort him to another interrogation, or had the corporate suit decided Orion simply wasn't worth the trouble? He measured the distance to Javin with his eyes for a moment, calculating how quickly he could cross it.

"Go ahead," the other elf challenged him. "Try it."

Orion looked Javin full in the face and saw a tight smile. He saw that the barrel of the gun was held steady. Clearly, Javin meant it. He was hoping Orion would try something, give him an excuse to kill him. Orion considered that reason enough to wait for a better opening.

He walked through the door and into the hall. It

was nondescript enough to be any corporate facility anywhere in the world, but Orion assumed he was in the Telestrian Habitat. That assumption didn't tell him much, since the habitat was itself the size of a small town. Javin escorted him down the hall to an elevator, which he opened by slotting something that looked like a credstick. The interior didn't have the usual panel of buttons, just another port, where the elf slotted the stick, causing the elevator to ascend.

At least we're not headed down, Orion thought. If Javin was sent to finish him off, he wouldn't take him upstairs to do it, but down to a basement or outside. Orion glanced at the digital numbers counting off the floors, and decided for sure that they were in the habitat, and near the top floors, too. Not many buildings in Portland could have more than one hundred and twenty floors.

The elevator doors opened onto a hall paneled in what appeared to be beautifully stained and polished oak. Though Orion had very little basis for comparison, having seen mostly synthwood and plastics his whole life, he felt sure it was all real. The carpet was a deep forest green, and the air carried a faint scent that Orion found comfortable and familiar, despite having never smelled it before. He thought it smelled like the forest, but the aroma was richer and more complex in a way he couldn't describe.

Javin gestured with his pistol, and Orion preceded him out of the elevator and down the hall, where they stopped in front of a set of double doors. Javin knocked.

"Enter," came Telestrian's voice from the far side. Javin opened the door, motioning for Orion to go in, then following him into the room.

The office had a spectacular view, not of the city of

Portland, but of the private estates of the elven nobility toward the west. From the tall windows, Orion could see out over the Portland Wall toward the distant sparkling lights of Royal Hill. Looking at that view, with the silhouettes of castles and estates cloaked in primeval forest beneath a silvery moon and a sky filled with stars, he could almost believe in the faerie tales about the elven Land of Promise. Out there was the Tir Tairngire people imagined, outside the wall, protected from the incursion of the city that was not meant to be a part of their world.

Telestrian was sitting behind a finely carved desk decorated with an oak-tree-and-ivy motif, looking calm and composed. But Orion barely noticed him; his attention was immediately drawn to the other people in the room, one of whom towered above the rest.

"Lothan?" Orion said, in spite of himself. "What the frag—?"

"Orion," the troll mage interrupted. "I'm glad to find you alive. There is little time for explanations, so you must trust me." He nodded toward the Asian man in dark clothes standing next to him. "This is Toshiro Akimura. He has something to tell you, but first, we need to know everything that you know about what Midnight has been doing."

Orion looked from Akimura to Telestrian and back to Lothan. G-Dogg was standing just behind Lothan, and he nodded encouragingly to Orion. He tried to process what Lothan was saying. Was this for real? Was it some sort of interrogation technique—a trick to get him to tell them what he knew?

"Javin," Telestrian said, "wait outside." With a curt nod, the security man withdrew. Now there was no gun trained on his back, but Orion still felt confused.

"Orion," Lothan repeated insistently, "where is Midnight?"

"I don't know," he said, abruptly deciding to trust Lothan. "She got away with Kellan." He saw from their faces that it had been the answer they feared.

"We have to find them," Akimura declared. "Midnight set you up. Now she's trying to finish what she started twenty years ago, when she betrayed me and Kellan's parents."

16

The Cross Applied Technologies main system was in the independent nation of Québec, but distance was no factor in the virtual world of the Matrix. While Eve was still on a plane to the Cross main offices, Jackie Ozone was outside the company's host system in the blink of an eye.

The blocky white towers of the system soared high overhead in the virtual world, topped with lights like shining beacons. A near-constant flow of traffic came and went through the massive double doors situated at the base of the largest tower, the gateway into the Cross system.

Over the doorway, carved from the marble of the tower wall, was a fantastic, life-sized relief of an angel, head bowed in humility, feathered wings furled around his body. His hands rested on the pommel of a sword, its point at his feet, and white robes flowed around his body. Though it looked like nothing more than a fine piece of graphic design, to Jackie's trained eye, the relief was a representation of the first hurdle to overcome: a sentinel program set to watch the system's gateway for intruders. Though the stone angel appeared lifeless, its eyes closed, she knew full well it was carefully and tirelessly examining everything and everyone entering the system.

The decker withdrew a shimmering cloak from one pocket. Its silvery material seemed to flow and reflect the surfaces around it in a way that made it difficult to look at directly. Draping it around the shoulders of her persona, Jackie drew up the hood, causing her Matrix-self to vanish from view, blending perfectly into the background of the surrounding system. Thus concealed, she headed for the Cross gateway, keeping a careful eye on its watcher program.

Traffic moved at a brisk pace in and out of the system, and Jackie merged with it, planning for the system traffic to help conceal her presence. She remained ready to take action at the first sign of trouble from the system's security, but the stone angel did not stir as she passed through the doorway and into the Cross Corp host.

That's step one, Jackie thought with a sigh of relief. She knew there were plenty more opportunities for her to get caught, and that the longer she remained inside the system, the greater the chances it would notice her unauthorized access, and react. She needed not only to work subtly, but quickly.

Beyond the main doors was a great rotunda. Columns supported layer upon layer of balconies, soaring high overhead to the massive dome capping it off. The inside surface was covered in a fantastic mural, a reproduction of a Michelangelo, Jackie believed, or a Da Vinci, maybe—she couldn't quite place it. All around the circular balconies, figures moved from place to place. There were honeycombs of shelves and cubbyholes, storage nodes for information, and access to different parts of the system.

The floor was designed in the corporation's circled-cross logo using different colors of marble inlaid with gold. Corridors led off in all directions into other parts of the system. Jackie broke off from the streams of traffic moving toward one or another of the passages, and approached a rectangular brass plaque attached to the wall. It displayed an index of system nodes: a directory for visitors.

In the real world, Jackie's fingers flew over the keys of her cyberdeck, its interface translating her thoughts and macro commands into action in the virtual world. Her persona waved a hand in front of the plaque like a magician, and the fine lettering "engraved" upon it changed, as she executed a search program to find the file directory she sought.

It came as little surprise when NO MATCH appeared in small block letters in the center of the plaque for a moment before it reverted to its former appearance. The directory provided information for the top-level, public part of the system, and what Jackie needed had to be deeper, beneath additional layers of security. *Or higher, actually,* she thought, glancing up at the levels rising above the rotunda floor. She turned away from the directory and headed for a set of stairs off to the side of the entrance.

At each landing of the stairway spiraling around the central core, Jackie passed an alcove containing another statue, each gazing out over the stairs, standing composed in positions of meditation or prayer, but she could feel virtual eyes following her progress, watching her as she passed by. As she went up through each level of the system, their eyes were upon her. She huddled in the cloak drawn over her persona, relying on the masking software to conceal her presence just a while longer.

On the fourth level of the system, she headed down a long corridor lined with what looked like the work cubicles of monks and scribes, some of them occupied by robed figures carefully illuminating manuscripts—representations of the data management and storage subsystems. She paused at a heavy book placed on a reading stand, and waved a slim wand over it. In a glittering sparkle of faerie dust, the book flipped open of its own accord. Pages fluttered past, as if blown by a nonexistent breeze, then stopped on a particular page. Jackie ran a finger down the page until she found the right spot.

She immediately turned and headed down the hall, nearly running into the figure that stepped out to bar her way. He was heavily robed and cowled, leaving his features entirely in shadow, but the tabard he wore over his robe bore the circled-cross logo. Jackie came to a stop just in front of him.

"Password," the figure said in a deep and emotionless tone; more security ice, limiting access to the personnel and executive files. There was no way she could pass without responding. Jackie's persona reached underneath her cloak, producing a scroll that she handed to the sentinel. The hand that took it was flat black, like a living shadow. It unrolled the scroll and a tiny point of red-orange light appeared at the center of the parchment. It quickly spread outward, eating away at the paper and leaving only charred black ash in its wake. In an instant, the scroll was consumed and vanished.

"Password," the figure repeated, lowering its arms.

Damn! Jackie thought. Her spoof program hadn't managed to fool the password protection on the directory. Cross Corp probably had some new upgrades, so now she would need to take a more direct hand in getting past this thing. Quickly calling up the spoof program, Jackie's fingers flew over the keys, tapping commands into the cyberdeck like a musician expertly taking well-worn chords to improvise a new tune. She adjusted the program's parameters, compensating for the reactions of the security to her first attempt, aware that the ice was awaiting a response.

In a moment, her persona handed another scroll to the sentinel, this one inscribed with fine calligraphy. He unrolled it without comment, and Jackie held her breath as the robed figure paused.

Damn! There was another puff of virtual fire and the scroll was consumed into ashes, then nothingness. The robed figure was unmoved.

"Password," it said again. Jackie knew she had already heightened the security program's scrutiny, and it was only a matter of time before it decided to take more stringent measures to ensure her credentials. She was running out of time.

Kellan floated, surrounded by light. It was the most peaceful, calm sensation she could remember, like a memory of being safe and warm in her mother's arms.

My mother, she thought. *Who was she?*

A beautiful woman, a voice whispered in her mind, *so fierce and passionate, so unsuspecting of the power of love.*

Who's there? Kellan wondered.

I am here, the voice said. *I have always been here, Kellan.*

Who are you?

Kellan suddenly felt as if she was falling. Gravity seemed to reassert itself with a vengeance, and she screamed as she fell into a dark void. The warm, comforting glow of the light gave way to darkness—cold, hard and unforgiving. The light shining around her was a mere glimmer of what she had known, providing just enough radiance to cast dark shadows against walls of stone.

The light illuminated the face and figure of a man, an elf. He stood in front of her, dressed in jeans, hiking boots and a dark sweater. Over it all he wore an open robe, like the one Lothan wore, its edges embroidered with graceful elven script in silver thread. His hair was honey-auburn and worn long, like Orion and other elves she'd met wore theirs, and his face seemed strangely familiar to her, though she was certain she'd never seen him before. He held out a hand, fingers spread wide in a gesture of forbidding.

"Hold," he intoned. "By the power of this circle you are bound, by the power of your name do I compel you, by the rites and powers of the elements, I bid you now be manifest to do my will."

Kellan felt like a weight was pressing down upon her. She tried to move, to speak, but it was as if invisible hands held her fast, clamped over her mouth, muffling her and resisting her struggles. She saw shadows move in the darkness behind the elf as he reached into the pocket of his robe with one hand, and withdrew something he clutched in his fist.

"As a sign of your obedience," he said, "place your life within this stone." He opened his hand to allow a familiar amulet to spill out, dangling from its chain, which gleamed in the light. The jade stone seemed to glimmer from within, and Kellan recognized the amulet she wore, the one that belonged to her mother.

It was as if the green stone pulled at her heart and

soul, and Kellan could feel them drawn away, a glowing mist swirling, spiraling through the air. Her life was pulled into the stone like smoke, and the jade glowed faintly from within.

"By this token you are bound," the elf intoned, "and so you shall remain, until by it you are freed."

Kellan felt cold and tired, her struggles weakening. Then she saw the shadows move again in the edge of the light. Something stepped forward, a dark shape emerging. She was clad in form-fitting dark leathers, and a slim hand raised a small pistol, its surface flat black in the dimness, the cylinder of a silencer attached to the barrel.

Look out! Kellan thought, but she couldn't speak, and a part of her wondered if she should call out a warning at all. The gun chuffed: once, twice, and the elf jerked spasmodically as bullets tore through his chest. He didn't even have time to turn, instead pitching face-first onto the floor. The black-clad figure didn't hesitate, crouching by his side to scoop up the jade amulet that fell from his nerveless fingers. As she did, she glanced up at Kellan, face revealed in the light.

Midnight.

The look was only for an instant. Then she turned and ran from the light, disappearing into the shadows.

"Aerwin!" Kellan heard a distant voice call out, followed by, "Marc!"

A woman emerged from the darkness, dressed in sturdy street clothes and a close-fitting jacket of black synthleather. Her hair was cut short, her face a mask of concern and fear. She clutched an automatic pistol in one hand. Instantly, she dropped to her knees, fingers searching for a pulse at the elf's neck.

"Marc . . ." she whispered, rolling him over. "Oh, my God . . ." Blood had already begun to pool on the stone floor, soaking into the dark material of his sweater and robe, and the woman bit back a sob. She cradled his head, her free hand brushing gently along his neck. She felt for any signs of life, looking into his eyes, still wide open with shock and surprise. Tears began rolling unheeded down her cheeks, dropping gently onto his face.

Then she bent down and gently kissed his lips, lowered him to the stone, and closed his eyes. With a look of grim determination, she rose and turned back the way she had come.

"Wait!" Kellan called out. "Don't go! Don't leave me here!" she said, but the woman paid her no heed. She either didn't hear or didn't care as she rushed away, vanishing into the dark, leaving Kellan alone with the silent and still form of the elf lying on the stone floor.

"No!" Kellan called out, struggling against the bonds that held her, but her movements were weak and feeble. Then, suddenly, she opened her eyes.

"Take it easy, we're out," came a familiar voice from beside her, as Kellan raised one hand to rub her aching head and tried to get her bearings.

She was sitting in the passenger seat of a car as the road outside the tinted windows flashed by. The headlights illuminated a dark stretch of highway, surrounded on all sides by thick trees. In the distance, mountains loomed up, black shapes against the deeper black of the night sky, lit by the stars and the fullness of the moon. The hum and motion of the car were vaguely soothing.

"Are you all right?" Midnight asked from the driver's seat. She was handling the car smoothly, one hand resting on the steering wheel, eyes watching the road.

"*Unh.* I think so," Kellan said, still rubbing her head. "What happened?"

"You don't remember?"

"No," she said, trying to think back. "I remember meeting the Rinelle in Portland. . . . What happened?"

"They dosed you with a sedative," Midnight said.

Kellan thought back. Vague memories surfaced of being led, blindfolded, of the dank odors of the underground, and the smell of rust. She remembered the brief touch of a drug patch, the warmth of it spreading into her veins before she could react, then sinking down into darkness just as she realized what was happening.

"Why?" she asked.

The elf gave a slight shrug. "They tagged you as a mage," she replied. "Said it was the only way they could be sure their safety wouldn't be compromised."

"I don't remember," Kellan muttered. "Must have been strong stuff."

"I honestly didn't expect you to wake up quite so soon."

Kellan sighed. "I had this awful dream," she said. "Really weird."

"What was it about?" Midnight asked, and before Kellan thought better about it, she was telling her—until she got to the part where she had recognized the woman who shot the elf in the back, taking the amulet from him. She trailed awkwardly off into silence.

"Really? Then what happened?" Midnight asked.

"I'd . . . rather not talk about it," Kellan muttered. "Where are we, anyway?" She looked around at the dark landscape passing by, but nothing was familiar.

"Outside of Portland," Midnight said.

"Salish territory?"

"No, still in Tir Tairngire."

"How long was I out?" Kellan glanced at the car's digital clock. It showed it was past midnight.

"Over an hour."

"But we're still in the Tir?"

"Yes," Midnight replied.

Why were they still in elven territory? The border with the Salish-Shidhe Council was just on the other side of the river from Portland. Even if they left the city on the eastern side, why not head north and out of the country as soon as possible?

"Why are we slowing down?" Kellan asked instead, as Midnight slowed the car. She turned off the road, into what looked like a rest area to Kellan, coming to a stop once they were in the empty parking lot.

"We're here," Midnight announced. "Get out of the car, and do it slowly."

That's when Kellan noticed the gun in Midnight's other hand, pointed right at her.

17

"**K**ellan's parents?" Orion asked.

Akimura nodded. "At least part of what Midnight told Kellan was true. Kellan's mother was a shadowrunner in Seattle who went by the street name Mustang. What Midnight didn't tell her was that Mustang actually worked for Cross Applied Technologies, and I was her partner. We worked undercover, operating in the shadows, but also funneling information back to the company. It provided Cross with an insight into the shadows, as well as a useful resource for shadow ops. So naturally, when we heard rumors about a top-flight magical researcher in Tir Tairngire looking to defect, the company was *very* interested, even more when they found out who it was.

"Twenty-five years ago, Dr. Marc Thierault was one of the brightest new minds to come out of MIT&T's thaumaturgy program. Cross Applied Technologies helped pay for his education, but Thierault was an elf, and he was lured away from his corporate R&D job by an offer from Telestrian Industries."

James Telestrian gave an elegant shrug at the glance directed at him. "Thierault was a brilliant researcher," he said, "and Tir Tairngire needed people like him.

He understood that, and the importance of creating a homeland for our people."

Akimura allowed that observation to pass without comment. "Not surprisingly, Cross didn't see it that way. When Thierault absconded to Tir Tairngire, they protested, but the Tir government refused to acknowledge corporate extraterritorial rights, and declined to give him up. The company ultimately decided Thierault wasn't worth causing trouble with the Tir. At least, not then."

Telestrian spoke up, leaning forward with his elbows on his desk. "Dr. Thierault specialized in the study of conjuring, with an emphasis on powerful spirits and the astral metaplanes. His theories were cutting-edge; they were supposed to give us new insights into how spirits were summoned, and where they came from.

"One of the limits on conjuring is the difficulty in bridging the distance between the astral and physical planes. Dr. Thierault theorized that certain places and times offered stronger interfaces between the two planes, making it easier to conjure more powerful and capable spirits."

"A few years before the Kano hypothesis, too," Lothan murmured.

"His research even turned up an area in Tir Tairngire, in the Cascade Mountains, where the background mana was stronger than normal," Telestrian continued. "He wanted to test his theory, to see if it was possible to summon a more powerful type of spirit there."

"What happened?" Orion asked.

Telestrian shrugged. "Before we could plan the operation, the Council of Princes issued an edict.

Thierault's research was to be suspended, and the project scrubbed."

"Why?"

The elven executive smiled tightly. "We didn't ask. You don't question the Council's rulings, and they didn't feel the need to explain themselves. Thierault was supposed to be assigned to other, less sensitive research."

"And he didn't like that," Orion guessed.

"To put it mildly. He protested, but, as I said, you don't question the Council's decisions. I didn't know at the time why they cut off his research, but it was clear that the project was Thierault's passion."

"So he started looking for a way out."

Akimura picked up the story. "And that's where we came in. Cross offered to get Thierault out of Tir Tairngire, along with his research. All would be forgiven, and he would come back to the corp as a vice president of R&D, with the chance to finish his research. Mustang and I were given the assignment of getting him out of the country. There was just one potential hitch."

"The Council became aware of Marc's . . . discontent, shall we say," Telestrian added. "So they assigned him a bodyguard named Aerwin Dir Tanari to keep an eye on him for 'security reasons.'"

"Midnight," Akimura said, and Telestrian nodded. Akimura picked up the narrative again. "What the Council didn't plan on was Midnight having her own ambitions. She was supposed to be keeping Thierault safe from any outside influences, but she was also learning all about his research. Thierault was a magic geek, all too willing to discuss what he'd discovered and had been forbidden to talk about to anyone else. So, when we made arrangements to slip into Tir Tairngire and begin surveillance on Thierault to look for an opportunity to get in contact with him, we were surprised when his bodyguard got in contact with *us*.

"At first we thought we were fragged, but Aerwin offered us a deal: if we would help to get her out of the country, as well as Thierault, she would help us arrange it. Naturally, we were cautious, in case the offer was some kind of trap to lure us out into the open, but she gave us enough information to make us believe it was genuine, and she *did* arrange to put us in contact with Thierault.

"What I think Aerwin didn't expect was for Marc and Mustang to hit it off so well. She'd been leading Thierault on a bit, dangling the promise of some romance in front of him, I suspect, but from the moment he met Mustang, he didn't have eyes for anyone else. And the feeling was mutual. I know Mustang had a hard time of it, because she tried to stay professional and not get involved, but she couldn't manage it. The two of them became . . . involved. I really think Mustang was thinking of getting out of the biz once the run was over. At the very least, she knew they would be working for the same company, and that meant they would have a chance to be together."

"Wait a minute. Then Thierault—?" Orion interjected.

"Was Kellan's father, yes."

"Kellan's father was an elf?" Orion asked. "But how come—?"

"Not all the offspring of elf-human couplings are elves," Lothan said gently. "It does explain Kellan's considerable magical talent, however, among other things."

Akimura went on. "It took time to arrange things to get Thierault out of the country, and to clear an extra extraction with the company. We also had to set up the right opportunity, and Cross wanted proof of the value of Thierault's theory."

"What kind of proof?"

"The practical kind, of course," Akimura replied. "So we arranged to take Thierault to the Cascade Mountains so he could try his experiment, then immediately get out of Tir Tairngire, before we were discovered. Everything went smoothly until Aerwin turned on us. She shot Marc in the back and took the amulet he was using as part of the summoning ritual. I went after her. We struggled, and I managed to get the amulet, but then the Tir Peace Force showed up. We had to run. We barely made it out in one piece. Naturally, the whole mission was a disaster, and Cross disavowed us. We went to ground in Seattle, but kept moving, working the shadows. It was a couple of weeks later that Mustang found out she was pregnant.

"She decided she couldn't end the pregnancy, and I respected her decision. She did what she needed to do to protect her baby and, when Kellan was born, she gave her to her sister in Kansas to raise until she could retire from the business, set herself up with a new identity and raise her daughter herself.

"What we didn't count on was Midnight. Aerwin hadn't given up on getting Thierault's research, and she hadn't forgotten what happened in Tir Tairngire. She was in exile, on the run from the Tir authorities, but she found plenty of work in the shadows in Seattle and elsewhere. Eventually, she tracked us down and made her move.

"Mustang left Thierault's amulet with me for safe-keeping, which is what kept it from Midnight when she ambushed Mustang. I never heard from Mustang again."

"Midnight . . ." Orion began.

"Killed both of Kellan's parents," Lothan concluded, "and will do the same to her, if we don't act, and quickly. Toshiro, I think we've explained enough. We need to figure out where Midnight and Kellan are headed."

"I know exactly where they're going," Akimura said with a grim nod. "Where this all began, so Midnight can finish what she started." He turned to Telestrian. "We can get there on our own, but it would be faster and easier if we had help."

The elven executive gave the fixer an appraising look. Certainly, it would be easier for him if the whole affair never came to light, but would he try to keep it quiet by helping them, or by ensuring that they never got the chance to tell anyone else what they knew? He tapped a control on his desktop.

"Javin, have a VTOL standing by," he said.

"Yes, sir."

"Thank you," Akimura said, and Telestrian nodded.

"Aerwin manipulated my son to suit her ends," he replied, "and she turned on me back then, too. It's past time for some payback. And I'm sure I'll give you the opportunity to repay me at some point," he said with the hint of a smile.

"I'm sure you will."

"Were are we going?" Orion asked, as Akimura and the others headed for the door.

"To the Cascade Mountains—the place where Kellan's father died, where he summoned one of the most powerful spirits the world has ever seen, and where it has been trapped for nearly twenty years."

"Midnight, what the hell is going on?" Kellan asked.

"Get out of the car," Midnight repeated, gesturing with her pistol for emphasis. Kellan did as she was told, unbuckling her safety harness and opening the car door, as Midnight did the same on her side. Kellan slid out of her seat and stepped out of the car, Midnight mirroring her motions, keeping the gun trained on her the whole time.

"It was true, wasn't it?" Kellan asked. "The dream, what I saw, it was true."

Midnight didn't respond, moving around the front of the car, never taking her eyes off Kellan. They were as hard and cold as chips of black stone.

"Take off the amulet and hand it to me slowly," she said. "Now. Don't try anything foolish, Kellan. At the first sign of any magic, I *will* shoot you. I'd prefer to have you along for this, but it's up to you."

"The amulet," Kellan said softly. "You took it from him. . . ."

"Yes, and it was taken from me. Now . . . hand it over, unless you want me to take it from you the same way." Midnight held out one gloved hand.

Kellan reached up and slowly unfastened the chain, closing the clasp again after she'd taken off the necklace. She dropped the jade amulet into Midnight's outstretched hand, which closed around it in a tight fist, golden chain spilling out around her fingers.

"Good," she said. "Now, start walking toward the tree line." Midnight responded to Kellan's confused, frightened look with a tight, cold smile. "It's okay. As long as you behave yourself, you don't have anything to worry about. If I intended to shoot you, I'd have done it long before now."

"So it was the amulet all along," Kellan whispered, numb with shock.

"Of course. It's nothing personal, Kellan, just an opportunity too good to waste."

"I trusted you."

Midnight shook her head sadly. "Kellan, if I have taught you anything, isn't it that you can't trust anyone?"

The elven woman's head was perfectly lined up in the crosshairs of the targeting scope projected over his field of vision, zoomed in close enough to make out her features: the cool, confident expression, and the wary way she watched the younger, human woman who walked ahead of her. Though the full moon was the only source of light out in the wild lands, light-intensifying electronics made everything as bright as day to the sniper's cyber enhanced vision.

"I can take her from here," he said quietly, subvo-calizing into the pickups implanted in his throat.

"Negative," came the reply, transmitted through bone-induction speakers in his skull. "Not until we get a go order from the home office."

"I've got a clear shot."

"And you'll have others. We're to take *no* action other than surveillance until we get the order. Monitor their progress, but stay out of sight, and don't get trigger-happy. Understood?"

"I copy that," the sniper replied reluctantly. It was

such a good shot. He allowed the crosshairs to linger
for a moment, just enjoying the feel of having a target
dead to rights, knowing he could put a bullet through
her before she even knew what was happening: one
shot, one kill. Of course, that also took some of the
fun out of it, the target never knowing it was coming.

With a sigh, the sniper allowed the targeting lock
to slip, and shifted his weapon back to his shoulder,
hunkering down in the cover of the tree line. The
two women were definitely headed upcountry, which
suggested his unit's intel was right. Getting into elven
territory and into position hadn't been easy, but now
at least it looked like it was going to be worth it, once
they got the order to go ahead.

Then it would be over, just like that. They wouldn't
know what hit 'em. *Bang*.

The Cross Applied Technologies sniper slipped
back into the shadows of the trees to rejoin the rest
of his team, keeping a close eye on the two figures
headed up the mountain, and being careful not to be
seen.

Jackie retreated from the sentinel ice safeguarding
the subsystem she needed to access, in order to design
a better response to its demand for verification. Her
second attempt had been a makeshift effort, an improvisation. She needed a more carefully customized
response.

Though it added risk to her operation, she decided
to leave the Cross system for the relative safety of the
open Matrix, for as long as it took to put together a
better response. Her cloaking programs had gotten her
inside once, and, so long as nothing else compromised

the system to put it on alert, she was confident they could do so again, though she didn't want to test that theory too many times if she could avoid it.

Working in virtual space, she began assembling the components of the new program from the software she had on hand, using what she knew about Eve and the Cross systems. She had to work quickly, but not as fast as when the ice was looming directly in front of her. In less than five minutes she was satisfied with the result of her work, and reasonably confident it would do the trick. *There's only one way to find out.* She turned back toward the Cross host.

As expected, her cloak allowed her to slip past the watchful presence of the stone angel once more, through the main rotunda and up the stairs to the corridor off the main system. Once again, the guardian ice emerged from the shadows of its alcove to challenge her.

"Password," it intoned in its deep, cold voice.

This time, Jackie's persona reached into her pocket to produce a perfectly red and shiny apple, which she held out to the ice with a flourish. He plucked the fruit from her hand, and the decker held her breath, preparing to act. This time, if her spoof didn't work, odds were good the ice would trigger an alert and she'd find herself in combat.

The hooded figure raised the apple to the dark void of his face, as if smelling it. Then he suddenly engulfed the apple in his hood, and swallowed it with an audible gulp. There was a pause, and Jackie tensed.

"Password accepted," the ice said, stepping back into the shadows of his alcove. Jackie breathed a sigh of relief, and hurried down the corridor, looking for one particular cubicle. She scanned quickly through executive departments and meaningless names until she found the one she was looking for, about halfway along the subsystem.

The cubicle was unoccupied, writing materials laid neatly out on the angled surface of the desk—parchment, quills and ink—along with several envelopes, and packages wrapped in paper and twine or sealed with colored wax. All these items represented the personal storage node of her contact at Cross, the corner of the system where she'd placed her evidence of Toshiro Akimura's activities and movements.

Jackie ignored the materials on the desk itself, knowing they weren't what she was looking for. Even with the security of the company's host system protecting her files, Eve would hide her information deep in the node, for fear that an internal competitor would steal her coup. Sliding behind the desk, Jackie's persona felt along the underside of the edge. As she'd hoped, the angled desktop moved slightly, indicating that there was something below. She ducked her head and looked, and saw it was locked.

"We'll see about that," she muttered, withdrawing a silver key from her pocket and slipping it into the lock. She had to jockey it around a bit before the key caught. She gave a twist and the desktop popped open, the key vanishing back into the nothingness from where it had come.

The space inside the desk was a yawning black void, like the darkness inside the hood of the guardian ice. Jackie stared into the apparent nothingness, looking for a means of access. Suddenly a tendril of darkness erupted from the void, wrapping around the slim form of her persona. It was followed by another, and then another, as if a monstrous kraken of shadows dwelled in the depths of the storage node. Jackie struggled, her cyberdeck interpreting her movements as commands to disengage, but the ice program held her fast. She was trapped!

18

The Federated-Boeing tilt-rotor hummed through the night sky over Tir Tairngire, dark treetops rushing past below, the moonlit mountains in the distance toward the east. Black, ragged clouds had begun to veil the face of the full moon overhead, but the VTOL moved swiftly, its running lights dimmed to the absolute minimum, guided solely by its instruments and the mind of the pilot plugged directly into its systems.

Orion sat in the passenger compartment alongside Lothan, G-Dogg and Toshiro Akimura, watching the landscape below. Lothan was reading the Morningstar file on a dataslate, occasionally rumbling "hmmm" as he read something of particular interest. G-Dogg double-checked his weapons, while Akimura gazed out the windows without speaking.

"If you knew Midnight was after Kellan, why didn't you warn her?" Orion finally burst out. Akimura sadly shook his head.

"I tried," he said. "As soon as I tried getting in touch with Kellan through the regular channels, Midnight set up a run on Nightengale's, letting Kellan believe I was the client. Then she paid the Halloweeners to cause trouble and claim they worked for me.

She knew Kellan would have enough friends along to deal with them, and it made Kellan too suspicious to trust me when I finally did make contact."

"But why wait so long? Why didn't you get in touch with Kellan before now?"

"I did," Akimura said. Orion studied Akimura's face while he thought.

"You're the one who sent Kellan her mother's gear."

"Of course. When I didn't hear from Mustang after a certain period of time, I knew something must have happened to her, and assumed it was Midnight's work. I knew she would come after me next. So I used my connections to get work from a patron who was willing to invest in an ex-company man—a patron even Midnight didn't care to cross."

"A great dragon," Orion said. "Dunkelzahn."

Akimura smiled. "Yes. I was one of his most trusted fixers, which allowed me to build up a considerable reputation and network, but then things far bigger than me happened. My employer was killed, and though the inheritance he left me provided some security, I suspect Midnight saw an opportunity to make her move."

"Why didn't you deal with her first?" G-Dogg asked, and Akimura shrugged.

"I attempted it a few times, but Midnight wasn't an easy target, and, honestly, I had bigger things to worry about. Dunkelzahn's fixer network imploded, and a lot of people in the shadows didn't like learning that they could have been working for a dragon any time I hired them. I hadn't heard anything about Midnight for years—I didn't even know her by that name. She wasn't working under the name Aerwin, and I'd lost track of her—same as the Tir authorities, I imagine. I had stopped expecting trouble from her, and when I realized she was still on my trail, it was almost too late. I was very lucky to avoid her first attempts to get the amulet.

"When I realized that she was really after the amulet, I knew I needed to keep it away from her. I didn't know what destroying it would do, and I wanted a safe place to hide it—someplace from which I could eventually retrieve it. So I went to Seattle to deal with Midnight, and I sent the amulet to Kellan, along with a note and a few spare items of her mother's equipment I'd held on to. I figured it would be safe in Kansas City for a while. I didn't expect Kellan to come to Seattle looking for the truth—though I should have; she's her mother's daughter."

"If you knew she had come to Seattle, why didn't you contact her as soon as she got here?"

Akimura gave Orion a long look that spoke volumes.

"Oh—the clinic. The records Kellan saw. . . ."

"I found Midnight," the fixer said, "or, more accurately, she found me. I made the nearly fatal mistake of underestimating her a second time, and I almost didn't survive my error. Midnight left me for dead—hell, I *was* dead, technically—but I had backup plans in place. DocWagon tracked me down by following the signal from an implant Dunkelzahn had paid for, and delivered me to a discreet cyberclinic. My treatment was paid for in advance from a deeply buried escrow fund set up for just such an emergency.

"They practically rebuilt me," he said, slowly flexing one hand in front of his face as if seeing it for the first time. "Replacement tissue, cybernetic reconstruction,

backup organs, cloned parts, gene therapy—the works.
It took months of slow convalescence, surgery and
therapy, and it was necessary to let the world think I
was dead, or else Midnight easily could have showed
up to finish the job. As it was, I had to leave the clinic
immediately when she discovered I was alive. I suspect
that's when she put her plan into motion, with Kellan
at its center.

"She'd already gained Kellan's trust by then, and
was managing the situation so that Kellan wouldn't
trust me, so she could—"

Lothan's horned head suddenly came up, as if he
could hear a sound imperceptible to anyone else. He
held up one hand for silence, the other hand setting
aside the dataslate and closing around the Staff of
Candor-Brie.

"We have a problem," the troll mage pronounced,
nodding toward the front of the VTOL.

The four of them looked out the cockpit windows
to see dark clouds gathering to blot out the night sky.
Lightning tinged a bluish violet flashed between the
clouds, lighting up the darkness, followed by an echoing boom of thunder.

The pilot called back from the cockpit. "Make sure
you're strapped in!" she said. "This is going to get
rough!"

"This storm is not natural," Lothan said. "There is
magic at work."

"Can you do something about it?" Akimura asked,
already making sure his safety harness was in place.

"Let's see," the troll replied. He clasped both hands
around the staff planted on the floor between his
booted feet, and closed his eyes. The crystal atop the

Staff of Candor-Brie glowed faintly in the dimness of the cabin as the first blast of wind hit them.

The VTOL listed to the side, engines roaring against the force of the wind. The turbulence jostled the cabin, slamming the passengers against their restraining straps as the wind howled outside like a living thing, clawing to get at them. Another flash of lightning lit up the sky.

"We're not going to be able to keep flying in this! Damn, I wish we had Max at the controls," G-Dogg muttered.

The turbofan engines whined as the VTOL listed again. Lothan opened his eyes, the light within the crystal on his staff fading away.

"I've never encountered power like this before," he said. "There is a force behind the weather, but it's too great for even my arts to counter it—not from here, anyway."

"I have to find a place to set down before we get knocked down!" the pilot shouted. "Everybody hold on!" The lightning flashed again, this time perilously close to the vehicle, the smell of ozone sharp in the air as the crack of thunder rolled over the cabin, and the wind shook everything inside. The pilot struggled with the controls, using sheer muscle power to wrestle against the storm, in addition to the force of her will, which directed the VTOL's systems in the landing procedure.

They came in at a sharp angle, but their descent leveled out as the ground rushed up toward them. The clearing in the foothills of the mountains was barely large enough to hold the VTOL, but the pilot managed to set them down in it with only a few branches dislodged by their descent. They hit the ground with a rough bump, but it was a far better landing than reasonably could be expected under the circumstances. Everyone in the cabin simultaneously sighed with relief.

"Now what?" G-Dogg asked.

"We're grounded," the pilot answered, "until I can see if we took any damage, and until the weather decides to let up. I can try and radio back to headquarters for help, but . . ."

"Then we go it on foot," Orion responded with a look at Akimura, who nodded in reply, unfastening his safety harness. Lothan and G-Dogg quickly followed suit.

"Wait here for us," Akimura told the pilot, who shrugged.

"Not like I can go anywhere, anyway," she said.

"And maintain radio silence until we make contact, just in case there's someone listening in."

Jackie Ozone cursed as the trap ice squeezed her persona in an ever-tightening grip. The tendrils felt icy cold as the pressure seemed to squeeze the breath out of her. Jackie knew full well they were only false sensory impressions, but they *felt* entirely real.

Well, we can dispense with stealth. Jackie switched her deck from stealth to cybercombat mode. The silvery cloak around her persona dissolved, replaced by gleaming armor of polished chrome with flat black highlights. She pulled one hand free, and a slim silver sword materialized in it, blazing with light.

A slash of the blade severed one of the black tendrils, sparks crackling from exposed circuits within, the broken end dissolving into a shower of pixels before vanishing altogether. Several more of the tentacles waved and grabbed at her as Jackie struggled to get free. She slashed again, but watched with dismay as the first tendril she severed began to grow back.

Self-repairing, she thought, *great.* She couldn't afford to dance with the ice program. If she didn't take it out quickly, its repair subroutines would allow it to keep fighting until either the system allocated more resources to dealing with her, or she got tired enough to make a mistake. She needed to end things quickly and decisively.

Fingers flashing over the keyboard, thoughts moving faster than even she could register, Jackie shifted processor capacity from her persona's defense to offense. It was risky, but she couldn't fight a defensive battle. She made some adjustments to her attack programs, taking what she knew about the host system into account, along with the particular model of ice. If she could just hit the right section of its code. . . .

The chrome armor receded to become a simple breastplate and gauntlets over her silver-white clothes, while her gleaming sword slashed through the restraining tentacles. Several of them dropped away, and Jackie's persona was free. She could have used this chance to log off the system before the ice could entrap her again, but if she left now, there was no chance of getting the same level of access in time to accomplish her goal. The system was on alert, and there was no time to waste. It was now or never.

Jackie's sword morphed, becoming a silvery recurve bow, shot through with circuitry. She drew back the string, and a gleaming arrow appeared across it. As her persona took careful aim, Jackie was adjusting the program, tweaking its parameters on the fly, synching it up with the target. The black tentacles drew back, writhing, then launched themselves en masse at her as she let fly.

The shot went straight and true into their midst, disappearing into the black void from where the ice issued forth, swallowed up by the darkness. The tendrils slammed into Jackie like a dark wave, causing her to drop her bow, surrounding her in a crushing mass as they wrapped and squeezed. She saw black spots across her vision as she gasped for breath, fighting the urge to jack out of the system. She couldn't run, couldn't use all her defenses, otherwise it would all be for nothing. She had to hang in there. Just a little longer.

Come on, she thought, her vision starting to darken, *c'mon!* Then there was a crackling sound like glass splintering. From the depths of the void, a silver-white coating of circuitry spread out along the tendrils, from their bases to their tips, covering them completely and freezing them in place. They stopping moving as they were covered, and Jackie exerted the full strength of her deck's processor against them.

The tentacles shattered, gleaming shards raining down before dissolving into random pixels and then nothingness. It'd worked: she'd been able to use the IC's own self-repairing subroutine against it, introducing a flaw, like electronic cancer, disabling the program from the inside out. Where the ice once was, Jackie could now see a set of stairs leading down, the inside of the virtual desk now lit from within, rather than pitch dark. Cautiously, her persona slipped down the stairs to find out what lay beyond.

The VTOL landing did not go unnoticed. Some distance away, a man lowered a compact pair of electronic binoculars after the aircraft dropped down below the tree line.

"Crash?" a dark-clad figure at his side asked, and he shook his head.

"Unlikely. No smoke, so it's a safe bet they managed to put down."

"Who are they?"

He shook his head. "I don't know, but this party is starting to get crowded." He keyed the subdermal microphone implanted in his throat, transmitting on a scrambled frequency. "Gabriel to all points," he said, "we've got more company—a tilt-rotor with Telestrian Industries markings, put down a couple klicks from my position. Keep sharp and report in as needed, but do not, repeat, do not engage unless absolutely necessary. We wait until we get the go order, people."

Gabriel waited to get confirmation from the members of his team, and then signaled again.

"What's the status of our visitors?"

A voice replied through his subdermal induction speakers. "Headed up the mountain. I'm keeping them in sight."

Gabriel nodded. "It's a good bet the newcomers are headed the same way. We'll join up with you. Keep them in view, and give me regular updates on their progress, but stay out of sight." He closed the channel, than spoke over his shoulder to the other member of his team close at hand. "Let's move out."

Gabriel glanced back in the direction where the VTOL landed. This was hardly the first mission he'd carried out for Cross Applied Technologies where he didn't have all the information, but he was starting to get a bad feeling about it. This mission was looking anything but routine, and Gabriel didn't like unexpected complications. He stowed his binoculars, grabbed his gear and headed for the rendezvous. He hoped orders from HQ came through soon. The faster they got this over with, the better.

19

"If you intend to kill me, why don't you just get it over with?" Kellan asked.

"Kellan," Midnight replied in a tone of mock concern, "I told you, if I wanted to kill you, I would have done it by now."

Which means you need me alive for something, but what? She still didn't know what Midnight wanted with her amulet, or what they were doing out here in the middle of nowhere.

Kellan wanted to kick herself. How could she have trusted Midnight so completely? Dammit, how could she still trust *anybody* in this business? Lothan already had taught her, quite graphically, that no shadowrunner could be trusted, not even those closest to you.

Except maybe Orion. As Kellan thought about him, about the way they'd left him behind to suffer an unknown fate, she felt a cold fury welling up.

"You set it up, didn't you?" she accused Midnight, stopping to turn and face her. "You sent the Telestrian security to the safe house to take out Orion, didn't you? You set up this whole thing!"

"Keep moving," came Midnight's curt reply, emphasized with a wave of her gun.

"Or what? You'll shoot me? I don't think so. You need me for something."

"Not so much that I won't shoot you the minute you become more trouble than you're worth, Kellan," Midnight said coldly. "Don't overestimate your value. I'm perfectly willing to leave you here and take my chances. So don't be foolish, and *keep walking*."

Kellan looked Midnight in the eyes, and, this time, she was absolutely sure that she was telling the truth. So she slowly turned and began heading back up the incline ahead of them.

"You set up this whole thing, didn't you?" Kellan repeated. "I mean, it's no coincidence that we ended up here," she waved her hand, taking in the whole of the dark woods and mountainside.

"Perhaps I just saw a good opportunity," Midnight replied coyly.

"No," Kellan shook her head. "It's more than that. It's something about this place, about Tir Tairngire. Was the run for Telestrian even real?"

"In a manner of speaking," Midnight said. "Timothy Telestrian thinks it was real. I convinced him I could get information to blackmail or embarrass his father, and he wanted that badly enough to make certain arrangements and not ask too many questions."

"But what we took from the Telestrian system couldn't have embarrassed anyone."

"It certainly wasn't what Timothy thought I was going for, though I suppose the file could be embarrassing to the senior Telestrian if put into the right hands."

"Except you never meant to turn it over to him. Did you even set up a meeting with him to deliver the chip?"

Midnight's silence was all the answer Kellan needed.

"You wanted us to get out of there because you sold out Orion to Telestrian and knew they were on their way."

"I didn't particularly want him to come in the first place," Midnight said. "But it did prove useful to have some meat to throw to the dogs."

"You . . ." Kellan spun back toward Midnight.

She wasn't sure which stopped her faster, the sound of the gunshot or the swift kick that followed it, hitting Kellan in her midsection and doubling her over on the rocky ground. She heard the hammer draw back on Midnight's gun as she coughed and tried to catch her breath. Reflexively, she felt for blood, for any sign of a wound.

"Don't worry," Midnight said with a tone of contempt. "That was a warning shot. But that's your only one, Kellan. I'm not some fragging little girl playing shadowrunner. If you do as you're told, you might get to walk away from this. If not . . ." she shrugged, keeping the gun leveled at Kellan. "Now get up and keep walking."

Kellan struggled back to her feet, and they continued up the slope of the mountain.

"How far are we from this cave?" Orion asked as they hiked up the mountain.

"Not too far. We should be there pretty soon," Akimura replied, consulting a portable GPS. "Assuming the weather holds out," he added, glancing up at the dark clouds gathered overhead.

"I think it will," Lothan replied, breathing heavily. "I suspect it has accomplished what it was supposed to do. It's more a question of whether or not I'll hold out." The old troll was physically powerful, but not exactly built for climbing. He leaned heavily on his staff as they clambered along. Orion had taken point, and had to resist the urge to rush ahead. Only Akimura knew exactly where they were going—plus, there was no telling what other surprises might be waiting for them on the way.

"Do you know what Midnight is planning to do?" Lothan asked Akimura, and he shrugged.

"Something involving the spirit Marc bound in the cave. You're the expert, but I would guess that with Marc's research notes and the amulet he used as part of the ritual, she should be able to accomplish something, even though she doesn't have the Talent."

"Possibly," Lothan muttered. "It depends on a great many factors. I knew there was something nagging at me about that blasted amulet! I had never seen a focus quite like it before. Because it wasn't exactly a focus, merely invested with spiritual energy—and a considerable amount of it, at that. The ritual also is like nothing I've seen before. It's quite daring—shouldn't even be possible without the kind of interface between the astral and physical planes Dr. Thierault discusses. Under the right circumstances, it's just possible that Midnight might be able to use these components to some end. Assuming she hasn't also been concealing magical talents from me all this time."

"I don't think so," Akimura said with a bitter smile. "Midnight has her secrets, but I don't think she includes magic among them."

"Which suggests she'll leave Kellan unharmed for the moment."

Orion's heart leapt at that conclusion, and he turned back to glance at Lothan.

"Ya think?" G-Dogg asked, and Lothan nodded heavily.

"Midnight may be many things, but she's not stupid. If she needs a magician for whatever she intends to accomplish, she'll have Kellan along, and she'll try to convince her to do it, one way or another."

"And if she doesn't?" Orion asked. Lothan's look told him all he needed to know, and he turned and began heading up the incline again.

"And what's our plan when we catch up with them?" G-Dogg asked.

"We persuade Midnight to let Kellan go," Lothan replied.

"Forcefully, if necessary," Akimura added.

G-Dogg grinned. "Hey, fine by me."

Orion scanned the mountain slope ahead. The trees were still heavy enough to make it difficult to see very far, though the darkness posed little problem for him. Elven eyes could see a considerable distance, even by the light of only the moon and stars.

He paused and slowed his progress, allowing the others to catch up. As Akimura approached, Orion dropped his voice so no one could overhear them.

"I think I saw someone watching us from higher ground, around two o'clock," he said, careful not to look in that direction.

Akimura glanced down, as if consulting the GPS unit, then up ahead of them, eyes flicking in the direction Orion indicated.

"You sure?" he asked quietly, and Orion nodded.

"As sure as I can be."

Akimura called a halt, making it look as if he was showing the others something on the GPS readout as he spoke quietly.

"Orion says he thinks he saw somebody watching us from ahead near the tree line. I think we should head north-northwest to get out of sight, and try to circle back around."

"What about Kellan?" Orion asked. "We can't waste time playing games."

"We're not going to do her any good if we walk into an ambush," Lothan replied. "I may be able to do us one better once we get out of sight."

"All right." Akimura pointed off in their new direction. Hopefully, whoever was watching would assume they were making a correction in their course, still following their map or positioning system.

Orion fought the urge to look again at the place where he had spotted the watcher. He waited until they had moved off a ways before allowing his gaze to drift back in that direction, scanning slowly across. A few minutes later, he again spoke quietly to the rest of the team.

"I don't see anyone," he said, "and we're out of sight of the place where I spotted our watcher."

"A bit further, to be on the safe side," Lothan said. In a few minutes, they stopped near a large tree, the mage leaning on his staff.

"Now then," he said, "let's see what sort of company we have." He held out a hand, palm up, closing his eyes and whispering magic words just under his breath. Orion saw the crystal on the Staff of Candor-Brie glow faintly, and a similar glow appeared cupped in Lothan's palm. It grew into a faint, misty ball of light, shimmering in the darkness, before Lothan opened his eyes.

"Now we'll see what there is to be seen."

"Won't whoever it is notice?" Orion asked, and Lothan shook his head.

"Fear not," he replied. Then he gently blew the glowing light off his hand and it zipped off among the trees, fading as it moved until it vanished altogether. "It shall be unseen and unheard to mundane senses," Lothan pronounced. Orion watched it vanish from sight.

"Now what?"

"We wait," Lothan said.

"We should keep moving . . ." Orion began, but Akimura shook his head.

"Not until we have a better idea what we're dealing with. We could be walking right into trouble."

"How long is this going to take?" G-Dogg asked.

"Not long," Lothan said over his shoulder. "The watcher will do a quick recon and then report back to me."

"In the meantime, we should keep a lookout," Akimura said.

"An admirable idea," a voice said, "if a little late."

Everyone reached for a weapon, but paused at the same instant as dark-clad figures emerged from the shadows, their weapons trained on the shadowrunners. The faint red traceries of laser sights glimmered in the darkness around them, and Orion slowly removed his hand from the grip of his pistol, keeping it out where they could see it. The others did likewise.

"It's getting a little crowded around here," said the same voice. "So I agreed it was time to do something about it. Lay that staff down on the ground and step away from it, if you please," he said to Lothan.

The troll mage glowered, but did as he was instructed, setting his staff down and taking a step back as he straightened up. A moment later, the faintly glowing ball of light zoomed back toward him from the trees, bobbing excitedly near Lothan's horned head.

"Do ya think it found them?" G-Dogg asked in an acid tone, and Lothan's frown deepened. He dismissed the tiny spirit with a flick of his hand, making the light vanish with a barely audible popping sound.

"Who are you?" Orion asked.

Akimura, standing near the elf warrior, silently regarded the black-clad figure apparently leading this team. His voice was familiar, and it was a moment before Akimura was sure the man didn't recognize him. *After all, I've changed quite a bit since then.* Considering the reconstructive surgery and facial alterations he'd undergone, he didn't think he would be recognized as long as he kept quiet. It was vital that Gabriel not recognize him. In this place, even after so long, being recognized by a fellow Seraphim operative could easily be fatal.

"I think it's better for you not to ask too many questions," replied Gabriel, emphasizing his point by indicating his weapon. Orion ignored the man's advice.

"Are you working with Midnight?" he asked.

"I don't think so," Lothan answered thoughtfully, looking them over. "They're corporate shadow ops."

Akimura's face didn't betray his thoughts, but his mind was racing. How had Cross found out about what was going on in Tir Tairngire tonight? He considered and discarded possibilities at a rapid-fire pace, and wondered what he might be able to do about the situation.

"What are you going to do with us?" Orion asked. The elf was tense with barely pent-up energy, and Akimura wondered what the chances were that he would make a move. If he did, the whole team was dead.

"That's not my decision," Gabriel said. "But if you cooperate, then you have a chance to survive this. If not . . ." He shrugged slightly, his weapon remaining steady on its target.

"Surely it's not a coincidence that a corporate team is here in Tir Tairngire tonight," Lothan observed.

"We have our sources and our reasons," Gabriel said. "I could say the same about you. In fact, why don't you tell me what you're doing here?" The shadowrunners exchanged silent glances. "Remember what I said about being cooperative?" Gabriel added, emphasizing his words by inclining his head toward the other shadow ops.

The dark-suited executive assistant squinted against the backwash of the turbofans as the company VTOL landed on the pad atop the Cross Applied Technologies headquarters in Montreal, in the independent nation of Québec. The gold-circled cross logo gleamed from the craft's side in the reflected illumination of the same logo on the side of the building, shining out over the city skyline. He scampered toward the craft as the fans slowed, the wind started to die down, and the side hatch opened to allow the woman wearing fashionably conservative business attire to step out onto the landing pad.

"Ms. Henshaw!" he called. "I'm Carter LaValle, assistant to Monsieur Cross. Welcome to Québec." He spoke slightly accented English.

"Thank you," she replied with a nod.

"Arrangements for the meeting have been made," LaValle said. "If you'll come with me, I'll take you straight to the conference room."

Eve allowed LaValle to lead the way inside the building and to the bank of executive elevators that would take them to the conference room, where she would make her presentation. She allowed herself to savor the experience of passing through the uppermost executive levels of the corporate headquarters, guided by one of the CEO's personal assistants. If all went well, she could look forward to this sort of treatment as her due. She still hadn't decided whether she should ask to take over all covert operations in western North America, or focus on the more active eastern half, where Cross' primary rival, Ares Macrotechnology, was headquartered. Seattle offered opportunities, but beyond the UCAS enclave, Cross interests tended to taper off.

The elevator glided smoothly to the appointed floor, the doors opening with a faint pneumatic hiss and a musical chime. LaValle guided her along the carpeted hall to a private conference room, holding the door open for her to enter.

The room was larger than most apartments in Seattle. The far wall appeared to be floor-to-ceiling windows looking out over the vista of the city of Montreal, but Eve knew they were actually holographic crystal matrices layered over the walls, projecting an image of the view on the far side of the heavily reinforced exterior wall. Real windows, even bulletproof ones, were too much of a security risk in this part of the building.

The conference table was oak, stained with a warm

finish, surrounded by comfortable chairs covered in soft leather. A sideboard offered refreshments, while the opposite wall was dominated by a wide flatscreen display and wood-finish cabinets concealing sophisticated electronics: voice operated communications and multimedia equipment, all linked with the company's computer network and the building's internal systems.

"Please make yourself comfortable, and prepare whatever materials you need," LaValle told her as she was taking in the room. "Monsieur Cross will join you shortly for the meeting. If you should need anything, please let me know."

Eve thanked him, and the assistant withdrew, closing the door behind him. She allowed herself a moment to sink into one of the chairs at the table, enjoying the comfort of it after the long flight from Seattle to Montreal. She was tired, but felt elated, charged with excitement, and she quickly tucked her carryall under the table, withdrawing her pocket secretary and flipping open the cover.

It took only a moment to access her secure node on the company's main server in preparation for retrieving the data files she had prepared for the meeting. The system asked for her passcode a second time, so Eve entered it again—she must have mis-keyed the first time in her eagerness to get ready. This time, the system accepted it and gave her access. She pulled up the files and opened the program she needed to connect to the conference-room display. While she waited for Mr. Cross to arrive, she reviewed her notes. A few minutes later, the conference room door opened and Eve stood, pushing back her chair.

A woman wearing sunglasses and a dark suit entered the room. Her blond hair was short and slicked back, making her look almost plastic. She scanned the room with a quick but professional glance before stepping aside to allow LaValle and two other men to enter behind her. Eve didn't recognize one of them, but she instantly knew the other.

Lucien Cross, the founder and CEO of Cross Applied Technologies, had the distinguished and mature look appropriate for a man in his position, but his age seemed to hover at an indeterminate point somewhere between late thirties and late forties, thanks to the wonders of modern medicine and magic. His dark hair was immaculately swept back from a high forehead. The traces of gray at his temples and in his neatly trimmed beard could have been affectations, and were certainly there by choice. The same was true of the lines around his eyes, the corners of his mouth, and across his brow. His whole persona spoke of a man in complete control of everything around him, including his image. Cross wore a hand-tailored suit, a crisp white shirt and a silk tie. His only other ornamentation consisted of the heavy ring he wore on his right hand and the polished chrome of the datajack discreetly located behind his right ear.

"Ms. Henshaw," he said in a deep, unaccented voice. "You understand this meeting will be necessarily brief."

"Of course, sir," she replied respectfully, as Cross' bodyguard closed the door behind them and took up a position beside it.

"It wouldn't be happening at all," Cross continued, "if what you related in your proposal was not so promising."

"Yes, sir," she answered. Cross and his companion took up seats at the conference table directly across from Eve, facing the display screen on the far wall. LaValle stood behind and slightly to the left of Cross, dataslate in one hand. Eve remained standing and, at a nod from Lucien Cross, she began.

Akimura spoke up before any of the others could reply. He nodded his head toward the peak of the mountain. "There's a cave up there where a powerful spirit is trapped," he said in a voice that sounded far more like a native speaker of Japanese than his usual diction. None of his companions reacted to the change, as if they didn't notice it.

"And you're looking to free it?" Gabriel asked.

He shook his head. "Just the opposite. We're looking to make sure it stays there."

"On whose behalf?"

"I'd say it's in everyone's best interests," Akimura replied.

"I'd guess the two ladies ahead of you disagree."

"You've seen them?" Orion asked, and Gabriel seemed to notice him again. There was a fractional pause, then he nodded.

"We've been keeping the area under surveillance," he said, returning his gaze to Akimura. "So whom do they work for, and whom do you represent?"

A howl of wind blasted through the trees, shaking branches and scattering dead leaves in front of it. Gabriel's team didn't waver in covering the shadowrunners, but everyone in the clearing looked up at the dark clouds rolling across the sky.

"So you can see," Eve concluded, the screen on the far wall displaying a satellite map of the Pacific Northwest, with a slightly smaller inset focusing on the elven nation of Tir Tairngire, "we have a prime opportunity—" She paused when Mr. Cross held up a hand, indicating he had heard enough.

"Michael?" he said to the man sitting at his right hand. This second man had remained silent since entering the room, and Eve had ignored him, assuming he was another assistant or junior executive. Now she looked past the studiously bland exterior and saw a penetrating intellect. She felt sure that this man had missed no detail, no implication of what she had presented. He took a pocket secretary from inside his jacket and manipulated the controls for a moment. The wall display responded to what he was doing, and Eve watched as the information she had acquired was run at optical processing speeds through comparative analysis.

"The genetic map and physiological data is a match for our records, sir," Michael told Cross, poring over the palmtop, "but it has been altered to make it so. The signs of tampering are subtle, but they're there."

Lucien Cross' eyes narrowed. "Ms. Henshaw?" he asked in a dangerous tone of voice. "Do you have an explanation for this?"

"I . . . I don't, sir, but—"

"Did it not occur to you to confirm that your information was genuine before deciding to come all the way here to waste my time?"

"Of course!" she said. "I mean . . . yes, sir. I double-checked the information against the company records, and it was an exact match. There were no signs of tampering!"

"To the less experienced eye, perhaps," Michael said quietly.

"I checked these facts myself," Eve said angrily. "I trust my source. Maybe you're mistaken!"

The other man didn't react, but Cross leaned forward slowly, dark brows drawing together over his stormy gaze. "Are you saying, then, that the director of the Seraphim doesn't know his business, Ms. Henshaw?"

"The . . ." Eve began, the words dying in her throat. She glanced at Michael again—*Michael*—who was regarding her calmly, no emotion showing on his face. No one ever saw the director of the Seraphim. His identity was a secret closely guarded at the highest levels of the company. She turned back to her boss.

"Mr. Cross—" she began, but he cut her off, speaking to Michael as if she wasn't even in the room.

"So the data is a forgery?"

The Seraphim director nodded. "Almost certainly. A job this well executed means someone either had access to our records or to original genetic samples, but given the way the information matches up with ours, I'd say it's the first. The match is almost too good. Add that to the evidence of alterations in the file . . ." He laid the pocket secretary on the table. "I'd say someone *wants* us to believe he's still alive."

"And you authorized this operation?" Cross said to Eve, pointing to the map displayed on the wall screen. She mutely nodded her head. The CEO turned back to Michael.

"One of your agents is in place?"

"As usual."

"Get me a line," Cross said. "Now."

"As fascinating as all this is, I think it's going to become quite inhospitable out here quite soon," Lothan said, looking at Gabriel. "What is it exactly that you plan to do?" The team leader turned his attention back to the troll.

"I *should* just leave the lot of you to rot," he said, "take care of the other two up the mountain, and call it a night."

"Assuming that's what your employer wants," Akimura countered. "After all, we all know how . . . unforgiving companies can be when people fail to live up to their expectations."

The wind roared again, and a flash of lightning momentarily lit up the sky, the peal of thunder immediately following suggesting the strike was uncomfortably close by.

"Personally, I don't . . ." Gabriel began, then he trailed off, eyes focusing past the fixer, as if listening to something the rest of them couldn't hear. Orion gathered himself as if to strike, and Akimura practically prayed for the adept to wait. The rest of Gabriel's team didn't react, keeping their weapons closely trained on the shadowrunners, who would still be caught in a killing zone if they made any sudden moves.

The slight movement of Gabriel's jaw made it clear he was subvocalizing responses. He suddenly gave a short, humorless snort of laughter, and a sardonic half smile curled one side of his mouth. His thumb rested on the hammer of his pistol. Everyone tensed, but then Gabriel uncocked the gun and raised it so it was no longer pointed directly at the runners.

"The mission's scrubbed. We're moving out," he said to the rest of his team. "Seems you get to live," he said to the shadowrunners.

"Lucky us," Akimura replied quietly.

Gabriel suddenly leveled his gun directly at the fixer, its targeting laser painting a red dot squarely on his forehead, like a glowing caste mark in the darkness.

"Don't fool yourself," he said. "I could kill you right here and right now, orders or no orders, and be done with it. Who would even know?" There was a dreadful pause as he waited to see how Akimura would respond, but the fixer remained completely still, locked eye-to-eye with the Cross company man. After what seemed like an eternity, Gabriel raised his weapon again.

"But I'm a professional," he said, "and I don't want to waste the time or the ammo. Stay out of our way and hope our paths don't cross again, street trash."

He gave a hand signal, and his team went into motion, backing away into the shadows of the trees, their weapons still carefully trained on the shadowrunners. Another flash of lightning illuminated their retreat for just a moment before Gabriel, too, backed away. Then the Cross team was gone, vanished into the darkness.

"What the frag just happened?" Orion asked, glancing around to make sure the sudden withdrawal wasn't some sort of trick.

"We got lucky," Akimura said, drawing his gun. "Damn lucky. For the first time in a long time, I think somebody up there likes me. Let's move. I don't think we have a lot of time left." He glanced up at the sky just as the wind howled, shaking the trees, and a heavy rain began to fall.

Midnight guided Kellan unerringly to a ridge along the mountainside and the narrow entrance to a cave. The rocks and rubble scattered around the cave mouth still smoked from what looked like some sort of explosion. From the blackened marks, Kellan wondered if one or more of the lightning bolts they'd seen had struck there. Though the cave was cloaked in shadows, a faint, golden light shone from within the mountain.

"Inside," Midnight said curtly, and Kellan picked her way over the debris, ducking her head to step into the passage in the rock.

She somehow wasn't surprised to feel a sense of familiarity as she moved into the cave. It looked exactly like the place she'd seen in her dreams, only from a different perspective. At the widest point, where the ceiling was high enough that she could have reached up and not been able to touch it, Kellan saw the source of the light filling the cavern.

The glow came from a figure kneeling on the stone floor, as if in prayer or meditation, made up entirely of golden light, with white-gold wings furled around its body. As they approached, the shining head rose, crowned in a bright halo, and its eyes opened, their depths filled with white-hot light that seemed to look right into her soul.

"Kellan, say hello to Morningstar," Midnight said.

Hello, Kellan, came the voice in her mind. *I have been waiting for you for a very long time.*

20

Kellan looked at the fantastic, shining spirit, unable to comprehend what she was seeing.

Waiting . . . for me? she thought.

Yes, it replied. *Ever since the day your father summoned me.*

My father? Kellan remembered her dream of the elven mage calling and binding a spirit, and now she understood that in the dream, she had been the spirit. She had seen Midnight shoot her father!

Yes, said the spirit, *Midnight killed him. You and I have long been connected by the amulet, and it was my vision I sent you.* Kellan looked at the jade necklace now in Midnight's possession.

"Impressive, isn't it?" Midnight said, nodding toward the spirit, her eyes reflecting its golden glow. "Can you imagine what a spirit this powerful can accomplish?"

"Is it enough to be worth so many lives?" Kellan said.

"So, you've started figuring it out," Midnight mused. "All those and many more, Kellan. I hope now you understand that you should not cross me."

"Why did you bring me here?"

"Because I might need you," the elf replied. "I have

Thierault's notes, what I remember from the original summoning, and this," she held up the necklace, "but they might not be enough to command this spirit. I might still need a magician, perhaps even one related to Thierault by blood."

"My father," Kellan said quietly, and Midnight nodded.

"That's right. I figured as much from the timing. Too bad you didn't take after him in more ways than just inheriting his magical talent; you'd have made a good elf."

"Not if it means being a fraggin' slitch like you!" Kellan shouted, the anger she'd been stoking in her heart for the last twenty-four hours finally flaring.

"Temper, temper," Midnight said, pointing her weapon at Kellan's heart. "If you play it smart, you can still walk away from this, Kellan. Once I get what I want, I'll have no further use for you, and we'll call it quits, but if you force me . . ." She left the remainder of the threat unsaid, but her intent was crystal clear.

For a moment, Kellan wondered if Midnight was fast enough to kill her before she could get off a spell that would fry the lying murderer to a crisp. What did she have to lose, after all?

No, Kellan, Morningstar's voice came back into her mind. *There is another way. I can help you, if you will help me.*

Help you?

Help to free me, the spirit replied, *and we can both have our revenge.*

Kellan didn't look away from Midnight. *Why should I trust you?*

What choice do you have?

"So," she said to Midnight. "What now?"

"Now I perform the ritual, and you keep an astral eye on things and tell me what's happening. Any tricks and . . ." she waved the gun in Kellan's direction.

She will be vulnerable during the ritual, Kellan, Morningstar's voice whispered in her mind. *Just do as I ask. . . .*

Kellan felt completely empty and entirely filled with rage. She simultaneously understood that she could not trust either of them, and had no choice but to behave as if she did. Her mind was empty of any other options. "All right," she said out loud, answering them both at once, "let's get this over with."

"I knew you'd see it my way," Midnight said with a smug smile.

Outside, the storm intensified, until the shadowrunners were leaning heavily into the wind as they struggled up the mountain slope. Rain slashed down in driving sheets, with the wind slapping it in their faces, lightning flashing and thunder booming overhead. One bolt came close, splintering a tree and sending part of it crashing down near Orion, but the elven warrior rolled nimbly out of the way.

"There!" Akimura shouted, pointing to a tiny, glowing dot of light in a fold of the mountain's rocky flank. Orion squinted to see it, then broke into a run, the others close behind.

Kellan stood close to the wall while Midnight spoke the words of the ritual. If Midnight had any concerns about keeping one eye (and her gun) trained on Kellan while speaking the mystic phrases, she didn't show it. Much of the ritual was in Sperethiel, which sounded both lyrical and oddly familiar to Kellan's ears. She realized as Midnight spoke that the words she'd heard in her dream were in Elvish as well, but she'd somehow understood them at the time.

"Seterin'ranshae!" Midnight intoned, then switched to English, holding up the necklace in her free hand. "Known as Morningstar, by the power of your name do I compel you, by the rites and powers of the elements, I bid you, be manifest here to do my will and no other. By this token, you are so bound. Arise! Arise and do my bidding."

The necklace, Morningstar said to Kellan. *She must put on the necklace.*

"You have to wear the amulet to command it," Kellan advised her, speaking for the first time during the ritual. At Midnight's questioning look, she added, "The power is there, I can see it, but the amulet needs to be worn to gain its full effect."

Midnight gestured for Kellan to approach. "Put it on me, then," she said, "but don't get clever."

Kellan stopped in front of Midnight, and Midnight handed her the necklace. She could feel the muzzle of Midnight's gun pressing against her stomach, the elf's dark eyes as cold as stone. Kellan unclasped the golden chain, slipping it around Midnight's pale neck and smoothly fastening it in back before taking a step away from her.

"Now what—?" Midnight began, but the rest of her question was choked off. The jade amulet burned with a fiery light, and the elven woman staggered back as if struck. The gun slipped from her suddenly nerveless fingers to clatter onto the ground as light poured from Midnight's formerly dark eyes.

Yes! Kellan heard the triumphant call in her head, as Midnight gave a strangled cry.

There was a clap of thunder outside that echoed in the cave as the spirit Morningstar seemed to dissolve into a golden mist. It transformed from a glowing, angelic being of light into a figure out of nightmare: horns and claws and bared fangs, burning with the color of a forge fire. Kellan only saw it for an instant before it flowed into Midnight's eyes and open mouth, pouring into her as the amulet glowed and she stood, frozen. In an instant, the shining form of the spirit was gone, and Midnight stood alone, head bowed, dark hair veiling her face.

Kellan hesitated only a split second before going for the gun on the floor, but that hesitation was enough. As she crouched to reach for the weapon, Midnight's hand came up like a striking snake, grabbing Kellan by the throat in a grip like iron. Kellan looked up to see her eyes open, the cold black replaced by a hot, white-gold glow shining from within.

"Ah, Kellan," she said, and her voice vibrated in Kellan's head, a buzzing blend of Midnight's own voice and Morningstar's. "Still with so much to learn."

"I did what you said!" she rasped. "Finish her off!"

"I'm grateful. Unfortunately, you have heard my true name, and I cannot risk you ever telling anyone. You felt what I felt when your father bound me; you will understand that I can never allow myself to be so bound again. It's too bad your father isn't here for this, but you will have to do in his place." The hand gripping Kellan's throat began to squeeze, cutting off her air. Kellan's vision began to swim.

"Get the frag away from her!" someone yelled from

the mouth of the cave, the shout followed by the thunder of gunfire. Blood spattered over Kellan as the bullets struck Midnight, causing her to lose her grip and stagger back against the wall of the cavern. Kellan gasped and coughed, twisting as she fell to her knees to see Orion standing just inside the cave entrance, soaked to the skin, pistol in hand. Right behind him came Lothan, G-Dogg and an Asian man Kellan didn't recognize.

"Kellan—" Orion shouted, but G-Dogg called out.

"Look out!" he said, drawing his own weapon.

Kellan automatically rolled to the side as Midnight surged out from against the wall. Though her vest was dark with bloodstains, she could see the wounds made by Orion's shots already closing, fiery light burning in Midnight's eyes and from the jade amulet.

"She's possessed!" Lothan called out from behind the others.

Orion and G-Dogg both opened up on Midnight, guns roaring in the close confines of the cave. She jerked and danced like a puppet with broken strings, bullets tearing through areas of her close-fitting suit where the armor was weak, pounding flesh and bone where it was not. Midnight collapsed to the floor, dark blood pooling around her.

"Kellan!" Lothan called out, "Everybody! Fall back now!"

Orion ran forward to grasp Kellan's wrist, pulling her up and helping her out of the cave onto the ridge.

"We should have made sure she was finished!" Orion yelled at Lothan, who shook his head.

"Mere bullets can't kill something like that," he said. "She's possessed by a powerful spirit."

"It calls itself Morningstar," Kellan told them, and Lothan grimaced.

"I know. We need to banish it, but the file doesn't have the necessary—"

"Its true name is Seterin'ranshae," Kellan gasped out, careful to pronounce it correctly.

Lothan beamed like a proud father. "My dear, you'll be a master of the Art yet! We—"

"Incoming!" G-Dogg yelled.

Lothan instantly raised the Staff of Candor-Brie in a warding gesture, its crystal flaring in the darkness and pouring rain. They heard the dull roar of an explosion, and it seemed as if the very air was on fire. Kellan flung up her arms to shield herself as the force of the blast knocked her down.

She hit the ground, but quickly regained her feet as the flames cleared. Lothan stood unmoved, though his robes were singed and burned in spots.

Morningstar, in Midnight's body, stood just outside the entrance of the cave. Light streamed from her eyes as the remnants of mystic flames shimmered around her hands.

"Well done, magician," the spirit sneered in its combined voice, "but I wonder how long you can maintain such a defense against me."

"Long enough," Lothan countered. Planting his staff firmly on the ground in front of him, the troll mage pointed his other hand at Morningstar. "By the power of the elements, and by my will, Seterin'ranshae, you will be banished from this plane!" he shouted above the wind.

Rather than recoiling from Lothan's use of its true name, Morningstar merely laughed, rolling thunder echoing the sound across the mountains.

"I will *not* be bound again, and I will not be banished!" the spirit cried out, and raised Midnight's hands to the roiling sky. A bolt of lightning split the heavens and struck the ground at Lothan's feet with a tremendous burst of thunder, sending rocks, dirt and the troll mage flying. He collapsed in a heap on the ground, nearly sliding down the ridge.

"Lothan!" Kellan cried, rushing to his side. The others responded by opening up on Morningstar with a hail of gunfire. It drove the spirit back a step, bullets tearing into Midnight's flesh, but the damage healed before their eyes as quickly as it was done, the burning light growing brighter around Midnight's hands.

"Lothan, are you all right?" Kellan asked, crouching at her teacher's side. Lothan groaned loudly, pushing himself up and nodding.

"I shielded myself from the worst of it," he said. "Ye gods, it's powerful. We might not be able to stop it, Kellan." Lothan looked at the spirit as Morningstar raised Midnight's glowing hands.

"Shield the others!" he rapped out, and Kellan concentrated on extending her magical defenses around her fellow runners as the spirit lashed out with another shimmering bolt of mystic power. It stabbed into G-Dogg, who howled in pain, clutching the side of his head with his free hand and dropping to his knees.

With a battle cry punctuated by a rumble of thunder from above, Orion drew his sword, casting aside his pistol, and rushed Morningstar, blade held low in a two-handed grip. The spirit turned, but too late to unleash a spell against him. The enchanted blade slashed across Midnight's outstretched arm, laying it open almost to the bone. A dual scream of pain was torn from her throat, and the spirit retreated, but the wound was already starting to close.

"Orion's blade may be able to destroy it," Lothan

said to Kellan, climbing to his feet. "We must defend him against the spirit's magic long enough for him to accomplish it."

Kellan focused on cloaking Orion in a shield of protection against any magic Morningstar might use against him. So when the spirit lashed out at the elf with a sweeping hand that trailed a scythelike arc of mystic force in its wake, it dashed against the combined power of her and Lothan's spell defense, leaving Orion unharmed. He struck again with his sword, but this time Morningstar was prepared for the attack, apparently drawing upon Midnight's considerable agility and skill in hand-to-hand combat.

"Why didn't its true name compel it?" Lothan asked, brow furrowed, concentrating on the defense spell. "It should have been enough to banish it." He and Kellan looked at each other almost simultaneously. "The amulet!"

At that moment, the clouds split, and another massive bolt of lightning struck. This one hit Lothan directly. His magical shields sent most of the energy flowing around him and into the ground, but the troll mage was blasted to his knees by the force of the strike, and he nearly lost his staff. Morningstar dodged and weaved around Orion's attack. He managed to tag Midnight with a shallow cut along the shoulder, but the injury immediately began to heal.

"Orion!" Kellan shouted. "The amulet!"

Morningstar turned on Kellan, eyes burning with fury, and the moment's distraction was just long enough for Orion to lunge in and grab the amulet hanging around Midnight's neck with his free hand. With a howl of rage, the spirit flung out Midnight's hand, and an invisible force sent Orion flying like he'd been struck by a car. But the adept managed to hold onto the amulet, and the golden chain snapped, the two ends of it fluttering from his closed fist as he flew back, hit the edge of the ridge and rolled. He dropped his sword, but kept hold of the amulet as his free hand clawed for purchase in the rocky soil.

Kellan ran to Orion, as Morningstar, arms raised, shouted to the sky above. Kellan extended her defenses, bracing for another lightning strike, hoping she could protect them both against it. Then shots thundered in the dark as Akimura emptied his pistol's clip into Midnight. The rounds could do little more than distract the spirit, but that distraction apparently was enough to spoil whatever magic it had been planning. As Kellan reached Orion's side, he opened his hand and held out the amulet as she pulled him up onto solid ground.

"Are you alright?"

He shook his head, clutching his side with his free hand. "I will be," he said through clenched teeth. "Just do what needs to be done."

Kellan snatched up the amulet as Akimura's pistol clicked on empty. He ejected the spent clip and jammed in another, but the delay cost him. Morningstar lashed out again, and he, too, went flying from the force of the magical blow.

"Seterin'ranshae!" Kellan called out, brandishing the amulet like a talisman. The words she'd heard in her vision seemed to spring fully formed into her head. "By the power of your name, by the power of this token, by the power of my will, you are bound! I command you . . . begone! Begone from that body, and from this world, forever more!"

"*No!*" the spirit and Midnight cried out as one, and

suddenly Morningstar surged forward, its elven host crumpling to the ground. The spirit appeared in the form Kellan had last seen it: skin rocky and scaly, open maw filled with teeth, gnarled hands tipped with claws, eyes burning with hate and power. It swooped toward Kellan like a bird of prey, but stopped just out of reach, held back by the power of her will, joined with the magic of the banishing ritual and the amulet holding a portion of its essence.

I . . . will . . . not . . . be . . . banished! Morningstar howled in Kellan's mind. She could feel tremendous pressure—all the energy of the spirit bent on destroying her, defying her attempt to cast it from the material world. It fought like a cornered animal.

"You *will*!" she countered, pushing back with all her might. But even as she strained to impose her will on the spirit, Kellan wasn't sure it would be enough. Morningstar was like a raging beast, barely contained, and she didn't know how long she could hold it.

Lothan shook off the effects of the lightning strike, raising his head to see Kellan locked in magical combat with the spirit's astral form. The blazing Morningstar hovered before her, fiery wings spread, burning gaze trained on her. Kellan stood firm, holding the glowing jade amulet out in front of her, eyes narrowed in concentration, but it was like a tree standing against the fury of a storm. He felt a surge of pride in her abilities, but next to the unleashed power of Morningstar, she looked so small. . . .

Lothan, a voice whispered in his thoughts. *Lothan. . . .* It took a moment for the mage to recognize the voice when separated from Midnight's voice—Morningstar was speaking to him directly. Lothan levered himself to his feet, leaning on his staff.

Lothan, the spirit repeated. *Aid me, and you will be rewarded. I have power such as you have only imagined. I know secrets of the netherworlds, of realms beyond mortal imagination. I will grant you knowledge beyond your wildest dreams!*

Images filled his mind, of standing atop the highest pinnacles in the metroplex, commanding legions of spirits; reclining in a thronelike chair, surrounded by rare tomes and objets d'art; of fine wines, rare delicacies, the touch of a beautiful woman. . . . Lothan glanced in the gilt-edged mirror beside his throne and saw the handsome, distinguished, *human* face looking back at him, so very like the face of his father, but with the bearing of a king. All he needed to do was strike the amulet from Kellan's hand—or, better yet, take it for himself. . . .

"Ahhh!" Kellan cried out, dropping to one knee in front of Morningstar. She thrust out both hands in front of her to ward off the spirit, directing all of her will against it, slowing pushing back to her feet. Lothan took one lumbering step toward her, feeling the bulk of his metahuman body, the creak and ache of every joint, his age in the depths of each bone. How he hated the cruel humor of nature! How fondly he recalled his childhood, before the Awakening twisted his body as the price for his power.

I could restore you, were it your wish, said the voice in his thoughts. *You could be human, young and handsome. It is within my power.*

Lothan was no fool. He knew the spirit would say anything, promise anything, in order to save itself. He also knew such spirits were treacherous. They would go back on their word unless bound with certain rituals, and even then they would seek to use the letter of the agreement to escape from it, to find an opportunity to turn on their erstwhile "ally."

But with the amulet, and knowledge of Morningstar's true name, there was a good chance Lothan could bind the spirit, enslave it to his will like any other servitor, and freely command its powers. Such power would be his, and his alone, to wield. He would need to subvert Kellan's attempt to banish Morningstar, and then prevent her from ever doing so again. Of course, if he succeeded, would that matter?

In only a few steps, the troll towered over Kellan, who was barely maintaining her stance, wavering before the onslaught of the unleashed spirit shining like a fallen star before her, almost too bright to look at.

"Lothan . . ." Kellan breathed, looking up at him—no longer the lost girl G-Dogg brought to him, her face now lined with determination and experience, creased with pain and effort. Lothan reached out for the amulet with one massive hand, closing his fist over Kellan's.

"Not safely is such a servant taken on," he muttered. Then he intoned, voice carrying over the thunder and rain.

"By the power of this token, by the power of my will, and by the power of your name, Seterin'ranshae, thou art banished forevermore! Leave this world and trouble it no longer! We command thee, *begone!*"

As a surge of fresh power flowed into the struggle, Kellan straightened and pressed with all of her remaining will. Morningstar shrieked like a damned soul, recoiling from the combined power of the two magicians. Its shape flickered between its two forms, fiery wings folded in around it like a cloak, hands reaching out, as if pleading, trying to find anything to hold on to as it was pulled into an invisible vortex.

No, please! It cried out. *Please! I will give you anything you wish—anything! I will serve and obey you, please, I beg of you, do not . . . Noooooooo!*

The spirit's remaining pleas were cut off in a wailing cry as its astral form collapsed, swirling like glowing smoke drawn into a vent. White-gold streamers of light formed a whirlpool in the air, then suddenly winked out in a flash and a final booming crack of thunder from the clouds overhead.

Kellan slumped against Lothan's side, the amulet dangling from her hand by its broken chain. The jade stone was charred and cracked. A thin trickle of smoke rose from it, dispersed by the steady rain. She breathed a heavy sigh of relief and exhaustion.

"Is it . . . ?"

"It's over," Lothan replied. "It's gone."

Kellan raised her head and surveyed the area scarred by lightning, brushing rain-soaked strands of hair out of her eyes. Suddenly, her head whipped around.

"Oh, frag, where's Midnight?"

With the rain still coming down, the mountain slope was treacherous, but a slim shadow moved alongside the ridge, out of sight of the cave mouth, toward the northwestern side of the mountain. From there it would be a slow climb down to the relative safety of the tree line and a long trek back to civilization, but she still had contacts and connections, arrangements for a safe haven and an opportunity to recoup. From there it would just be a matter of time.

"Leaving so soon, Aerwin?" The voice stopped Midnight in her tracks as surely as the sound of a pistol being cocked. Toshiro Akimura stood nearby on the ridge, his weapon trained on her. She straightened up, hands held loosely out to her sides, and smiled, knowing Akimura could see as well as she despite the darkness. She slowly shook her head.

"That gun's empty, Silk, and we both know it."

"Are you sure of that?" he replied flatly.

"Don't be a fool," she said. "You know I've made arrangements, should anything happen."

"Things worse than you've already done?"

She only smirked. "You can't even imagine."

"Maybe I just don't care."

"You know I won't believe that," Midnight said. "We've both worked the shadows for too long. It wasn't personal, it was just business. I'm sure we can make a deal. . . ."

When Midnight whipped out the small holdout pistol, there were three shots in rapid succession. The first two caught her in the shoulder and arm, scattering sprays of blood in the rain. The third slammed into her midsection. She stumbled back a step, booted feet finding no purchase on the slick, wet slope; her arms windmilled, grasping at nothing, and she fell.

Toshiro Akimura stepped up to the edge of the slope, looking down into the darkness as a flash of lightning illuminated the still form lying far below. He slowly holstered the gun, rainwater running down his face and dripping from his nose and chin.

"You understand," he said into the darkness. "Nothing personal." Then he glanced up at the sky and sighed. "Rest easy, Marc, Mustang. Rest easy."

Epilogue

G-Dogg taped the box closed and rapped a hand on the top. "That takes care of that," he said. "Anything else, Jackie?"

The decker glanced over from where she was taking stock of the boxes, bags and furniture stacked up in the middle of the main room of the apartment. Her hair was pulled back, and instead of her usual slick street or business wear, she was dressed in a well-worn tee-shirt and jeans. She shook her head.

"I think that's it," she said. "Looks like we're ready to load up this stuff."

G-Dogg stacked the box on top of two others and crouched down to lift them all in his burly arms. "I notice Lothan didn't come by to help you move," he grunted.

"Lothan's rarely around when there's any kind of heavy lifting to be done," Jackie said with a smile, "but he is coming by my new place later to help out with some of the finishing touches."

"Magical security?" Kellan observed, stepping through the open door of the apartment with Orion in tow. Jackie nodded in response as Orion picked up a box and followed G-Dogg downstairs to where Silver Max waited with the truck. Kellan took a look around the now almost empty apartment, stripped to the walls and ready to be cleaned.

"Still can't believe you're giving up this place," she told Jackie, who only shrugged.

"It was time for me to move on," she said. "It's not a good idea to get too settled in this business, and my new place will keep people guessing."

"It's sure not as nice as this one," Kellan noted, and Jackie shrugged it off again.

"It's got other features that I need at the moment," was all she said, and Kellan decided not to press the matter. She got the distinct feeling that Jackie's move involved more than just a desire for a change of scenery, but the decker didn't volunteer any information, so Kellan didn't ask. She was frankly appreciative of the fact that Jackie trusted her enough to help her relocate; she knew the decker liked to keep her offline life as private as possible.

"So," Jackie asked, changing the subject, "how long before you and Orion are looking for a place?"

Kellan shrugged, blushing pink. "I don't think we're ready for anything like that yet," she said, and the decker laughed.

They each grabbed a box and headed down to the truck, passing G-Dogg and Orion on their way back up. The ork and elf were talking about recent conflicts between the gangs of the Seattle Barrens like any other two guys would talk sports scores. It seemed the war between the Spikes and the Ancients had heated up again, and G-Dogg was betting the Spikes were going to do some real damage this time, with Orion countering that the Ancients were probably getting help from someone of influence inside Tir Tairngire, since the elven nation had an interest in maintaining an underground pipeline into south Seattle. G-Dogg wondered if both gangs would recognize the growing threat of the Hellhounds, who claimed 405, and settle things out of mutual gain, or do enough damage to each other for the Hellhounds to make a move against one or both gangs.

Silver Max was down curbside with the truck, though when they go there, he was in the middle of checking over the sleek racing bike parked just in front of the truck's cab. The dwarf looked over the bike's engine with an expert eye, nodding to himself as he followed the twists and turns of the pipes and valves.

When G-Dogg and Orion came back down carrying Jackie's small couch, the elf called out over his shoulder.

"What do you think, Max? Can you fix it up?"

"Oh yeah," the dwarf replied, a smile splitting his bearded face. "The '59 Yamaha body is solid, you just need some new points and a tune-up, maybe an overhaul. I could probably put a nice charger in there for you, too." The rigger was clearly eager to tear into a new engine, take it apart and put it back together better than he found it. Orion grinned, helping G-Dogg heft the couch into the truck.

"Sounds wiz," he said. "Wouldn't mind helping you out with it."

"You're on."

In fairly short order, the truck was loaded up, Jackie's old apartment locked up, and they were on their way to her new place. Kellan and G-Dogg rode in the cab with Silver Max, following Jackie, while Orion followed close behind the truck. Along the way, they filled Max in on their adventures in Tir Tairngire, the dwarf observing that he could have gotten them through the storm over the Cascades if he had been flying the VTOL, and saying he was sorry that he missed the whole caper.

James Telestrian had been appreciative enough to arrange passage from Tir Tairngire back to Seattle in exchange for everything the runners learned, all copies of Marc Thierault's notes, and the promise of their silence on matters concerning Midnight and Morningstar. If the Tir government took any note of the "unusual meteorological phenomena" in the Cascade Mountains, no one chose to comment on it, leaving it as just another oddity of the Awakened world.

In the dim light of his study, Lothan finished entering the last of the data via the wireless keyboard, and tapped the command for the computer to encrypt and save the file to his personal datastore behind a protected password. He leaned back in his heavy chair with a creak of old leather. While he would never entirely trust computers, he had to admit they were far more secure than actually writing things down. The heavy encryption would keep the information safer than a locked box.

He had written down everything he could remember from Marc Thierault's ritual and experiment notes, and included his own observations of the spirit Morningstar, and, of course, its true name. Lothan had agreed to turn over the original datafile to Telestrian and to keep quiet about what he'd seen and learned during their excursion into Tir Tairngire, but he wasn't fool enough to simply forget about it. One never knew when such information would come in handy, after all.

The troll mage sighed heavily as he lifted the ruined jade amulet from the table in front of him, letting it dangle by its broken chain. It looked like a toy in his massive fist. The stone was cracked and charred, and only the faintest magical aura still clung to it. After Morningstar was banished, the necklace had apparently lost all magical power, and Kellan decided she wanted to bury it in the cave where her father had fallen; her way of honoring the man she never really knew, and putting the past behind her to move on to the future. She'd asked Lothan to teach her how to enchant a new amulet, something that could be truly hers.

She didn't know that Lothan had unearthed the amulet when he stayed behind to seal up the cave, or that he brought it back with him to Seattle. There was no need for her to know. Lothan understood Kellan's desire to put the past to rest, but he was too practical to allow such a potential resource to lie buried under earth and rock—not when there still might be a use for the lingering astral traces within the gold and jade.

Sighing again, Lothan opened the small teakwood box on the table in front of him, gently depositing the amulet within, folding its chain on top. He shut the lid and waved one hand over the box, causing a faint golden glow to flicker around it for a moment. Then, with another wave of his hand, he sent the box floating through the air to slide into an empty spot on the shelves lining the walls of his study, filled with books and the accumulated trinkets of a lifetime studying magic in the shadows. The computer signaled it had completed the encryption of the file, and Lothan looked at the message window for a moment before clicking it closed and shutting down the display. *That's that.* He rose from his chair, pausing for a moment in the doorway to turn off the light before closing the door, and consigning the room and its contents to the shadows.

Alone in her new space—actually a slightly converted warehouse—Jackie Ozone sat cross-legged in an overstuffed chair amidst a dark cityscape of boxes. Unpacking and organizing her physical space would have to wait until she had taken care of more pressing matters.

The only light came from the faint halogen and neon glow filtering through the closed blinds, but Jackie didn't need the physical light, since her attention was focused instead on the virtual world filling her skull through the thin fiber-optic cable that snaked its way from the cyberdeck in her lap to the chrome jack in her head.

She built up the new virtual image slowly, layer by layer, like a sculptor working clay. The design of a new Matrix persona was slow and painstaking work. Of course, there were prefabricated templates and virtual "puppets" you could quickly copy and paste, but it was the difference between buying off the rack at a second-hand store and the custom work of a fashion designer. No decker like Jackie would be caught dead wearing a prefab persona.

She was sorry to retire her old icon—it had served her well, and it was known throughout the Seattle shadows—but that was the problem, after all. If there was any possibility a description of her persona would find its way out of the Cross corporate system . . . well, it was better not to take chances. Her new Matrix identity would just need to be that much better than before, and she tried to look at it as a challenge rather than a setback.

She was so engrossed in the work that she barely noticed the knocking sound coming from the real world. When she did, she put the persona design and her deck on standby, switching off the simsense feed and allowing her senses to revert back to the real world. She nearly leapt out of the chair when she did.

Standing beside the door, knuckles rapping on the inside, was a slim Asian man dressed in a tailored leather jacket over a dark, close-fitting shirt and jeans. Gloves covered his hands and dark shades covered his eyes, so Jackie knew he must have optic enhancements to see clearly in the darkness of the room. Her first reaction was to reach for the bag sitting next to her chair where her sidearm rested in its holster.

"Don't," the man said firmly. "If I wanted to hurt you, I'd have done it already." Jackie paused. He was right about that, and, if he was armed, it was doubtful she could reach her weapon before he drew his.

"You could use a better security system," the man observed casually. A green light burned from the tiny box set in the doorframe at shoulder height.

"Know any good sources?" Jackie asked, and he nodded.

"Some. I still have a few connections here and there."

"And your skills clearly haven't gotten rusty, Mr. . . . ?"

That earned her a small smile. "Fox. You can call me Mr. Fox. Well, not too rusty," he countered. "I'm not here to make trouble," he reassured her. "I just came to talk."

"You could have called ahead," she observed, "or at least knocked." He shrugged.

"I did. You were otherwise occupied."

"What do you want?" Jackie asked, afraid that she already knew.

"Like I said, I still have a few connections here and there, including some inside Cross Applied Technologies. I wondered why a Seraphim ops team that had a shadowrunning team dead to rights would suddenly get recalled, and, for that matter, how they might have found out about what was going on in Tir Tairngire in the first place. So I did some checking. Rumors travel fast within a company, especially when it involves the CEO and a top-level meeting."

"And what did you find out?" Jackie asked him, trying to keep her tone no more than idly curious.

"That the information someone passed on to a Cross fixer here in Seattle—information Midnight stole from Nightengale's, which showed that a certain former operative was still alive and here in the Northwest—ended up being nothing but a wild goose chase. This suggests that someone managed to alter the data, either before it was sold, to convince the fixers it was authentic when it wasn't, or, more likely, after the fact to throw the company off the trail."

"And why tell me this?"

Fox shrugged again. "Professional courtesy," he said. "I figured a decker of your reputation—someone who has worked closely with Lothan and Kellan before—enough for Lothan to engage you in digging up information on that former corporate operative, would appreciate the kind of effort necessary to pull off a job like that."

"Couldn't have been easy," Jackie observed.

"No, I'm sure it wasn't. So you can understand how a fixer might appreciate finding someone willing to go to such lengths, regardless of their motivation. Somebody like that would be a valuable asset—one that bears watching, don't you think?"

"No doubt."

"I'm glad you agree. Here," he took small card from the inside pocket of his jacket and set it down on a nearby stack of boxes. "You might be interested in this. I'll be in touch about your security system real soon."

Jackie smiled tightly. "I guess you'll know how to find me."

Fox returned the smile in equal measure. "Count on it," he said, before silently opening the door and stepping out into the dimly lit hall. The door quietly clicked shut behind him, the light on the monitor box changing from green to red.

Jackie set aside her deck and unfolded from the chair, going over to pick up the card he left behind. She glanced over the few lines of neat type, nodding slowly.

Kellan and Orion arrived at Dante's Inferno together, and Newt the bouncer admitted them past the growing line of club-kids and other hopefuls, to the usual chorus of complaints and catcalls.

Purgatory, beneath the main levels of the club, was laid out with Dante's signature opulence, including a sideboard laden with indulgent hors d'oeuvres, chilled bottles of champagne, and a sinful selection of sweets. Sitting on the far side of an octagonal table was Toshiro Akimura, dressed in a finely cut dark suit, with an iridescent blue and gold silk tie highlighted with a trace of Japanese kanji. Lothan stood nearby talking quietly with the fixer, the Staff of Candor-Brie leaning against a chair. The troll mage was wearing his symbol-decorated overcoat, but also a fine dark tunic and newly polished boots.

"Come in," Akimura said, waving them toward the table. "Help yourselves to something."

Not long after, several others arrived: G-Dogg looked sharp in a pin-striped suit and dark vest, complete with watch fob and chain; Liada wore a dark green cloak over a short-sleeved top and black slacks; the dwarf Silver Max even changed out of his usual grease-stained overalls into a trim coat worn over a collarless shirt and neatly cuffed trousers. Kellan was only a little surprised to see Jackie Ozone arrive; according to her clients, the decker preferred to attend meetings and get-togethers virtually. But Kellan understood that her friends saw her in the flesh much more often.

"How's the new place coming?" Kellan asked Jackie.

"Settling in," she said. "I just got a new security system that's better even than the one at my old place. Gotta keep an eye on the neighbors," she added with a wink, and Kellan laughed.

They turned their attention to Akimura as he stood and pushed back his chair.

"You all know me," he said, once he had their attention. "Some of you better than others," he added, glancing in Kellan's direction. She gave him a tiny smile in return. "But you all know that I've been in the biz for a long time."

"By some people's standards . . ." Lothan muttered,

just loud enough for everyone to hear, drawing some chuckles.

"After recent events," the fixer continued, "I find myself looking to cut some old ties and reestablish myself in the shadows. So Mr. Fox is opening up shop in Seattle. Even though I've been out of circulation for a while, I assure you that I can still put together a deal. Liquidating my old assets gives me material resources to work with: What I need to find is people I can rely on—professionals who know their business and get the job done, who want to take an opportunity and make something of it, on their own terms."

A loud pop caught everyone's attention as G-Dogg opened a bottle of champagne. Kellan smiled at the way hands reached for weapons that were all checked in the Inferno's cloakroom or else simply left at home. The ork simply offered a tusky grin in response to startling a few people, and started passing out glasses and pouring.

"So," Akimura said, taking a glass and holding it up. "If you are interested, I'd like to be able to consider all of you as potential resources in this new enterprise, the core of a pool of talent I can rely upon to get the job done. Naturally, you are also free to simply enjoy the evening and leave it at that. . . . What do you say?"

Before anyone else could answer, Kellan cleared her throat, and suddenly all eyes in the room were on her.

"I just wanted to say, I've made my share of mistakes since I got to Seattle," she said, pausing and swallowing, looking at the faces gathered around the table, "but I've been lucky to have friends willing to back me up, even when I mess up, willing to do more than just get the job done. I came to Seattle to find

out more about my family and to make a name for
myself in the shadows, and I hope"—she glanced at
Orion, who smiled—"I think that I've found both family and opportunity here—not just professionals I can
work with, but people I can trust."

Akimura raised his glass in acknowledgment, and
everyone else quickly followed suit.

"To trust and honor among the shadows," he said,
and everyone clinked glasses in response.

"I'll drink to that," Jackie said, just loud enough
for Kellan to hear. She caught the decker's eye, nodded, and the two of them touched glasses with a ring-
ing chime.

ABOUT THE AUTHOR

Steve Kenson stepped into the shadows in 1997 with the *Awakenings* sourcebook. Since then, he has written or contributed to more than two dozen Shadowrun® RPG books. His first Shadowrun novel, *Technobabel*, was published in 1998. He has written five other Shadowrun novels (*Crossroads, Ragnarock, The Burning Time, Born to Run,* and *Poison Agendas*) in addition to MechWarrior® and Crimson Skies™ novels. Steve lives in Merrimack, New Hampshire, with his partner, Christopher Penczak.

STEPHEN KENSON

SHADOWRUN BOOK #1: BORN TO RUN

Earth, 2063. Long-dormant magical forces have reawakened, and the creatures of mankind's legends and nightmares have come out of hiding. Megacorporations act as the new world superpowers, and the dregs of society fight for their own power. Sliding through the cracks in between are shadowrunners—underworld professionals who will do anything for a profit, and anything it takes to get the job done.

Kellan Colt has come to Seattle to make a name for herself. But her first run proves that in her line of work, there's no such thing as a sure thing, and that in her world, there is only one law—survival.

0-451-46058-8

Available wherever books are sold or at penguin.com

Stephen Kenson

Shadowrun Book #2:
Poison Agendas

Earth 2063. Shadowrunner Kellan Colt
thinks she's ready to strike out on her own
when she discovers the location of a secret
cache of military weaponry—right in the heart
of the supernatural creature-infested
Awakened wilderness.

0-451-46063-4

Roc Science Fiction & Fantasy
NOW AVAILABLE

DEATHSTALKER CODA by Simon R. Green
0-451-46024-3
As prophesied, Owen Deathstalker has returned to
save the Empire from the mysterious entity known
as the Terror—leaving his descendant Lewis
with the task of leading an army against the legions
of the madman who has usurped the throne.

NIGHTLIFE by Rob Thurman
0-451-46075-8
In New York, there's a troll under the Brooklyn
Bridge, a boggle in Central Park, and a beautiful
vampire in a penthouse on the Upper East Side.
Of course, most humans are oblivious to this,
but Cal Leandros is only half-human. His father's
dark lineage is the stuff of nightmares—and he
and his entire otherworldly race are after Cal.